THE
HATBOX
MURDERS

THE HATBOX MURDERS

An Elliott Bay Mystery

JENNIFER BERG

LEVEL BEST BOOKS

Historia

To my wonderful and patient family

Contents

Chapter One: Miss Margaret Baker   1

Chapter Two: Pike, Roberta Ester. Case closed.   8

Chapter Three: Michael and Amy Riggs   14

Chapter Four: Uncle, Jacob Greenleaf   19

Chapter Five: Cousin, Sadie Greenleaf   29

Chapter Six: Boyfriend, Sylvester Finnegan   34

Chapter Seven: Half-Brother and Former Friend   40

Chapter Eight: The Heartbroken Landlady   48

Chapter Nine: Ruby's Boss, Maxim Blackwell   57

Chapter Ten: The Reluctant Request   62

Chapter Eleven: The Banker, Bruce Steele   69

Chapter Twelve: A Late Night Fire   74

Chapter Thirteen: Inspector Riggs Re-Opens the Case   77

Chapter Fourteen: A Country Club Garden Party   87

Chapter Fifteen: Sunday Dinner and Double News   93

Chapter Sixteen: Sadie Gets Pensive   97

Chapter Seventeen: The Police Chief Puts on the Brakes   102

Chapter Eighteen: Maxim Blackwell's Secret   108

Chapter Nineteen: Former Lovers   110

Chapter Twenty: A Break-In   114

Chapter Twenty-One: Tracking Sylvester Finnegan   120

Chapter Twenty-Two: The Disappearance of Sadie Greenleaf   123

Chapter Twenty-Three: Murder   127

Chapter Twenty-Four: Roberta's Green Hatbox   130

Chapter Twenty-Five: Sadie Greenleaf's Secrets   137

Chapter Twenty-Six: Sadie's Trail   142

Chapter Twenty-Seven: The Boyfriend's Last Stand 147

Chapter Twenty-Eight: Eastlake Coffee and Cakes 153

Chapter Twenty-Nine: The Blackwell Estate 159

Chapter Thirty: Sylvester's Unlucky Shadow 163

Chapter Thirty-One: Patricia Mooney's Hard Work 166

Chapter Thirty-Two: Eddie and Ann Marie 169

Chapter Thirty-Three: One Flies Away and Another One... 174

Chapter Thirty-Four: The Consultation That Never Happened 179

Chapter Thirty-Five: The Last Will and Testament 184

Chapter Thirty-Six: Ann Marie's Quandary 189

Chapter Thirty-Seven: The Boiling Point 194

Chapter Thirty-Eight: A Confession 201

Chapter Thirty-Nine: Dresses and Murders Explained 207

Chapter Forty: The Calm After the Storm 213

Acknowledgements 219

About the Author 220

Also by Jennifer Berg 221

Chapter One: Miss Margaret Baker

Michael Riggs froze in the hallway outside his office.

He didn't mind Mondays as a rule, but he preferred to start them with a cup of coffee and a closed door. He had the coffee—terrible as it was, but there was a stranger in his office.

She had light brown hair that was pulled up neatly under her blue felt pillbox hat. And whoever had designed her dress—with its scooped neckline and full skirt–would have felt gratified to see her wearing it.

Riggs observed her through the glass windows that connected his office to the department hallway. He didn't like her stiff posture. He didn't like the distressed look on her face. And he didn't like the way she was clenching the morning newspaper.

Riggs checked his watch. It was only half past eight. Whatever was troubling this woman, Riggs had no way of escaping it. No reasonable way, that is. Riggs sighed, took a deep breath, and walked into his office.

The woman turned to look at him.

Riggs didn't say good morning. One, because he hadn't had his coffee yet. And two, because if it were a good morning, this woman wouldn't be here.

Riggs took off his gray fedora and hung it on the coat rack.

To the woman's credit, she waited.

Her perfume smelled like lilacs—not unlike the stuff his wife wore. Riggs sat down at his large wooden desk, set down his mug, and rubbed his mustache.

The woman was just about to say something when a seagull landed on the ledge outside the window. As she glanced at the bird, Riggs sized her up at closer quarters. She was about twenty-seven years old, five foot seven, with two inches coming from her fashionable shoes. Her eyes were brown, and her lipstick was rose. The skirt of her dress fell just below her knee, and besides the newspaper, she held a glossy smooth handbag. Her hat matched her dress and was decorated with felt flowers and thin netting swept wistfully above her eyebrows. She wore a strand of modest pearls around her neck and a small pearl earring on each ear.

When she pulled off her gloves, Riggs wasn't surprised to see a diamond on her left finger. Based on the early hour, she was probably a secretary at one of the bigger firms or a sales girl at one of the better department stores. And based on the size of her diamond, Riggs guessed that her future husband was successful as well.

She turned back at him. Riggs was aware of two things. Firstly, he was sure he had never met this woman before. And secondly, he was equally sure that although he'd never met her, something about her was familiar.

She shifted the newspaper between her hands. Riggs could see a headline about Marilyn Monroe's recent marriage, but it wasn't a Hollywood story that brought this woman to the police station on a Monday morning. Most young women had never met a policeman, let alone barged into a Sergeant Inspector's office.

He indicated one of the wooden chairs. "Please have a seat, Miss...."

"Baker." She answered in a voice that was steady but not overly confident. The room was so quiet he could hear the fabric of her skirt rustling as she sat down. "My name is Margaret Baker," she continued, "and I understand you're Sergeant Inspector Riggs. You're the man in charge of murder investigations."

Riggs took a swig of his coffee. It tasted worse than usual. Murder Investigations. "That's right. What can I do for you, Miss Baker?"

She unfolded the newspaper and laid it out on his desk.

"Are you familiar with Roberta Pike? She died on the fifteenth of July, just over a week ago."

Riggs glanced down at the article.

"My colleague is handling that investigation, Miss Baker," he said. "Inspector Fisher is the man you want to talk to. His office is just–"

"I know where his office is," Miss Baker interrupted. "The secretary told me. She also told me you were the best inspector in the department. And if Inspector Fisher is the man who's been handling the investigation so far, he's gotten it all wrong. I need to talk to someone else."

Riggs rubbed a worn groove on his wooden desk. He objected to meddling in other officers' cases. This woman was bold, but Fisher would have to learn to handle that side of his job too. Besides that, Riggs was familiar with the Pike case, and he didn't want to go near it.

"In the newspaper," Miss Baker continued, "The Seattle Post claims that the police believe Ruby jumped off the University Bridge. That's not right."

Riggs leaned back in his chair. "What makes you say that?"

Margaret Baker took a deep breath. "Because I knew Ruby. And she wouldn't jump off that bridge. Never. Not in a million years."

Riggs brought his subpar coffee near his face until he could feel the steam. "Was Roberta Pike a relative of yours?"

Miss Baker shook her head. "We worked together. I'm the head stenographer at Blackwell Enterprises. Ruby was the new girl."

"I see. How long had you known her?"

"She started working there three months ago, in April," Margaret admitted. "It was her first time working as a stenographer, and it was my job to train her."

"And you and she became friends?"

The woman nodded. "The other girls are friendly enough, but they're not very interesting; Ruby was different. She was so outgoing and confident and she learned her job quickly. She was new to Seattle, so she didn't know very many people. Since my fiance was away on business, I had lots of free time, so Ruby and I started meeting up for dinner or to go to the cinema together."

"When did this start?"

"She started working there three months ago."

"When did you and she start socializing outside of work?"

There was a pause. "About six weeks ago."

3

Riggs took a deep breath, but he kept his tone soft. "And did you know, Miss Baker, that Roberta Pike was in a tight spot financially?"

Margaret's brow furrowed. "No. Well, not exactly. That is, well, I had the idea she wasn't very good with her money, but Ruby was young, and she liked nice things. I earn four dollars more a week than the other girls, and I noticed that Ruby sometimes spent more money than I would have been able to afford, but I just assumed that she had savings or some money set aside. Besides, it wasn't my business."

Riggs leaned forward and asked, "And did you also know that on the night of the fifteenth, Miss Pike had a heated argument with her boyfriend, and he broke it off with her?"

Margaret Baker frowned.

Riggs rested his elbows on his desk. "See here, Miss Baker, how about if you talk to Inspector Fisher, and tell him what's on your mind. He's a good inspector, and he'll listen to what you have to say. Sometimes these things can be more complicated than they seem, and things don't always work out the way they were intended; an accident—"

"No, Inspector," Margaret objected. "I'm not just saying Ruby didn't *mean* to commit suicide. It wasn't an accident, either. Ruby Pike was murdered."

There was a long silence.

For the first time in months, Inspector Riggs didn't have any active cases. And all he wanted was to take off his shoes, enjoy his terrible coffee, and catch up on all the reports that had been piling up on his desk. Roberta Pike's death was tragic, but it was Fisher's case, and it was suicide, and it was closed. Inspector Fisher should be talking to Miss Baker. Fisher was no match for her, of course, but that was his problem.

But here was Miss Baker saying "murder," and even though she was wrong, that was a big word. And while Fisher was no match for Margaret Baker, he was certainly no match for Margaret Baker if she happened to be right about her friend's death.

But she wasn't right. Riggs reminded himself. Roberta Pike wasn't murdered.

"I know I didn't know Ruby very long," Margaret Baker was explaining,

4

"but I can tell you that Ruby wasn't the sort of girl who got down. She loved life, and she lived on top of the world. She was always having fun and looking forward to the next adventure."

"Sometimes even the happiest people–"

"Not Ruby," Margaret objected. "Problems were never real to her. Ruby relished a problem like it was a game, a challenge to be overcome. I don't know how to explain Ruby properly, but she was very confident. Some people might have said she was a little selfish, and she was in a way, but she wasn't the bad kind of selfish, where someone hurts other people. Ruby was just determined to enjoy life. Do you see what I mean? She wasn't the sentimental sort of girl who suffers from melancholy or gets overlooked in life; she was the sort of girl who thought for herself and got what she wanted."

"Miss Baker, do you have any actual proof—or evidence—to support your suspicions?"

Margaret Baker slowly shook her head. "My only proof is Ruby's character. I know that you need more than that, but I knew Ruby, and because of who she was, I know that I'm right."

Riggs glanced down at the newspaper, the article of the tragic death of Roberta Pike.

"I've talked to her family," Margaret Baker said, "Her parents died before the war, but Ruby had a cousin and an uncle. And they both feel the same way about it as I do; it's just not possible that Ruby could have committed suicide; it wasn't in her nature."

"What about Ruby's other friends, Miss Baker, and your fiancé? What do they think?"

"Ruby didn't have many friends. I only knew her boyfriend, Sylvester, but I didn't know him well, and I have no idea what he thinks. My fiancé never met Ruby because his company sent him to Europe for the last four months, and I met Ruby while he was away."

Riggs opened his mouth, but Margaret went on talking, "Ruby's death wasn't an accident because she wasn't a careless girl. She wouldn't have climbed over the railing on a dare or anything like that, not in a million

5

years. And it couldn't have been suicide because Ruby simply wasn't the type. And that leaves only one possibility, Inspector. Someone killed her."

Riggs took a deep breath and finished his coffee. What he really needed was some peace and quiet, and what Miss Baker really needed was a sympathetic shoulder to cry on. Death is never easy, and suicides are among the most painful in the business. But Riggs had read Fisher's report, and there was no hint of foul play.

So Ruby Pike had been the new girl in the company. And Margaret Baker was the head stenographer in charge of training her. She's a couple years older and more established; she may have even felt responsible for the younger woman. They hit it off, and everything was great. Then suddenly, Ruby jumps off a bridge. No one saw it coming, and everyone is devastated. Margaret is deeply upset. She was one of Ruby's only friends, but she didn't see the signs. Ruby was vulnerable, now she's gone. Margaret has a good job, a fiance, and a promising future, but Margaret doesn't know how to go on. So she does what so many people do; she looks for another explanation. She convinces herself that Ruby was murdered, it's still horrible, but it's not Margaret's fault. And now Margaret can do one last thing for her friend; she can demand justice.

Riggs turned over the newspaper and was surprised to see a photograph of Margaret Baker smiling at him from the social page.

There she was in a floor-length gown beside a tall dark-haired man in a tuxedo. The caption read, *Mr. Otis Jenison & his fiance, Miss Margaret Baker, at the Art Museum reception last November. Mr. Jenison, vice president at Jenison Co., returned yesterday from London, where he has spent the last four months supervising the opening of the London branch of Jenison Co.*

Riggs looked at the young woman in front of him. The photograph was charming, but it didn't do her justice. Margaret Baker was beautiful. And no wonder she had seemed so familiar; she wasn't just a successful stenographer, she was one of the fortunate class of citizens whose comings and goings were published in the social column. Margaret Baker may be just a stenographer, but she was a very well-connected one. Most people in her position would have used their social connections to make demands at the top.

"Inspector Riggs, please," she appealed to him, "could you just look at the case? You're a sergeant inspector—you might notice something someone else missed. I don't know why, but I'm telling you, Ruby Pike was murderer. Please, will you look into it?"

Riggs frowned. Going over Fisher's work wouldn't change anything. Roberta Pike jumped off a bridge, and nothing could change that painful reality, no matter how badly Margaret Baker longed for it. Then again, it wouldn't do any harm either—provided the police chief didn't find out about it–and it might just give Miss Baker a sense of closure.

Chapter Two: Pike, Roberta Ester. Case closed.

Riggs stood by the filing cabinet and looked down at his colleague's file. Inspector Fisher was the youngest inspector in the department and the greenest. He had plenty of flaws, but he also showed promise. The last thing Riggs wanted was to give Fisher or anyone else the impression that Riggs doubted his work. He had no justifiable reason to check this file. And the chief would fly off the handle if he caught Riggs wasting department time. Michael Riggs looked down at the letters which had been typed only a couple of days ago.

PIKE, Roberta Ester
    BORN: May 13, 1935
    DIED: July 15, 1956
    CAUSE OF DEATH: probable suicide

Reluctantly, Riggs tucked the file under his arm. If Fisher were here, Riggs would have to explain himself, but if he didn't... At that moment, the young inspector came striding through the office toward the back staircase. He was moving fast, but Riggs grabbed his gray hat and hurried after him.

"Hey, Fisher," he said when he was close enough not to shout, "you mind if I have a look at that Pike case?"

He'd expected the younger officer to stop, but Fisher just shrugged his complacence as he ducked into the stairwell.

Riggs followed him.

He had to hurry to keep up with Fisher's descent. "By the way," Riggs asked, "was there anything suspicious about Pike's death?"

"Nope," Fisher said, turning a corner to descend rapidly down the next flight. "Pike was in town for less than a year. She took a few temporary jobs, then she landed a stenographer position at one of the big companies on Fifth Avenue."

"What about her family?"

Fisher was breathing heavily but kept moving. "Her folks were long gone. But she had a rich uncle over on Queen Anne Hill. I gather he's an old business tycoon, not that he looks like it now, if you know what I mean. His place was practically a mansion. Apart from him, Pike had a cousin and a half-brother, but they weren't close. Pike lived alone in a little place in Eastlake."

Fisher reached the ground floor, but before he could exit the building, Riggs grabbed his arm. "Hey, what's the big rush?"

Fisher glanced back up the stairwell as though a tiger might be tailing them. He moved toward the door and lowered his voice, "Didn't you hear? Chief's on the warpath again. A few of us forgot our expense reports last month, and he's on his way down. I don't know about you, but I sure don't want to be sitting at my desk waiting for the bomb to drop."

Thankfully, Riggs hadn't botched up an expense report for fifteen years, but that wouldn't amount to a hill of beans. Once the chief got going, he would ball out any officer in sight.

Riggs glanced up the stairway and stepped out onto the street. He matched his pace to Fisher's. "Which way are you heading?"

"Pike Place Market," the young man said. "I've got some important work to do. And I could use your help if you can spare the time."

Riggs agreed, and the two inspectors began heading north. After a couple blocks, their pace slackened, and Riggs asked, "So how did she die?"

Fisher raised an eyebrow and gave Riggs a side glance. "Roberta Pike? She jumped off the University Bridge almost two weeks ago."

"What else?"

"She'd been out drinking with her boyfriend at a bar in Eastlake, a dive called the Blue Bay Tavern. The boyfriend's a dive, too, as far as I can tell."

"Anyone I know?"

Inspector Fisher shook his head. "His name is Finnegan, and he doesn't have a record, I checked. He and Pike were regulars at the bar, so folks recognized them. Anyway, that night, they both had plenty to drink, then there was a row. Finnegan told Pike to go to hell, and she stormed out. That was the last time anyone saw her."

"What about the boyfriend?"

"He stayed in the bar," Fisher explained. "It was only a few blocks from her apartment, but Pike had to walk past the bridge on her way home. The way I figure it, she was angry and heartbroken—"

"And drunk," Riggs added.

"Yep. When she got to the bridge, it all must have seemed like too much, so she jumped. The water didn't carry her very far. A sailboat found her the next morning on the rocks further down along the cut. She had a couple small bruises, but Doctor Hara's guess is that she drowned first and got the bruises from the rocks. The medical cause of death was drowning."

"What time did she jump?" Riggs asked.

"Around eleven o'clock. The boyfriend stayed in the bar until it closed at one."

The two men walked in silence until they reached the market. As always, the open-air market was bustling. Over the shouts of the fishmongers and vendors, Riggs could hear a street musician fiddling for spare change. He followed Fisher under the umbrellas. The daily catch from Puget Sound was spread out over tables of ice. Sleek fish bodies of every shape and size glistened in shades of pink, silver, and blue. There was a row of produce and flower vendors down the main alley, and the air smelled like a strange mixture of saltwater and roses.

Fisher turned at the stairs and made his way to the market's lower levels.

They walked down three stories, following the hillside of the market, until Fisher turned into a small bakery wedged between a curiosity shop and a shoe cobbler.

Fisher took his place in line and waited to place an order. He pointed at the file in Riggs' hand. "So, Sarge, why all the interest in the Pike case?"

Riggs rubbed his mustache. "I'm not interested," he explained, "but I promised a young woman I'd have a look."

"A young woman?" Fisher glanced at his superior doubtfully. "Are you on the level?"

"It's not official," Riggs assured him. "She's one of Pike's friends, and while I trust your work, she's convinced Pike was murdered."

"Well, I'm afraid she's wrong," Fisher said. "It was suicide, plain and simple. If this distressed woman would like to discuss it with me, I'd be happy to reassure her–"

"I already tried that tack," Riggs admitted reluctantly. "She didn't bite. But you may still end up meeting her before this is over."

"Is she a looker?"

Riggs nodded. "Unfortunately for you, she's also sharp," Riggs added. "Not to mention engaged."

Fisher huffed with disappointment.

"I should have sent her packing," Riggs grumbled. "No evidence or motives, and the chief will blow a gasket if he finds out."

"Then why are you doing it?"

Riggs frowned. "She has a head on her shoulders, and she's absolutely positive that Pike was murdered."

"Yes, but murders are prompted by motives," Fisher reminded him, "and there weren't any motives in the Pike case. Just a young woman who was drunk and feeling hopeless. It's horrible, but it's true. I investigated every angle for a full week. Roberta Pike jumped off a bridge."

Fisher stepped up to the counter and ordered a blackberry jam-filled doughnut. The woman handed him a small but bulging paper bag, and the two men left the bakery. They wandered outside and sat down on a faded bench overlooking the bay. Two massive ferries drifted past each other off Coleman dock. One was coming back from the Kitsap Peninsula, and the other one was headed over to Bainbridge Island.

Riggs set the file down and asked, "What was she like?"

"Roberta Pike was glamorous," Fisher said. "I never knew one girl could own so many dresses, and she seemed to have a souvenir photograph of herself wearing every dress."

"So she was attractive?"

"Bombshell was more like it," Fisher sighed, leaning back. "And her apartment was something out of a movie: pink curtains with ruffles, loads of mirrors, and more bottles of perfume than a girl could use in a lifetime. And it wasn't cheap stuff either; those bottles had high price tags. And not just her perfumes; Roberta's hats, shoes, all of it."

"On a stenographer's salary?"

"Her uncle kept her stocked with dough. Pike didn't earn that much, but she sure liked to spend it."

"How bad were her finances?"

"Her account was negative when she died, but her banker said her balance would occasionally jump to five hundred dollars or more."

Riggs whistled. "Did she have any other vices? Gambling, dope, anything like that?"

"Anything that could mix her up with the wrong sort?" Fisher shook his head. "I didn't see any evidence of it, and I looked. Of course, it's always a possibility, but the only low-life she seemed to know was the boyfriend, Finnegan—and like I said, he stayed in the bar."

Riggs leaned forward so that his elbows were resting on his knees. He poked the brim of his hat upward so that it tilted farther back on his head. After several minutes he glanced over at Fisher. "So when you said you had work to do, were you referring to that jam-filled doughnut?"

Fisher glanced at the paper bag and grinned. "I'm going to ask out the brunette who works at the Chowder House. She mentioned that she loves these things, and a buddy of mine says you can impress a girl if you listen to her."

Riggs shook his head and chuckled. "Well, thanks for the scoop." He stood up. "It sounds like you covered all the bases. I'll put the file back and relay the bad news to the friend."

"It was just a rotten deal," Fisher said, "of course, it shouldn't happen to anyone, but in the Pike case, it was completely senseless."

"Senseless is a good word for it."

Riggs started walking away, but Fisher stopped him. "Hey, Riggs, there was one thing that really didn't make sense," he said with a frown. "Pike was wearing one of those summer jackets over her dress. You know, a pink thing with big white buttons and pockets, and her little handbag was still stuffed into one of the pockets. She had three C notes and a loose key."

"That's a lot of cash for a girl with no money in the bank," Riggs agreed. "But it shows she wasn't mugged."

"Yeah, but I never figured out the key," Fisher said. "It didn't fit her apartment. In fact, we never found her apartment key. It should have been in her handbag, but it wasn't."

Inspector Riggs frowned.

"All the same," Fisher said, "an extra key couldn't have anything to do with Pike jumping off of that bridge."

Inspector Riggs rubbed his mustache. "Yeah, just like it couldn't have anything to do with Pike having been murdered."

Chapter Three: Michael and Amy Riggs

Michael Riggs was still mulling over the case that night after dinner. His wife came down the stairs carrying her apron. Amy Riggs was a slender woman with a few wisps of gray in her autumn-red hair and a warm smile that appeared often, even after a long day with the kids. She smiled at her husband as she hung her apron by the automatic clothes washer. The action signaled that the day's work was over. And even if the work wasn't finished, Amy was finished with it.

"I was beginning to think that little boy would never fall asleep," she said with a sigh. "Two stories, then a drink of water, then his teddy bear, and when I insisted it was time to sleep, he admitted that he was afraid Dr. Frankenstein's monster was hiding in his closet."

"That huge monster would never fit in his tiny closet," Riggs pointed out as he poured two small glasses of port. Michael found the port too sweet, but Amy adored the stuff.

"The logic of an eight-year-old isn't always as sound as yours," Amy turned on the lamp beside her favorite red chair and took the glass her husband was offering her. "Thank you, dear. And last night, do you know what he was afraid of? He thought the Mummy and a wild lion were under his bed—together."

"You make it sound scandalous," Michael chuckled as he sat down beside her. "So, do you still think the Saturday matinee is causing Willie's sleep problems?"

She nodded. "Forty-five cents for the privilege of a double feature that gives our little guy nightmares for the rest of the week." Amy picked up her book and put her feet on the brown ottoman. "I just don't think it's worth it."

"Whatever you decide is all right by me," Michael said as he took off his shoes and picked up the newspaper. "But he likes tagging along with the big kids."

Amy leaned back in her chair, came up with a plan for dealing with the Willie-Matinee-Problem, and opened her book. She adored Jane Austen, Emily Bronte, and almost anything else that carried her out of the city and off to the English countryside.

Michael sat down in his own chair and opened the newspaper to the sports section. "Maybe it's time to move Willie in with George," he said after a few minutes. "Willie wouldn't be so scared at night, and then you could have the little bedroom for your sewing again."

Amy looked at her husband until he remembered why that wasn't an option. Even though their youngest boy was nearly nine years old, he still needed the bedroom closest to the bathroom. To move him any farther down the hall would be to risk nighttime disasters.

"Right," Michael said with a nod.

Amy went back to her book. "Well, don't worry about it, dear. I have a plan."

Michael nodded and turned back to his paper, but he hadn't read two minutes before Amy interrupted him.

"Oh, I forgot to ask you. Is your mother coming to dinner on Sunday?"

"Hmm," Michael said as he looked at the page. The Seattle Rainiers were having a rough season.

Amy understood it was her husband's 'Distracted-but-Affirmative-Hmm' and not his 'Not-Listening-Hmm.' No matter, she would ask her mother-in-law to bake some bread for Sunday's dinner. The Riggs' home slipped into the quiet peacefulness that happened only when the children were asleep.

A ginger cat dashed through the room, catching Michael's attention. Officially, the animal belonged to him since he had brought it home one day on a sentimental whim. The children had fallen in love with the creature, and Amy had forbidden him from repeating the offense. In light of the cat's particular skills at stealing food, he had been named Criminal. The only reason Amy tolerated Criminal was because he periodically redeemed himself by killing a mouse. And if there was anything Amy hated more than a food-stealing cat, it was a mouse.

From Michael's chair, he could see into part of the kitchen. There was Criminal, tail twitching, stalking across the floor. Riggs glanced at Amy. She couldn't see into the kitchen from her chair, so he pretended nothing was happening. Amy turned the page of her book and sipped her port.

When Criminal pounced, Michael cleared his throat and rustled his newspaper.

A minute later, he could see the cat settling down with his catch. Michael's mind went back to the Pike report nonsense.

"Amy, what sort of keys does a young woman carry around with her? This one was twenty-two years old. We only found one key, but it doesn't match her apartment."

His wife frowned and closed her book on her finger. This sort of question was never as nice as the English countryside, which was the only thing that interested her at the moment. She considered for a bit before asking, "I don't suppose she owned a car?"

Her husband shook his head.

"Maybe the key goes to her parent's house-"

"No family, we checked."

"Well, then, a friend's apartment, or maybe her office. Did she have a boyfriend?" It was more of a suggestion than a question, and while Riggs considered the habits of young people, his wife went back to Jane Austen's gentle humor. She got to the bottom of the page and glanced up. Michael was still frowning.

"The young woman is dead?" Amy asked.

Her husband nodded. "She jumped off a bridge last week."

Amy sighed. "And are you sure that the key is important?"

"Could be," Michael shrugged. "I just don't see how."

"Well, someone once said that a good investigator never dismisses a detail until he understands it."

"My brother said that." Michael smiled.

"And he was right." Amy shrugged. "So if something doesn't fit, you'll just have to find the explanation."

Michael rubbed his mustache and scowled at nothing.

Amy finished the page and turned it. "Of course, if you're really stuck," she said without looking up, "you could always ask—"

"I'm not stuck," Riggs objected miserably.

Amy looked at him over her book. "But it's not even your case, and you can't stop thinking about it."

Riggs frowned. "Even if I were stuck, I couldn't go to her."

"Hmm." Amy's gaze returned to her novel.

Riggs frowned at her. That wasn't her 'I'm-not-listening hmm,' it was definitely her "you're-being-stubborn hmm."

But Riggs wasn't being stubborn at all. In fact, he was being very accommodating. Riggs was accommodating Miss Baker even though he agreed with Inspector Fisher's conclusion; Roberta Pike had killed herself. And yet, there was no explanation for the key. And that wasn't the only thing. There was also Miss Baker herself, a smart woman who knew she didn't have any evidence, and yet she had come to him anyway. The chief would blow a gasket if he knew Riggs was wasting time following such a weak lead, but the key.

Riggs would talk to the dead girl's family—Margaret Baker said Pike had an uncle and a cousin. One way or another, he had to find out about that key. If he could just eliminate that detail, he would be able to drop the case for good, no matter what Miss Baker thought.

Amy shifted in her chair, and Michael remembered that Criminal was still in the kitchen with a mouse.

He stood up and stretched. "Well, I think I'll take out the trash before I forget."

Michael dropped the newspaper on his chair and strolled into the kitchen so he could deprive Criminal of his trophy. Fortunately, Amy was too engrossed in her book to notice him. Riggs carefully closed the kitchen door behind him.

Amy shuddered and turned the page. "Oh, I hate mice," she muttered.

Chapter Four: Uncle, Jacob Greenleaf

Michael Riggs got out of his 1949 brown Plymouth and looked up at the large house. With its covered wraparound porch and oversized gables, it was a perfect specimen of the style that had given this upscale neighborhood its name. An architect would have called the house a Queen Anne mansion, but as far as Inspector Riggs was concerned, it was an elaborate monstrosity.

Coming from an immigrant family of modest means, Riggs couldn't help but imagine the heating bill, let alone what his wife would say to the idea of cleaning all those rooms, even without the wall-to-wall carpeting. And the thought of painting the mansion's intricate facade almost made his shoulders ache. But that probably wasn't the way things worked in this neighborhood. So Riggs tried it again, and this time he imagined living in this mansion as a rich man instead of as a man on a policeman's salary; a housekeeper, a gardener, a handyman. He shook his head. It was still a monumental headache.

He walked up four wide steps and through the yard to the second set of stone steps that lead up to a wide covered porch. A polished brass plate on the door read, *Mr. Jacob Greenleaf*. Riggs touched the loose key in his pocket and mentally checked it against the keyhole on the front door, but it only took a glance to give him his answer. The key from the dead woman's pocket didn't match this lock, either. Riggs turned the old-fashioned bell so that it jingled on the other side of the wall. A moment later a disinterested woman in her late fifties wearing a gray dress and white apron opened the door.

She was holding a mop and she looked at Riggs as though he were just another chore. But as soon as she heard the words "inspector" and "Seattle Police," her eyebrows went up, and she quickly stepped aside.

"Come in, Sir. If you'll just wait here a minute, I'll go and see if Mr. Greenleaf is accepting visitors today." She started to walk away, but she stopped and turned back with a hopeful glint in her eyes. "Unless, of course, Mr. Greenleaf doesn't have a choice in the matter?"

Riggs wondered if there were a lot of housekeepers who would secretly enjoy having their employers harassed by the police. He decided there probably were. This particular woman seemed so agreeable to the idea it was almost a shame to disappoint her.

"I only want to ask him a couple questions," Riggs explained.

The crestfallen housekeeper nodded and left the room.

The large foyer was paneled in a dark wood, and the furniture was heavy and ornate. The room smelled of wood polish. A massive brass and crystal chandelier hung over his head. It wasn't Riggs's style, but there was a certain appeal to the decor. It had an old-world elegance. The woman returned, still carrying the mop.

"Mr. Greenleaf will see you, Inspector. This way."

Riggs followed her into a large, dark living room with tall ceilings. A crackling fire danced in a grand stone fireplace. In front of it sat an old man in a wheelchair. He was dressed in a gray house suit. A plaid wool blanket was draped over his lap, and his thin white hair was neatly combed. His pale skin looked like it had not seen sunshine for years, but his blue eyes and his expression were alert. He scrutinized the policeman's face.

"I'm Jacob Greenleaf. I assume you're here because of my poor niece, Roberta? But I already spoke to the other man, Inspector Fisher. I told him everything I know."

"Yes, Mr. Greenleaf. I'm sorry."

The old man nodded. "Why don't you sit down? Mrs. Lamar, would you ask Miss Sadie to make some coffee?"

The housekeeper nodded and left the room, taking her mop and her lingering hopes with her.

Riggs sat down on a massive velvet sofa. "Mr. Greenleaf, I realize you've already spoken to Inspector Fisher about this. I've read his report, and I don't like to bother you, but I was hoping you could just tell me a little bit more about your niece."

"What is it you want to know?"

Riggs leaned forward and rested his elbows on his knees. He could smell the old man's peppermint. "What sort of a girl was your niece?"

Mr. Greenleaf crossed his arms. "What can a man say, Inspector? My niece Roberta was as lovely and as charming a young woman as you could ever hope to know." He reached over and took a picture from the small table beside him. He glanced at it for a painful moment, then handed it to the inspector.

Riggs studied the portrait. "Yes, she was very pretty," he agreed.

"Roberta was my younger sister's child," the old man said. "My sister, Isabelle, was an angel from the ground up. She was the kindest and the most generous woman imaginable." He cleared his throat. "I made a couple of friends in the army–during the first war. Good men with families in business. While we were overseas, we came up with all sorts of plans and business schemes. I resented the war. By the time it was over, I was determined to catch up for the lost years, to really make something of myself. I couldn't bear the thought of coming back to my old life empty-handed. I settled in Chicago, and things started going well. Very well. My business grew, and my partners and I worked hard, year after year. We got into steel, transportation, and catalog shopping. I was the oldest child but I didn't feel a strong connection to my family, or maybe I was just too caught up with my own ventures. I sent money home, and I was happy to let Isabelle take care of our parents." A log snapped, and the old man looked at the fire. "But I never considered what Isabelle was giving up. Our brother, Paul, was supposed to be managing the finances. Every month I sent an allowance so Isabelle could take care of the house and look after our parents. In my mind, I was doing my duty, and I was happy to let Isabelle do the work."

Riggs nodded. "You were helping out."

"I was being a fool!" the old man snapped. "Paul squandered most of the money on himself. He gambled and womanized and he left poor Isabelle with practically nothing. But I was so obsessed with my own affairs I never even bothered to ask Isabelle how she was. Of course, she didn't know how rich I was, and she just made do with whatever Paul gave her. They lived in a little house on the east side, and all the time, my parents were getting older and weaker. That went on for years!"

"She never told you what your brother was doing?"

"She didn't know. Neither of us realized that Paul was a gambler, and Isabelle thought I was sending what I could; she never would have dreamed of complaining or asking for more. And all the time, I was practically rolling in money in Chicago while my own sister was pinching every penny to keep food on the table and the house warm. Of course, times were hard for most folks, and Isabelle was never one to complain. That's what I mean when I say my sister was a saint." He leaned back and closed his eyes for a few moments before continuing. "After being away for twenty years, I came home the last months before my parents died. I couldn't put it off any longer. But I tell you, Inspector, when I saw the state of things, I was shocked! Of course, I had it out with my brother. I disowned him entirely, and I never spoke to him again!"

"And your sister?"

"She forgave him, of course. Isabelle always forgave everyone. But it was only when I came back that I understood Isabelle's sacrifice. She had given up her best years to take care of our parents. I tried to make things right. I bought this house and moved the family here. Both my parents died within six months. And before I knew it, Isabelle had fallen in love with a man, Pike. He was a widower with one son, and he was as poor as a mouse. Maybe I should have objected to the marriage, but I just couldn't. Isabelle had never lived for herself, and I just wanted her to be happy."

Mr. Greenleaf took a deep breath and leaned back. "She was almost forty when she got married. Naturally, she didn't expect any children, but a year later, she was pregnant. She was so happy. Then her husband caught pneumonia that winter; he died just after Christmas, leaving poor Isabelle with a son from his first marriage and a baby girl."

"Roberta?"

The old man nodded.

Inspector Riggs lowered his voice, "It must have been very difficult for your sister."

"The shock almost killed her," the old man admitted. "And she never really recovered. Her health started to fail, but she carried on as best she could. She cared for that boy like he was her own son. And, of course, sweet little Roberta was the joy of her life." He sighed and shook his head sadly. "She died when Roberta was still a little girl."

The inspector waited while the old man took a deep breath. "I vowed to give little Roberta everything Isabelle would have wanted for her. I sent Roberta to the finest boarding school in New York. I spared no expense for her. She came home for Christmas, but she spent most of her summers touring Europe and the East Coast with her governesses. When she was old enough, I sent her to a proper finishing school in New England."

"A finishing school," the inspector repeated. He was pretty sure that it had something to do with etiquette and fancy stuff. He would have to ask Amy. Whatever it was, it didn't sound fun.

The old man smiled with pride. "You think that's an old-fashioned idea, don't you? But I'm an old-fashioned man. I believe a lady should be a lady, and I've never wanted to spare any expense, not where Roberta was concerned. She was a lady like the best of them."

Inspector Riggs took a cherry wood pipe out of his pocket and turned it over in his hands. "Did your niece enjoy her education?"

"Roberta loved every minute of it!" The old man beamed. "Her teachers and her governesses all adored her. I tell you, that girl never made an ounce of trouble for anyone. She was just as sweet as could be, like her mother. Last year, she finished school and, naturally, I wanted her to live here with me, but you know how girls are these days. They watch those motion pictures, and they think a young girl should have her own job and her own apartment. It's silly nonsense, of course, but girls nowadays want to feel independent. Oh, I tried to convince her that it was a waste of time. After all, I was prepared to give her a handsome allowance so she would have been very comfortable here. And I would have let her change the curtains, or whatever it was that she wanted to do."

"But she refused?"

"She said she wanted to make her own way in the world. Can you imagine? She even wanted to live in New York at first, but I put my foot down. She was too old for a governess, so I wanted her close. A girl needs some supervision, after all. But I finally allowed her to have her own apartment. I know it doesn't seem appropriate for a young woman to live alone, but she was so headstrong that I just couldn't say no to her. And I'll admit I was secretly proud of her determination. Besides, it was only a matter of time before she changed her mind. As soon as the thrill of independence faded, I knew my dear Roberta would decide to make her home here with me."

"So you weren't supporting her financially?"

"Not at all! The girl was determined to make good on her own. She wasn't afraid of hard work. I tell you, she was just like her mother, and everyone admired her for it."

The policeman considered his next words carefully. "But wasn't she occasionally..." He shrugged and rubbed the pipe on his trousers. "I mean, she must have occasionally needed a few extra dollars, just here and there?"

The old man smiled and said, "Well, Roberta was only twenty-two. I suppose she may have overspent her salary once or twice, or maybe she forgot to write down a withdrawal in her account book. Girls sometimes do, you know. But it wasn't anything serious, just a little bit now and then. If she'd any real financial problems, she would have come to me, but I wanted her to be comfortable."

There was a brief tap on the door, and a redhead came in with a tray of coffee.

"Oh, there you are, Sadie," the old man announced sternly. "I wondered what was taking you so long."

The woman regarded the visitor with mild curiosity, but her voice was controlled and even. "I'm sorry, Uncle, I didn't realize we had company. I'm afraid I was taking my time."

There were three cups on the tray.

"Well, no matter." The old man waved his hand. "But sit down and join us,

24

dear. This is Inspector Riggs of the Seattle Police. He came to ask us more questions about our dear Roberta."

The woman addressed the inspector. "I already told Inspector Fisher everything I know." She glanced at her uncle, smiled sadly, and sat down to pour the coffee.

"This is my brother's child," the old man explained without any particular enthusiasm. "Miss Sadie Greenleaf."

Sadie Greenleaf nodded, recited the customary 'how-do-you-do', and began pouring the coffee. She was older than Roberta had been, but it was difficult to fix her age. Riggs guessed she was somewhere in her early thirties. Her hair was intensely red. She wore black cat-eye glasses with small jewels on the outer tips. Her eyes were set wide, and her nose was so short it seemed as though it had been added to her face as an afterthought to prop up her glasses.

When she handed Riggs his coffee, he noticed that she was wearing an expensive gold wristwatch. Her demeanor was somber, but Riggs had the distinct impression of an actress playing a part. He wondered what part it was. While every other woman in town was wearing colorful clothes, Miss Sadie Greenleaf, who could afford nice clothing, was dressed in a plain dark brown skirt, a well-tailored dark green blouse, and a charcoal cardigan.

When she had finished pouring the coffee, she leaned back with her own cup. When her uncle looked at her, Miss Greenleaf was smiling and attentive, but as soon as his attention went back to Riggs, Sadie's expression changed. She was curious, and something else that Riggs couldn't identify.

Riggs glanced between the two of them. "Can you tell me who was close to Miss Pike?"

The old man lifted his chin. "She considered me a father figure. And she was extremely close to Sadie here." He pointed at his other niece. "Roberta was more than ten years younger than Sadie, but they were very close... almost like sisters."

He didn't look at Miss Greenleaf, and she made no sign of agreeing with him.

The old man continued, "And of course, there is Roberta's half-brother,

Eddie, her father's boy from his first marriage. But if you mean people outside the family...." He turned to his niece and pointed to a drawer in the end table. "Sadie, open that drawer, will you? There's a photograph Roberta gave me from the Art Exhibition in May."

Miss Greenleaf obliged, and a moment later, Riggs was gazing at a photograph of four people. Roberta Pike was easy enough to recognize; she was dressed in a fashionable silk dress with spaghetti-strap shoulders. Roberta was the sort of woman who knew how to flatter her curvaceous figure, and she had been lovely. Beside her was a man who must have been closer to forty. He was rugged and moody-looking, the sort of man some women find attractive; fair-haired with a strong jawline, broad shoulders, and dark, brooding eyes. Like Roberta, he was smiling at the camera, and his arm was wrapped around her waist.

"That was her beau," Mr. Greenleaf explained, pointing to the man. "Sylvester Finnegan is his name. Roberta told me he worked for the county, the building codes department, I think it was. But if you ask me, I think he was just a pencil pusher. No real ambition. I'm sure it was just a matter of time before Roberta realized she was too good for him."

"Was your niece very fond of him?"

Jacob Greenleaf chuckled. "I may be an old bachelor, but I'm not a complete fool! If you tell a young girl a fellow's no good, she'll turn right around and marry him just to prove you wrong. Roberta had a heart of gold, and she wanted to see the good in people."

Riggs thought about all the men he'd sent to jail while some loyal woman kept insisting that he was just a misunderstood soul who only needed love. But Roberta Pike didn't strike him as the rescuing type. And according to Miss Baker, Ruby Pike was no second fiddle or shy violet. If she was running around with a low-life like Sylvester Finnegan, chances were that was exactly what she intended to do.

Riggs looked back at the photograph. "And what about this other couple?"

Mr. Greenleaf pointed to the other woman. "That was her friend, Miss Ann Marie Lewis. She's a pretty little thing, isn't she? Not compared to Roberta, of course. No one was as pretty as Roberta. But Miss Lewis was charming in her own quiet way. I understand she has a small coffee shop on Eastlake."

Mr. Greenleaf pointed at the other man in the photograph and closed his eyes. "Let me see, what was that man's name?" He rubbed his fingers on the wheel of his chair as he tried to recall the information. "He's a banker; I remember that. Roberta said he works at Puget National Bank downtown. His name sounds something like 'Stale.' Was it 'Stark'...?

"His name is 'Steele,'" Sadie said.

"That's right," the old man snapped his fingers and nodded at his niece.

"And he works at Puget National Bank?" Riggs asked.

"That's right." The old man spoke, and Miss Greenleaf nodded.

"May I hold onto this photograph for a while?"

"If you think it will help you," Mr. Greenleaf agreed. "I have several lovely photographs of Roberta," he explained. "Dear Roberta always loved to have her photograph taken. I suppose she may have had a little streak of vanity. But what can you expect from such a pretty young lady? Besides, I'm sure she couldn't afford to go out very often on a secretary's salary; it must have been a real treat for her to have those little souvenirs."

Without looking directly, Riggs could see Sadie Greenleaf glaring at her uncle.

Riggs slipped the photograph into his coat pocket and asked, "Mr. Greenleaf, when was the last time you saw your niece alive?"

The old man frowned and cleared his throat. "Four days before she died." He whispered. "It was just an ordinary day like any other, but now I will never forget it." He dabbled his eyes with his handkerchief and cleared his throat again.

Riggs turned to Sadie Greenleaf. "Was that also the last time you saw your cousin, Miss Greenleaf?"

Sadie adjusted her glasses. "Yes."

"But Sadie, dear." her uncle turned to her. "You saw Roberta while you were out, didn't you?"

"What? On the night she died?" Sadie adjusted her glasses as she considered. "No, I'm afraid you're mixing up the days, Uncle Jacob. That night I stayed at home and read my book."

Her uncle furrowed his brow, and was about to say something else, but the door opened, and the housekeeper interrupted them. "I'm sorry, Mr. Greenleaf, but the doctor is here now for your check-up."

"Ah, yes. I hardly know why he bothers to keep an old man like me alive. There isn't much joy in living when I have to watch everyone I love die." He sighed. "You two will have to excuse me. I don't like to keep the doctor waiting. I hope that I've been some help to you, Inspector Riggs, but I doubt it. It was just a terrible accident, that's all." Jacob Greenleaf began rolling his chair towards the door, but Riggs stopped him.

"So you don't think your niece could have deliberately—"

"Certainly not!" the old man cut in sharply. He paused and took a deep breath. "Inspector, you must understand that Roberta was carefree and full of hope. She would fly to the moon before she would ever take her own life. Her death was nothing more than a tragic accident, and you can take my word for that." He waved to his housekeeper, and she wheeled him out of the room.

Chapter Five: Cousin, Sadie Greenleaf

After Mr. Greenleaf left the room, Riggs turned to Miss Greenleaf. She picked up a dish of hazelnuts and offered him some. When Riggs declined, Sadie took two of them, crushed them with the nutcracker, and popped them—one at a time—into her mouth. The crunch of her chewing joined the crackling of the fire.

"Miss Greenleaf, are you sure that you were at home on the night your cousin died?"

"Yes," she said with a nod. "And you shouldn't mind my uncle, Inspector. He's very old, you know, and…" She lowered her voice. "He gets confused about dates and things. He even mixes people up sometimes." She waved her hand in a lazy circle to indicate her uncle's unreliable mental process.

Inspector Riggs managed not to frown. "The last time you saw Roberta was…."

"On the 11th, four days before she died." Sadie smashed another nut. "Roberta came over to see Uncle Jacob. She never came here to see me."

"And was she her usual normal self that day?" Riggs asked.

"I never spent much time with Roberta." Sadie turned and looked out the window." How should I know what was 'normal' for her?"

Riggs rubbed his mustache. "But you do live here, too. Don't you?"

"I've lived here for twenty years." Sadie's voice had the note of a challenge. "Ever since my father died. I graduated from a public high school down the road. Now, I run the household, and I look after Uncle Jacob and make sure that he remembers to take his medicine." Her face suddenly relaxed. "Now, I'm the only family he has left."

"Roberta has a brother."

Sadie Greenleaf shrugged. "We don't see much of him. He works in his auto garage most of the time, but he does come by the house every now and then when Uncle Jacob needs him to fix something. Of course, Ruby never helped with anything."

Inspector Riggs set down his coffee and leaned back in his chair. His job usually required him to be tactful, but in this case, it seemed tact wasn't necessary. "Miss Greenleaf, were you and your cousin on good terms?"

Sadie glared at the inspector. "You might as well ask me if Roberta and I were on any sort of terms at all. The answer is no. There was nothing I could offer her. So as far as she was concerned, I didn't exist. Oh, she would say things to Uncle Jacob to make it *sound* like we were dear friends, but that was just for appearances, to maintain her perfect facade."

"Her facade?"

Sadie nodded. "Uncle Jacob adored Roberta, and she knew it. You heard how he talks about her; to him, Roberta was a saint. He practically worshiped the ground she walked on."

"But you didn't see her that way."

"What did she ever do that was 'saintly'?" Sadie demanded calmly. "Uncle Jacob gave her everything: the best presents, the best education, the best opportunities. He sent her to Europe. She never earned a thing for herself. In her whole worthless life, Roberta never did anything for anyone except herself."

Riggs finished his coffee and smoothed his mustache. "Miss Greenleaf, it doesn't sound as though you liked your cousin."

"Should I lie just because she's dead?" Sadie shrugged. "I don't see any point, do you? I'd have said the same thing before she died, if anyone had asked me." She refilled the cups and sipped her coffee. "Not to Uncle Jacob, of course; he never would have listened, anyway. But it was obvious: all Roberta wanted was to keep Uncle Jacob eating out of her hand."

"Why?"

Sadie Greenleaf scoffed. "For money, of course."

"Did Miss Pike ask your uncle for money?"

"Ask? Roberta never had to *ask* Uncle Jacob for anything." Sadie huffed. "No, she was 'too proud' for that. Too saintly. But Roberta didn't have to ask. All she ever had to do was hint that she wanted something, and my uncle would slip cash into her handbag. And she certainly wasn't too proud to accept gifts from her adoring uncle! Uncle Jacob is so absorbed in his own guilt about the past that he never could see Roberta for who she really was—a spoiled girl who only cared about herself."

Riggs softened his voice. "Miss Greenleaf, if your uncle treated Roberta so well, why didn't she live here?"

Sadie shook her head. "Because she didn't want Uncle Jacob's benevolent oversight. She went on and on about her precious independence, but what she really wanted was her own job, her own apartment, and her own life." Sadie scowled at the fireplace. "She always had to have excitement. She was too good to sit around here, keeping an old man company."

That's exactly what you do. Riggs thought to himself.

"Uncle Jacob fixed up an apartment for Roberta," Sadie continued. "I had to help him arrange everything, of course, but he paid for it all. The only thing Roberta had to do was earn enough cash to buy her dresses. I'm sure she got men to pay for her cocktails. And as long as Uncle Jacob believed she was a saint, Roberta would get a fat inheritance. She hid who she really was; a boozy floozy running around with low-life men. Believe me, Inspector, my cousin was no angel."

Riggs nodded and made a sound that he hoped sounded like an agreement. "She was so good at deceiving your uncle, how did you learn the truth?"

Sadie smiled triumphantly. "Because Roberta wasn't the only one with a key to the boat."

Riggs tapped his coffee cup. "What boat?"

Fisher's report had not said anything about a boat.

"It's a beautiful thirty-foot sailboat," Sadie said. "It's been moored in the Eastlake Marina for years. Of course, but Uncle Jacob hasn't been able to sail it in ten years, not since he started losing the strength in his legs. A couple years ago, he decided to sell it, but then Roberta started going on about how pretty it was and how she'd always dreamed of a boat. So, he kept it for her, and as soon as she moved out here, he paid for her to have sailing lessons and he gave her a key to the marina." She leaned forward and whispered. "But, I have a key, too. And I've stopped by the marina, and I've seen the state of things in that cabin."

"What sort of things?"

Miss Greenleaf shrugged. "Empty liquor bottles, cuff links, men's ties. My darling little cousin was no saint. And I'm sure that wasn't the worst of it. She probably took dope too."

"Did you see drugs?"

Sadie shook her head. "I don't know what dope even looks like." She frowned. "But I don't think anything was too low for Roberta."

"And now, unfortunately, she's dead."

Sadie Greenleaf gave a short laugh. "Yes, now Roberta is dead." She looked down at her coffee cup, and her forehead suddenly relaxed. "You know, that was probably the first thing in her entire life that didn't go her way."

Riggs frowned. "But it's a significant thing, Miss Greenleaf."

He found Miss Greenleaf's obvious disdain for her cousin both appalling and enlightening. And even though he disliked Miss Greenleaf more and more by the minute, he wanted her to keep talking. Miss Greenleaf paused for a moment; then she seemed to remember something.

"Inspector, there was a woman here last week, a friend of Roberta's...."

"Do you mean Miss Baker?"

Sadie's eyes brightened. "Yes, yes, that was her name, Miss Baker. She came to give her condolences, and she went on and on about how wonderful and friendly Roberta had been. But just before she left, she asked me something funny, and it keeps replaying in my mind."

"And what did she ask?"

Sadie lowered her voice to almost a whisper. "She asked if I believed Roberta jumped."

Inspector Riggs watched her face. "And what did you say, Miss Greenleaf?"

Sadie Greenleaf didn't respond at first. She touched the edge of her glasses and pulled a wisp of her red hair behind her ear. Then she leaned back in her chair and said, "I read the newspapers, Inspector. And they think Roberta did herself in. Suicide. And that's what the policeman said. Uncle Jacob doesn't believe it, but of course, he wouldn't believe Roberta capable of that, no matter how obvious it was."

"But what do you think, Miss Greenleaf?"

Sadie bit her lip for a moment and turned her attention back to the inspector. "Somehow, I just…I guess I don't really believe it either." She stared at him. "I hated the way Roberta pretended to love my uncle when the only person she loved was herself. But I guess that's why I just can't make myself believe Roberta would commit suicide."

"Why, exactly?"

Sadie huffed but didn't answer at first.

Riggs waited for several moments, then he suggested, "She had money problems…"

Sadie laughed. "Never! Uncle Jacob would have bailed her out of anything!"

"She quarreled with her boyfriend, and he called it off," Riggs said.

"Did he say he was her boyfriend?" Sadie shook her head. "I don't think Sylvester Finnegan was anything special to her. And I guess that's the part that bothers me about Miss Baker's question…."

"What do you mean?"

"Well, if Roberta didn't jump off that bridge, then that means someone must have pushed her. Maybe Sylvester or maybe someone else." Sadie's expression contorted as she sorted through her thoughts. "My cousin was a liar and a cheat, but everyone adored her anyway. It's scary to imagine that someone murdered Roberta, but at the same time, it's comforting to know I'm not the only one who hated her."

Chapter Six: Boyfriend, Sylvester Finnegan

From his office, Sylvester Finnegan walked along 4th Avenue until he came to Rosie's Corner Diner. Most of the customers were the typical lunchtime crowd, gathered into the window booths so they could enjoy the view of the sidewalk. Finnegan walked past them and sat on an isolated stool near the back of the sandwich counter.

When the waitress, Darlene, came over, Sylvester ordered the daily special without asking what it was. Darlene knew her regulars well enough to raise an eyebrow, but he didn't notice. While she was repeating the order to the cook when another man came in and headed back to the telephone. Darlene gave Sylvester the meatloaf special. He took it without looking at her. She leaned against the counter.

"Hey, Sylvester," she lowered her voice, "you doing all right?"

Sylvester Finnegan glared at her. "Course I'm alright," he snapped. "What kind of a question is that?"

Darlene shrugged and wiped a drop of coffee off the bar. "It doesn't have to mean anything. You just never talk to anybody anymore. You used to chatter up a storm. I thought maybe you had something on your mind."

Sylvester grumbled, "Why the hell should I talk to people if I don't want to? It's my lunch break, after all. Maybe I just want some peace and quiet."

He returned to his sulking and started eating his mashed potatoes. Darlene set the salt and pepper in front of him, and he grabbed the salt without saying a word.

As she walked away, she grumbled, "It's always the same with the good-looking ones. Think they're too important for manners." She glanced back at him and shook her head. "Well, I'd take my Billy over a fellow like him any day. A handsome cad is nothing next to a plain good man. " Darlene smiled and moved on to her happier customers.

Sylvester kept his handsome face downward except when he had to raise his head to down another slug of coffee. The man at the telephone must have used up his nickel because he took off his hat, sat down two stools over, and muttered something congenial about it being lunchtime.

Sylvester ignored the man and the remark, but the man didn't seem to notice. After half a minute of reading the menu, he leaned toward Sylvester and asked, "Hey pal, you don't happen to know what's better here, the roast beef sandwich or the pastrami?"

Sylvester scowled at the stranger. "Look, buddy, I'm sitting here to avoid company. You see that social crowd at the other end of the diner?" He pointed with his fork. "Why don't you go bother them?" He turned back to his plate and forked his next bite.

The man didn't move but he didn't speak either, and for a few moments, the problem seemed to be resolved. But a few minutes later, the man laid his menu on the counter and announced in Sylvester's general direction, "Well, I think I'll go with the Reuben. It's hard to go wrong with a good old-fashioned Reuben, don't you think?"

Sylvester didn't even bother to turn his head or swallow his potatoes before saying, "See here, Mister, you can have all three sandwiches, and you can pour hot coffee in your lap, too. I don't care, but I sure as hell don't want to pass the time of day with you."

The man moved his gray fedora to the stool right between them and ran his fingers through his hair. "I don't really want to discuss sandwiches either." His voice was quiet but authoritative. "But I would like to talk to you about your late girlfriend, Roberta Pike."

Sylvester stopped chewing and turned his head toward the stranger. He scowled. "Who are you? Police?"

The man nodded. "I'm Sergeant Inspector Riggs."

"I've already talked to the police," Sylvester informed him. "And aren't you supposed to show me a badge or something?"

"If you'd like," the inspector acknowledged.

Sylvester thought for a moment, then he shrugged and went back to eating his lunch. "There's no point anyway. I already talked to the other guy, and I don't have anything new to say, not to you or to anyone else. Ruby's dead. It's a shame, sure. But I didn't have anything to do with it."

"So I understand," the inspector said.

Sylvester Finnegan cut his meatloaf with the side of his fork. "So there's not much point in us getting acquainted."

Darlene came over and addressed the newcomer. "And what can I get for you, sir?"

"I'd like a cup of coffee and a Reuben sandwich with extra kraut, please," Riggs said.

"Oh, a gentleman," Darlene exclaimed with an approving wink. "It's so nice to have customers who haven't forgotten how to use manners." She gave a sideways glare to Sylvester, but he missed it. "I'll get that sandwich started for you right away, Mister. And I'll be right back with your coffee."

As soon as she was out of earshot, Riggs resumed. "Mr. Finnegan, maybe you could tell me about the last time you saw Ruby?"

"Nothing to tell." Sylvester swallowed hard. "Ruby was drunk."

"What else?"

"We were at the Blue Bay Tavern. It's by the University Bridge on Eastlake. We were having a good night until Ruby had too much and got in one of her moods. She stormed out, and I let her go."

Darlene returned to hand Riggs his coffee. After she left, Riggs asked, "How long had you been dating Roberta Pike?"

Sylvester huffed and shook his head. "Look, me and Ruby weren't exactly 'dating.' We were just seeing each other now and then. It was casual. Sometimes she'd be a pill, and we'd call it off. But Ruby knew how to have a good time, and she was a good-looking woman. So I'd forget what a pain she was, and we'd go out again."

Riggs raised his eyebrow. "How long had you known her?"

Sylvester gulped down a bite of meatloaf. "I met her at the Blue Bay Tavern about ten months ago. She said she was new in town, and I bought her a beer. By the end of the night, she gave me her telephone number, Eastlake 243."

Riggs poured some milk in his coffee. "What did you argue about that night?"

"I don't know," Sylvester groaned. "Ruby was short on cash, as usual, and she had some crazy scheme to raise some easy dough. She was excited. It was something to do with her friend, Ann Marie."

"What was the plan?"

"I told you, I don't know! Ruby was always inventing crazy stupid plans. Something with her friend, or she was going to be able to use her friend to pull it off. Ah, I don't know; I don't listen to that sort of junk. I'd already had a couple beers, and I wasn't paying attention. I told her if she was hard up for cash, she should just go ask her rich uncle."

"Is that when she left?"

"Yeah, I guess so. Maybe. She told me I could go to hell, and she grabbed her handbag and left." He looked down and whispered, "I never saw her after that."

"You stayed in the bar?"

Sylvester leered at Riggs. "I said so, didn't I? I ordered another beer if you want to know. And another one after that, and if you don't believe me, you can go ask the bartender 'cause he was there all night. He can tell you that I stayed 'til closing. So I couldn't possibly have killed Ruby Pike."

Riggs sipped his coffee. "The newspaper reported that Roberta Pike committed suicide."

"Then why are you pestering me?" Sylvester demanded. "I'm not stupid."

"No one has accused you of murder, Mr. Finnegan. And it's easy to answer a few questions. "

Sylvester Finnegan turned angrily back to his lunch and chewed hard. Between mouthfuls, he eventually muttered, "Well, I know how you cops are. You pick a guy and go after him, whether he's guilty or not. I wasn't Ruby's only…. Did you ever consider that there could be another man?"

Inspector Riggs ignored the bait, and a few seconds later, Sylvester whispered through gritted teeth, "Damn it, you don't know what she was like!"

"No. I don't," Riggs agreed, "but I'm listening."

Sylvester pushed his plate away. "Ruby played games with people, dangerous games. She was no good. I don't mean she wasn't pretty; she was beautiful, and she had class. She was charming and elegant, and she could control a room. And it wasn't just an act; her family has money. She went to fancy schools and traveled around Europe and everything. But she had a mean streak; she liked to mess with other people's lives." Sylvester Finnegan stood up and laid some money on the counter. Then he turned to the policeman. "Ruby did whatever she wanted, and she always got away with it."

Riggs kept sitting, but he pulled the photograph from his pocket. He set it on the counter.

Sylvester glanced down at the black and white photograph. "Yeah, that's me and Ruby. So what? She must have had dozens of stupid souvenir photographs, six from every bar and nightclub in town, fifty cents a pop, and they're not all with me, either."

"But this one is," Riggs said. "Do you remember when this was taken?"

"It was in June, no, May. The art exhibit on Memorial Day weekend. Ruby's uncle was one of the sponsors, so she had free tickets."

"Who are these other people?"

"The guy is a banker, Bruce something or other. I don't really know or care. And that girl was Ruby's friend, Ann Marie. She works in a coffee shop off Eastlake Avenue."

"Thank you, Mr. Finnegan."

Sylvester grabbed his hat off the bar and was just about to go when the inspector added, "Oh, one last thing, Mr. Finnegan. This key was found in Ruby's pocket, but it doesn't match her apartment. Do you happen to know what it goes to?"

Sylvester barely glanced at the key.

"I have no idea. It sure as hell doesn't go to my apartment, if that's what you're wondering. I'd never give a dame a key to my place, not even Ruby. Maybe it goes to the marina. She had a boat, you know." And with that remark, Sylvester Finnegan put on his hat and left the diner.

Michael Riggs slipped the key and the photograph back into his pocket before giving his full attention to his Reuben sandwich. Of course, he knew the key didn't match Sylvester's apartment because he'd already tried it.

Chapter Seven: Half-Brother and Former Friend

Riggs headed north and crossed the bridge until he arrived in the neighborhood of Fremont. It was a quiet residential area with neat bungalows on tree-lined streets. The neighborhood's main street was a modest cluster of small shops and restaurants.

Riggs traveled east until he found Pike's Garage. It was a modest establishment with four garage bays, an office on one end, and a little table out front with an umbrella and some chairs. Above the garage was a small second-story apartment which, according to the police report, was where the proprietor lived. It certainly wasn't a grand establishment, but it had a fresh coat of paint, clean windows, and a neatly trimmed rhododendron hedge on each side.

Riggs got out of his old brown Plymouth and walked up to the only mechanic who was still at the garage during the lunch hour. The young man was wearing blue coveralls and a matching hat. He wiped down the oil cap of a Kaiser Darrin before securing it back in place.

"Hello there," Riggs called out. "I'm looking for Edward Pike."

"Call me Eddie," the man said as he wiped a smudge of grease off of his hand, "everyone does." and held it out to the newcomer. Pike was a good-looking man, about thirty years old, with a solid jawline and a tall frame. His dark hair was trimmed but it didn't have any hair treatment in it. And although it was obvious that the young man owned a razor, he apparently didn't use it daily.

The two men shook, and the mechanic nodded his head in the direction of Riggs's car. "1949 was a good year for Plymouth. Is that one giving you trouble?"

"Nope. It's a good car." The policeman shook his head. "My name's Riggs. Inspector Riggs, of the Seattle Police. I'm investigating your sister's death."

Eddie frowned and stuffed the rag into his pocket. "Police?" He rubbed the back of his neck. "But they already—oh well, I'm not busy at the moment. Come inside."

He led Riggs into a little office. The furniture was worn but sturdy. The plain white walls were decorated with Mr. Pike's personal effects. There was a bowlers' league certificate and three, no four, photographs of a bowling team smiling happily in their matching shirts. On a small shelf behind the desk were two bowling trophies. A framed certificate from the Automakers of America recognizing Mr. Edward Pike as a qualified mechanic. Another certificate showed that Edward Pike had been a mechanic for the U.S. Army.

"Is this your garage?"

Eddie indicated an empty chair for the visitor. "Yep, as long as I keep up the mortgage payments, this is my place." He smiled proudly.

Riggs nodded approvingly and sat down. "Have you had it long?"

"Almost eight years," Eddie answered as he sat down. "I always wanted to have my own garage, ever since I was a kid. I just like the idea of being my own boss. I started saving up when I was sixteen. Even during The War, I saved every cent I could. When I had enough saved up, I got a loan for the rest and I bought this place. It had been vacant during the war, so it was in pretty sorry shape when I got it, but the price was right. And it's given me a hobby outside of work; when I'm not fixing cars, I'm fixing the garage." He grinned.

The inspector nodded. Coming from a working-class family, he respected the young man's approach to hard work and patience.

"I'm sorry to bother you," Riggs began tactfully, "but I'm hoping you can tell me a few things about Miss Pike."

"I suppose you already know what I told the other guy, Fisher?" Eddie asked. He waited for Riggs to nod before continuing. "Then I don't understand what else you want to know."

"I'd like to know what your sister was like."

Eddie's brow furrowed. For a moment, he seemed bothered, maybe even distressed. Finally, he took a deep breath and sighed. "I'm afraid I don't really know, Inspector."

Riggs waited.

The young man let his shoulders relax. "You see, Roberta was only my half-sister. My father died when I was twelve, and Roberta was just a kid. Roberta's mother, my step-mother, sent me to a boarding school in San Francisco—that's where my father was from, and his sister and father still lived there, so I was near his family. She didn't know anything about raising boys, and I think she wanted me to be close to my own people. It was great for me, but I didn't see much of Roberta. A few years later, my stepmother died, and after that, I only saw Roberta during the Christmas holidays. As soon as I was old enough, I joined the Army, and then I didn't see her or Uncle Jacob for some years."

"But you saw her after her schooling? I understand she moved out here last year."

"I've seen her twice," Eddie nodded. "Once at Uncle Jacob's house, when I was there fixing a leak in the bathroom sink. And I saw her another time when she came by here to drop off Uncle Jacob's Studebaker for a tune-up."

Riggs chose his words carefully. "That's not very often."

"We weren't close." Eddie shrugged. "I invited her to come bowling or to go to the cinema a few times, but she always had other plans."

"But she was your nearest relative?"

"Going by blood, she was my only relative," the young man said. "My aunt died during the war. Now, all I've got left is Uncle Jacob, and he's not my real uncle, Roberta's cousin, Sadie."

"Did you and Roberta get along?"

"We got along about as well as any two people who don't know each other. We didn't have any conflicts, if that's what you mean. She smiled at me, called me Edward, and gave me a kiss on my cheek when she saw me. But somehow…"

Riggs waited a few seconds and asked, "Somehow what?"

Eddie rubbed the back of his neck and frowned. "I guess I never really knew what she thought of me. I don't know if she had any real affection for me or if she was doing what was expected. Does that make sense?"

"Very much," the inspector nodded.

"It never used to bother me, but now that she's gone, I feel like a jerk," Eddie confessed. "I could have done more. When she moved out here, I was glad, but I thought there would be time to get to know each other. I didn't want to rush it. I offered to help her find an apartment and get settled, but she said Uncle Jacob had taken care of everything. In fact, I didn't even know where she was working until..." He gazed out the window and took a deep breath. "...until I read about her death in the newspaper."

"What about your uncle and your cousin, Miss Greenleaf? Are you close to them?"

"I wouldn't call it 'close,' but we're on good terms. Uncle Jacob invites me over for Thanksgiving, and three or four more times a year, they telephone me when they need something done around the house or when one of his cars needs an oil change. Uncle Jacob always pays me when I work for him; he's a fair man."

"Do you know how they felt about your sister?"

Eddie Pike smiled. "Uncle Jacob was totally devoted to Roberta. As far as I can tell, he adored my stepmother—she was his younger sister—Isabelle. I'm no head doctor, but from the way Uncle Jacob acted, I have the impression he felt guilty about something. When she died, I'd say he spoiled Roberta to make up for it."

"How did he treat you and Miss Greenleaf?"

"I'm not blood," Eddie said as he shook his head. "And don't get me wrong; he's always been decent to me. He always insisted that I call him 'uncle,' but that was for his sister's sake. But with Sadie, it's different. She's his real niece, just like Roberta was, but he never treated them the same." Eddie furrowed his brow. "Uncle Jacob is good to her, but Sadie was his brother's kid, and I don't think he got on with his brother."

"It's not fair to Miss Greenleaf," Riggs said.

Eddie shrugged in agreement. "As far as Jacob Greenleaf was concerned, the sun practically rose and set around Roberta. I don't think he ever thought much about Sadie."

"According to Fisher's report, you were out on the night your sister died."

"I was bowling with my friends." Eddie nodded. "We have a league at the Ballard Lanes. Normally, I'm home by ten, but that night was Charlie's birthday, and we stayed out later than usual. I didn't get home until just after midnight."

A little red Crosley pulled up to the garage, and Eddie glanced up. "It looks like I've got a customer." Eddie stood up. "I'll only be a minute or two."

Riggs turned to see an attractive young woman getting out of the car. Eddie Pike left the office door open and headed out to meet the woman. She was about twenty-five, average height, and she wore a pale green blouse with white polka dots, blue cigarette pants, and penny loafers. Her dark blonde hair was pulled back into a ponytail. She had poise. Riggs was just thinking that she looked like the sort of woman who could pull off a pair of overalls as well as a cocktail dress when he suddenly realized that he'd already seen her in a cocktail dress. He was looking at the other woman in the photograph. This was the woman who Jacob Greenleaf and Sylvester Finnegan had identified as Ruby's friend, Ann Marie.

Inspector Riggs pulled the photograph out of his pocket. He moved to the chair that was nearest the open door. He could overhear Eddie Pike introducing himself and asking how he could help the woman with her Crosley.

"I'm sorry," the inspector heard the woman reply, "it's not the car. It's just that—well, you see, I was a friend of Ruby's...." There was a pause, and the woman's voice resumed, "I only just read about it in the newspapers yesterday, you see. I didn't know what happened. And I wanted—well, I know you're her brother, and I...I wanted to tell you how sorry I am."

There was a short pause before Eddie said, "Thank you, Miss... "

"Lewis. My name is Ann Marie Lewis."

"You're Roberta's friend with the coffee shop on...Capitol Hill, isn't it?"

The woman smiled, and her face lit up. "Not quite. It's right off Eastlake

Avenue and Pine."

"Roberta mentioned you." Eddie cleared his throat. "I'm sorry we didn't meet before. I didn't know any of Roberta's friends."

"Nobody really does nowadays. I mean, everybody seems to have so many friends that it's almost impossible to keep track of anyone else's." Ann Marie swept a lock of hair behind her ear. "Anyway, I don't suppose Ruby would have mentioned me. We hadn't seen much of each other lately."

Eddie cleared his throat. "I hadn't seen Ruby for almost three months."

"Oh."

The woman seemed surprised—or maybe she was relieved. Riggs stood up and grabbed his hat. As he approached them, he could see that Ann Marie had small, neat features, brown eyes, and a small scar near her left ear. If she was wearing any makeup, Riggs couldn't see it.

"Miss Lewis?"

Ann Marie lowered her eyebrows at him. "Do I know you?"

Riggs touched the brim of his hat. "Inspector Riggs of the Seattle Police. I'm just tying up some loose ends regarding Miss Pike's death." He reached in his pocket and handed her the photograph, adding, "I'm sorry for interrupting, but I recognized you from your picture."

"I see." Ann Marie glanced down at the photograph. "That was taken at the opening of the new art exhibit at the end of May."

"Could you please tell me about the other people in this photograph?"

"Well, the man next to Ruby is—or was, her boyfriend, Sylvester Finnegan."

"Do you know him well?"

She shrugged. "Well enough to dislike him."

"Why?"

"There wasn't much to like." She took a deep breath. "He could be nice enough when he wanted to, but he wasn't sincere about it. And whenever he got drunk, he was moody and temperamental and even downright mean. Sure, he was good-looking and he had a job, but that's not enough, is it? I mean, if someone isn't a nice person, what else is there? And Sylvester was the sort of man who would do something awful and then blame the other person."

"But he was Miss Pike's boyfriend?"

Ann Marie stopped, and an expression passed over her face. Then it was gone, and she nodded.

"Did you ever tell Miss Pike what you thought of her boyfriend?"

Ann Marie glanced over to Eddie and then back to Riggs. "I told her that Sylvester was no good. Any woman would be better off alone than being with a man like him."

"How did she take it?"

"Ruby? Oh, she just laughed and said Sylvester was fun, but she wasn't going to marry him."

"I see." Riggs glanced down at the photo. "And what about the other man?"

Again, that strange expression passed over Ann Marie's face. "His name is Bruce Steele." Ann Marie said. "He works at Puget National Bank."

"Are you friends with him?"

"No."

"Do you remember the last time you saw Ruby?"

"That was it," Ann Marie said, pointing to the photograph. "The art exhibit in May."

Riggs was slightly surprised. "That exact night?"

"Well, more specifically, the next morning was the last time I saw her." Ann Marie absently touched her ear, then she took a deep breath and announced, "Ruby and I had a falling out the morning after this photograph was taken. We didn't see each other after that."

"I see," Riggs replied. "Do you mind telling me what the argument was about?"

Ann Marie shot a brief glance toward Eddie. "As a matter of fact, I do. It was strictly personal." Ann Marie looked at him with a calm determination.

Riggs softened his voice. "I appreciate that it's personal, Miss Lewis. But I'm trying to solidly rule out the possibility of any irregularities in regards to your late friend's death. Any detail could be important."

"Irregularities?" Eddie repeated. "What do you mean by that?"

"I want to establish the exact circumstances surrounding Miss Pike's accident." They both stared at him, and Riggs added, "Specifically, I want to establish that her death definitely was an accident."

"You're suggesting that Ruby was murdered?" Ann Marie said.

"I'm not suggesting it, but I am trying to rule it out."

"I see." Ann Marie turned pale. "Our falling out had nothing to do with Ruby's death," Ann Marie insisted. "It was between us, and it was entirely personal."

Riggs pulled out his business card and handed it to her. "I hope you're right, Miss Lewis. Please let me know if you change your mind."

She handed the photograph back to him. Riggs glanced at the black and white image. Ann Marie, with her brown hair, wearing a simple short-sleeved dress, and beside her, Roberta, fair and gorgeous in a fitted cocktail dress that followed her every curve. It had thin spaghetti straps, and she had a wrap draped over one arm.

"Oh, Miss Lewis," Riggs said, glancing back up at her. "You don't happen to remember what color Roberta's dress was, do you?"

Ann Marie grimaced. Then she frowned slightly and took a deep breath. Her face was relaxed. "It was yellow."

"Are you sure?"

She nodded. "Lemon yellow. Yes, I'm positive."

Chapter Eight: The Heartbroken Landlady

No evidence of murder.

Riggs hung his hat on the stand and stared at his desk. No indication of foul play. And yet, Riggs still couldn't prove that Margaret Baker was wrong. Roberta Pike had been drinking at the Blue Moon Tavern the night she died. Of course, the most likely solution was that, in her inebriated state, had deliberately jumped—or mistakenly fallen—off that bridge. Suicide or accident. No foul play. And that was precisely what Fisher had concluded. That's what the report said. Verdict: suicide or accident. Case: closed.

Riggs sat down. And Pike's case would still be closed if Miss Baker hadn't appeared at his office on Monday, insisting, without an ounce of proof, that her friend had been murdered.

And like the soft, sentimental sap he apparently was, Michael Riggs had started snooping. Michael Riggs opened up a closed file, and he started poking around, asking questions and stirring up trouble. And if the chief found out, it would be his neck. Riggs was good at his job, he was a solid detective, but he wasn't so good that the chief would overlook his mistakes.

Michael Riggs was on thin ice. The file was on his desk. And he tried to busy himself by writing out his other reports.

And yet, there was something about Pike's death that wasn't explained: the key. That single key that didn't belong to her apartment, her best friend, or her boyfriend. He could take it back to Jacob Greenleaf, but if he met with her family again and it got back to the chief…. No, he couldn't change it. But he could take it to the marina. It would fit the gate, and the problem would be solved. The case was closed, officially, but he wouldn't need a search warrant just to slip a key in a lock.

"You've got to let it go," Fisher said when Riggs brought it up again. But Riggs insisted, and Inspector Fisher finally agreed—off the record—to accompany Riggs to Ruby's apartment. And as they walked, Fisher explained that Miss Pike's landlady, Mrs. Mooney, was a widow who had looked after the apartments since her husband died in the war.

201 East Louisa Street was only a block off Eastlake. It was in a charming residential neighborhood, on the east side of Lake Union and about a mile north of downtown. There were small houses, two-story apartment buildings, and bungalows, most of which had at least a modest view of the lake. Number 201 was a collection of six tiny, attached bungalows wrapped like a "U" around a trim little green lawn and lavish flowerbeds. The houses were brick, small, and orderly.

Riggs stopped and looked at the property from the sidewalk. With the grassy courtyard in front of him, there were two units on the left, two directly across from him, and two more on the right. It was like a miniature village with six cottages wrapped around a common green. The windows and shutters were white, and each of the six front doors was painted bright green. A letter by each door labeled the apartment, A through F.

Fisher pointed slightly to the left. "Apartment C; that was Pike's."

"And where does Mrs. Mooney live?"

"Her apartment is E," Fisher said, "but the lady herself seems to be in the rhododendrons." He lowered his voice and added, "She acts in the community theater group."

Riggs looked to the right and saw an ample behind, covered in a faded floral print, protruding from a rhododendron bush.

Fisher cleared his throat as the men approached. "Excuse me, Mrs. Mooney?"

The bottom swayed from side to side as the owner reversed herself out from under the bush. Once she was out, Mrs. Mooney set down her trowel, stood up with a stretch, and removed her dirty gardening gloves.

"Oh, Inspector Fisher, isn't it?" she asked with some surprise. She was short, plump, and somewhere in her mid-fifties. Her graying hair was in a messy bun, and she wasn't wearing any makeup. She seemed more amused than annoyed at seeing the policeman again. "You're lucky to have caught me at home," she informed him happily. "In another hour, I'll be off to the theater. We're rehearsing our new play, 'Murder Will Out.' It's written by a Canadian playwright, Tschannen. She's very talented."

"Sounds interesting." Fisher smiled. "May I introduce Sergeant Inspector Riggs? Inspector Riggs, this is Mrs. Mooney."

The woman looked Riggs up and down with blatant admiration. "I suppose you want to see the poor girl's apartment?"

"Yes, I would."

Mrs. Mooney smiled. "You have a voice like Gary Cooper," she nodded. "It goes very well with your dark mustache."

Riggs blushed and smoothed his mustache. "Mrs. Mooney, I wonder if I could ask you a few questions first?"

"Yes, of course." Mrs. Mooney nodded. She led them over to a wooden bench and some chairs that were arranged nearby. She sat down, and the men did the same.

"Now, what would you gentlemen like to ask me?" the widow asked.

"I want to know if you liked Miss Pike—personally, I mean."

Mrs. Mooney seemed slightly taken back. She frowned. "My mother always said it was unlucky to speak ill of the dead, Inspector Riggs."

Riggs leaned forward and lowered his voice. "It could be important."

Mrs. Mooney reconsidered. "Well, since this is official?"

"Of course," Riggs assured her. "And it's your civic duty."

Mrs. Mooney raised her chin and announced. "Well, in that case: I thought Miss Pike was a sneak and a thief, and I didn't like her at all."

Fisher's jaw dropped. "What? Why didn't you say that before?"

"Because it's wrong to speak ill of the dead," she repeated. "And besides, you never asked me what I thought of her."

The junior inspector blushed.

Riggs leaned forward. "Please, Mrs. Mooney, tell us everything you can."

"Well, at first, she seemed like such a nice, sweet, young thing. She told me how she was new in town, and her uncle wrote me a nice letter about her, and he paid her rent in advance, so I didn't expect any financial problems."

"Her uncle paid her rent?" Riggs repeated.

"Only at first," Mrs. Mooney explained. "He was helping her to get settled in her new life. After Miss Pike came and had a look at the place, he sent over a check for a nice big deposit and the first four months' rent. I should have realized that a girl on her own couldn't afford the rent on a secretary's salary; most young girls have to share apartments, you know. And Miss Pike wasn't even working yet. But it all happened so quickly. And with her uncle helping her out, I just assumed it must be all right. The first several months were fine, but then things began to go badly."

"In what way?"

"Well, after the first four months, Miss Pike was always late with her rent every month. And on Saturday nights, she would come home very late. Of course, we're hardly in the Victorian age, and I'm not one to judge a fellow woman. It's not easy for a girl these days, and I know it. But she was so noisy, she could have woken the devil himself! Now I'm not saying it's not a crime to enjoy a cocktail every now and then. But when Miss Pike comes home singing and making a ruckus at four o'clock in the morning, drunk as a sailor and swearing like one too, the rest of the tenants are bound to get upset! This isn't that kind of a neighborhood, you know. Down in Pioneer Square, things get a bit rowdy at night, but this is a quiet neighborhood, and folks around here expect their neighbors to be civilized."

"And then there were little things," Mrs. Mooney went on. "Sometimes, Miss Pike played her radio so loudly that no one else could think straight. And when any of the neighbors complained, she would apologize so sweetly and bat her pretty eyelashes to high heaven until everything was forgiven. But twenty minutes later, what do you think? She'd have her radio up again just as loud as you please!"

"Inconsiderate," Riggs agreed. "And what about her being a thief?"

"I'm coming to that," the landlady informed him. Mrs. Mooney was not one to be rushed through a good story, especially a story that she'd been asked to tell. "So then, Miss Pike starts bringing her friends over, and they were certainly a mixed bunch! Some of them were nice, but a couple of the girls talked like dance-hall floozies, and I don't mean the nice dance halls," she added significantly. "And most of the fellas talked like thugs and used rough language, even in front of Miss Pike!

"But, like I say, I'm no angel myself. So I'm not one to judge, normally. 'Judge not lest ye be judged,' I always say. But Miss Pike and her friends were downright offensive. They were drunk most nights and noisy. Well, as you can imagine, that Pike girl was a general nuisance to the neighbors. I kept telling her she'd have to be more considerate. I was afraid she'd drive away my nicer tenants. Then, it happened!"

Mrs. Mooney closed her eyes, and a pained expression contorted her face. When she opened her eyes again, she had to blink away some tears. She took a deep breath and patted her chest two or three times as though her heart needed the support. "Well, there was a certain fella who Miss Pike had seen quite a lot of. I admit that I didn't like the look of him. I know they say you can't really spot a criminal by his face, but I tell you, he was a bad one! His eyes were quite close together, you see, and he had a sort of shifty way about him as though he was always checking over his shoulder. It may not be scientific to a properly trained doctor, but if you ask me, doctors don't know half as much as they pretend to. And I can tell you, that man—Finnegan was his name—he was a bad lot. He gave me the creeps every time I saw him." Mrs. Mooney shuddered and clenched the folds of her skirt.

"Of course, I should have known better," she went on. "But I've always been a trusting soul. My dear husband used to say I was as naive as a baby. He was exaggerating, of course. I'm not as naive as all that. But I'm sure you see my meaning. I'm just a naturally trusting soul. I always want to see the good in my fellow man. It's noble, but it's a curse, too. It really is! My husband may have laughed about it, but my mother warned me a thousand times: 'Patti dear, you mustn't be so trusting, or you'll end up a fool.'

Mrs. Mooney took a deep breath. "So, there I was, working in the garden one day, and Ruby came over and asked me if I happened to have a screwdriver. She said her friend had come over to fix a clock for her, and they needed a screwdriver. Well, I love to be helpful whenever I can, so I marched to my front door, took my spare key from its hiding place, and opened the door."

"Where was it hidden?" Riggs asked.

Mrs. Mooney pointed to her front stoop. "Just behind that little blue flower pot. And Ruby even said, 'Oh, I didn't know you hid a key. That's smart of you.' And I unlocked my front door and got her my best screwdriver. Then, as I handed it to her, I noticed her friend was waiting for her at her door, and who do you think it was?"

The policemen gave each other a side glance, but neither of them dared to interrupt a good flow.

"It was him!" Mrs. Mooney declared. "That shifty man who I never trusted in the first place! And I should have remembered my mother's words, but I didn't. I just thought about how it made me a bit uncomfortable to see him standing there watching me. I told you, he always gave me the creeps. But I told myself I mustn't be so judgmental because that's what it says in the Bible, doesn't it? So, I put it out of my mind. I went back to my gardening, and not three days later, I came home to find that I'd been robbed! Of course, they didn't take the silverware or the crystal vase, no." She shook her head and wiped a tear away. "No, they went right for the only things that could never be replaced!" She groaned and closed her eyes. "I wish they'd taken all my money instead. But no, they broke into my house, and they took my great-grandmother's ruby ring and my grandmother's pearl brooch."

"I see," Riggs said. "Did you report the robbery to the police?"

"The first thing I did was to march straight over to Miss Pike's door. I'm not a woman who believes in making a scene, no sir, but when your cherished family heirlooms have been stolen from your own bedroom dresser, well, even a good Christian has some limits!"

"Yes, they do," Fisher piped in, but Mrs. Mooney didn't notice him.

"And when she answered the door, I demanded that she return my heirlooms!"

"What did Miss Pike say?" Riggs asked.

"And do you know what she said?" Mrs. Mooney continued as if Riggs hadn't just asked her the same question. "She denied the whole thing. She said she didn't know what I was talking about. Hah! Oh, I never should have trusted her or that shifty boyfriend of hers. I'll never really know which one of them did it. Maybe they even did it together, I don't know. But, I tell you, I went to every jeweler and pawn shop in town, nothing! No one ever saw them. They were the only things I had from my dear grandmothers, and they may not have been the nicest pieces of jewelry; I mean, they weren't fit for a queen or one of these glamorous movie actresses, but they were treasures to me! And now I've lost them forever. And I blame myself for my stupidity, and I blame that terrible Pike girl for her horrible lies and her wicked friends!"

Riggs took a long solemn breath. It was best to proceed slowly when blame was being established. When it was safe, he asked, "So, what happened after that?"

Mrs. Mooney took a huge breath, and her large bosom heaved as she regained her composure. "What happened? Nothing. I told that selfish girl to find another place to live. Two days later, I found out she was dead."

"Wait," Fisher interrupted, "you mean all of this happened right before she died?"

"Of course it did. That's why she was still living here. You don't think I'd have a tenant rob from me and then just let them go on living here, do you? No, her rent was paid through the month, so I had to let her stay that long. But then, of course, she died, so it didn't matter, anyway," the landlady concluded. She stood up with a sigh of exhaustion and took her collection of keys from her pocket. "Well, you asked about Roberta Pike, and that's all I have to say about the girl. I wish I could forget all about her. And if I've done wrong to speak ill of the dead, I'm sure the angels will forgive me for all the pain and misery that awful girl put me through." She sniffed.

She took a key from her collection and handed it to Riggs. "This one is to Apartment C. Miss Pike's uncle wrote to me that he'll have her things removed before the end of the month, but for the time being, everything is still just the way she left it."

54

Riggs pulled the other key out of his pocket and showed it to her. "By any chance, are you familiar with this key?"

Mrs. Mooney took and examined it before shaking her head. "It doesn't match any of my locks here." And with that, she rolled up her sleeves and headed back to her flowerbed.

Inspector Fisher led the way to Apartment C and unlocked the door. The two men stepped into the little house.

"I hope the chief doesn't find out we were here," Fisher said.

Riggs looked at Roberta Pike's apartment. It was beautifully furnished. The mantel, the dressing table, and the bookshelves were sprinkled with various souvenir photographs taken at every restaurant and nightclub in town. There were theater tickets, movie tickets, and more photographs in the drawers. Apparently, not all of them were good enough for framing. Airplane tickets showed that Miss Pike had managed to take a couple of vacations while she was unemployed: one to Las Vegas and another one to San Francisco.

Riggs said as he began searching the massive closet. There were five stylish suits for work, complete with shoes, hats and handbags, and several glamorous evening dresses. He opened the next closet door—and discovered more party dresses. There were over two dozen.

Riggs began rifling through them.

Fisher glanced at his watch. "What are you looking for?"

"A yellow dress," Riggs said, "with spaghetti straps and a chiffon skirt."

"Spaghetti straps?" the younger man's brow furrowed for a moment. "Oh, you mean the little skinny straps at the shoulders?" Fisher smiled appreciatively.

Riggs stopped searching, frowned, and carefully pulled out a slender, off-the-shoulder, scarlet red satin dress. He held it up and hung it on the door.

The younger inspector whistled. "That's pretty."

"And it's been worn before," Riggs answered. "So why isn't Pike wearing it in any of those photographs?"

Fisher raised an eyebrow, scrutinized the dress, and began looking through the photographs more carefully. Riggs reached the end of the wardrobe and started checking the drawers. When he couldn't find what he was looking for, he started searching the hat boxes.

"Look, Riggs, I know this suicide thing is tough, and Pike's friend must have been pretty convincing to have got you all worked up like this, but there's nothing here."

"But something doesn't add up," Riggs said. "Even if we assume that Jacob Pike was bank-rolling his niece's lifestyle, even if we assume the key goes to a marina, that doesn't explain why Roberta Pike died."

"She was drunk," Fisher said. "It's awful, and I don't like it either, but facts are facts. You're pushing your luck if the chief finds out you're wasting—"

"Where's her yellow dress?" Riggs demanded. He took the black and white photograph out of his pocket and pointed. "Where is this dress?"

Fisher looked at the photograph and shook his head. "I don't know." He sat down on the bed. "You're going to get reprimanded–or suspended without pay."

Riggs frowned. "I have to get to the truth."

Fisher sighed and glanced back down at the photograph. Then he raised his head and smirked. "You know who's good at getting to the truth?"

Riggs paused and glanced at the junior officer. "She won't touch another case." He resumed his search. "And if I go anywhere near her, she'll probably skin me alive."

"Because of a few racy headlines?" Fisher snorted through his nose. "But it wasn't your fault! It was just the newsboys trying to sell more copies."

"And nicknaming her Seattle's Sultry Sleuth," Riggs reminded him.

"She's damn attractive," Fisher said. "And I looked up the word "sultry;" it fits. Besides, I think the chief may have coined that one himself. It's a real shame, too, cause I liked working with her. I liked the way she–" Fisher stopped and cleared his throat. His face was flushed.

Chapter Nine: Ruby's Boss, Maxim Blackwell

Mr. Blackwell smiled politely. "I'm sorry, Inspector Riggs, but I don't think I'll be able to help you much." The president of Blackwell Enterprises, Inc. was wearing a three-piece suit and sitting behind his grand mahogany desk. His office enjoyed a singularly fantastic view that stretched over Elliott Bay and Puget Sound all the way to the Olympic Mountains on the western horizon. Blackwell Enterprises was one of the largest privately-owned companies in the state. The man himself was tall, clean-shaven, in his early fifties, and he smelled of expensive cologne. Mr. Blackwell straightened a pen, then he regarded the policeman. "When did you say the girl worked here?"

"She worked here through the fifteenth of July—eleven days ago," Riggs informed him.

The president raised his eyebrows. "Did she now, as recently as that?" He adjusted his tie and leaned back in his leather chair to contemplate the situation. "And you say her name was Pike?"

"Roberta Pike, Miss. She was twenty-two years old, light blonde hair, average height, and she dressed fashionably."

Maxim smiled gently. "I'm sorry, Inspector Riggs, but this company employs nearly two dozen stenographers, and most of them are young, average height, and fashionable. But I see each of them so infrequently, I can hardly be expected to remember any particular girl."

"As president of the company, you don't have a regular stenographer?"

Mr. Blackwell frowned and shook his head. "My private secretary manages that sort of thing, Inspector. Of course, she occasionally calls one of the staff girls up when she's busy, but I don't really pay attention to which girl is which."

Riggs handed Mr. Blackwell the photograph. "Do you recognize either of these women?"

The president put on square, black-framed glasses and studied the photograph carefully. "I suppose Pike was the woman on the right? She seems like she might be vaguely familiar. But then again, all young women look alike, don't they?

"Mr. Blackwell, you're telling me you don't recognize this woman?" he repeated.

The man shrugged regretfully. "I was afraid I wouldn't be able to help you, Inspector." He cleared his throat, checked his watch, and began to get up. "She seems vaguely familiar, but of course, I read about the incident in the paper. It's a very sad business, but I guess that's how girls are these days. They argue with their boyfriend, and then their hearts are shattered. It's very unfortunate, but life does go on." He was standing now, and he pushed in his chair, indicating that the interview had ended.

Riggs didn't move.

Mr. Blackwell paused and added diplomatically, "Of course, if you want to talk to someone who knew her, I would suggest Miss Baker. She is the head stenographer here at Blackwell Enterprises, so she would have been personally acquainted with this particular girl."

"I'll do that," Riggs said. "It's important that I talk to everyone who was connected with the murdered woman."

The color went from Blackwell's face, and he blurted, "Murder, did you say? But surely not. No, I'm sure that's quite impossible!" He cleared his throat and tried to resume his professional manner. "I mean that murder, in general, is highly unlikely, isn't it? I'm sure as you learn more about the situation, you're bound to see it was just a tragic accident. It had to be." He nodded his head in agreement with his own prediction.

The intercom on the desk buzzed, and his secretary informed him that his wife had arrived. Mr. Blackwell opened the door, and a lovely woman in her mid-forties came into the room. She was dressed all in white, with a beautiful fur-trimmed wrap, a white turban hat, and an abundance of pearls. She looked as though she had just come from the salon, although Riggs suspected that Mrs. Blackwell was the sort of woman who always looked as though she'd just come from the salon.

"Hello, my dear," her husband said, kissing her cheek rather mechanically. "May I introduce Inspector Riggs of the Seattle Police? He was just tying up a few loose ends about that girl who used to work here."

Mrs. Blackwell shook Riggs's hand. "How do you do, Inspector? So, you're investigating someone who used to work for my husband?" she asked lightheartedly. "How interesting. I hope she hasn't joined the Communist Party or done anything too scandalous."

"No, dear," her husband corrected her as he slipped some papers into his desk and locked it. He lowered his voice. "He's investigating the death of that stenographer, the one who—who jumped off University Bridge."

"The suicide?" his wife groaned miserably. "Oh, I remember! How absolutely terrible. I suppose it must have been drugs. That's how they do it nowadays, isn't it? It's all the nasty dope that young people are always using. They think it's just grand, and then they take just a little too much, and it's all over."

Riggs asked, "Mrs. Blackwell, do you know any young people who have taken drugs and killed themselves?"

Mrs. Blackwell blushed. "Oh, no, of course not. I only meant that's how young people *in general* seem to behave these days. But, of course, I don't have any personal knowledge of that sort of thing. I merely meant that I've read about it from time to time in the newspaper. And that sort of thing often happens in the movies."

Her husband frowned and said, "Yes, well, fortunately, tragedies are very rare in the real world. Hollywood favors drama over accuracy."

But Riggs ignored the man. "Mrs. Blackwell, I don't suppose you were acquainted with Miss Pike?"

Mrs. Blackwell's gaze darted to her husband before she looked down at her velvet handbag. She unlatched it and re-latched it twice. "Miss Pike? Was that her name? No, no. I never met her, but I can imagine the type well enough."

Riggs looked at her. "Can you?"

"Well, I daresay they're all pretty much the same; silly and somewhat selfish young girls, who are trying to make out that they're better than they are. Anyway, that's the kind who always seems to come to a bad end."

Mr. Blackwell stepped up to his wife and gently took her arm. "Well, dear, we'd better get going or we'll be late for our lunch reservation." He turned to Riggs. "I'm sorry I wasn't able to help you more, Inspector, but as I said, I employ so many young women." He opened the door, and Mrs. Blackwell led them to the outer office.

Mr. and Mrs. Blackwell shook Riggs' hand, but instead of walking with them to the elevator, Riggs stooped to tie his shoe. The Blackwells paused awkwardly, then when Riggs started re-tying his other shoe, the couple wished him a good day and left.

After the elevator doors closed, Riggs finished his shoe-tying and turned to Mr. Blackwell's secretary.

"Oh, Miss…"

"Stuart," she informed him.

"Yes, Miss Stuart." Riggs smiled and reached in his pocket. "I probably should have asked you in the first place. Women tend to have the best memories," he said with a smile.

Miss Stuart smiled back as Riggs handed her the photograph. "Miss Stuart," he said her name softly, "do you happen to recognize the brown-haired woman in this photograph?"

The secretary took the photograph and scrutinized it before shaking her head. "I'm sorry, I don't. She was a friend of Miss Pike's, I suppose."

Riggs nodded. "Yes, that's right. I was hoping you would be able to tell me who she was or when this photograph was taken."

Miss Stuart studied the photograph and frowned. "Well, when Miss Pike first started here in April, she used to wear her hair all one length. She didn't have her bangs cut short like this until a few weeks later, probably about the first of May. And these pearl earrings were a gift from someone."

"Are you sure about that?"

Miss Stuart nodded proudly and said, "Oh yes, because she wore them for the first time on Tuesday morning, just after Memorial Day. She was wearing a white blouse, so the earrings stood out. And Mr. Blackwell noticed them too, and he said something like, 'Why, Miss Pike, those are beautiful pearl earrings you're wearing. Are they new?' And she blushed and said that they were a gift from a gentleman friend, but she refused to say anything more about it, even to the other girls."

Riggs smiled. "And was Mr. Blackwell happy with Miss Pike's work?"

"Oh, yes. A few weeks after she started working here, Mr. Blackwell started requesting her specifically. Between you and me, he said she was the sharpest girl in the group."

"And didn't that cause any...." Riggs paused to indicate delicacy, "problems?"

"With the other girls, you mean?" Miss Stuart asked in a confidential whisper. "Well, maybe a little; you know how girls like gossip, and Miss Pike was a very pretty girl. Personally, I never thought anything of it. Mr. Blackwell isn't that sort. But I think it made things a little difficult for Miss Pike. If you ask me, the president of a company really shouldn't show blatant favoritism like that; it's not good for morale."

Chapter Ten: The Reluctant Request

Riggs took a deep breath and stepped into the public library. This certainly wasn't city hall. Everything was quiet and still; the building smelled of books. In his hand, he carried a paper bag. As he walked, the bag crinkled slightly, violating the silence. But it was important. Inside the bag was a red satin dress and a can of smoked oysters.

It wasn't much, but it was his best chance.

He circled around the main floor, but he didn't see what he was looking for. On the second floor, he checked down each aisle, but she wasn't there either. Finally, he went up to the third floor, and that's where he saw her. She was standing between two bookshelves, talking quietly with another librarian.

Riggs stood well back and waited. When she had finished, the younger woman went off with a cart of books. Riggs watched her resume her work. She was wearing a light green tweed suit with a scoop neckline and three large white buttons, and the matching pencil skirt was set off with a white ribbon. Her gray high heels were raised just enough to be fashionable for a woman in her late thirties. And her dark hair was pulled up and held together by at least three pencils.

As Riggs watched her, she pulled one of the pencils out of her hair and made a note on a small card. Then she tapped it to her lip several times, shook her head, and he could just hear her whisper, *"List sollte nach Klang sein, nicht nach Magnetismus. Aber, warten Sie, ist das Recht?"* She checked the call letters on a thick book and sighed. *"Ah, ja, Funfhundertfunfunddreizig...."*

Riggs rehearsed his plan of attack again. Then he cleared his throat, and the woman glanced over at him, frowned, and went back to her work.

Riggs frowned, too. It wasn't a promising start. But she wasn't shouting at him either.

"Bell—" Riggs began.

"Don't call me that!"

"Okay, Victoria—"

"Don't call me that either! And you'd better be here for a book," she said firmly. "So, go find a book. Goodbye. Auf wiedersehen."

Riggs tried to stick with the friendly approach. "You know, it only just occurred to me that your name doesn't sound German."

"There's no reason it should." She frowned again and went back to her bookshelf. "But my complexion usually confuses people more than my name. I have family from the Persian Peninsula and family from a region that's now part of western Poland, and I'm an American, and I'm not in a visiting mood. So how about you get lost?"

"But I came here for something–"

"That's what I'm afraid of."

"It's important," Riggs said.

"A book for your kids?" She pointed down. "Children's literature is on the main floor."

Michael Riggs's brow furrowed. "How'd you know I have kids?"

She shook her head, turned back to the books, and slid one on the shelf, mumbling, *"Funfhundertseibenunddreizig."* She stepped up onto a stool.

Riggs smoothed his mustache and tried again. "Look, Bell, I need your help."

"No."

"Just your opinion."

"Inspector," she said in a hushed voice, "you have an entire department of officers to help you with that sort of thing."

"Just five minutes," he promised. "Nobody knows I'm here, and I'll keep it off the record."

She shelved the last book, got off her stool, and started walking away without another word.

Riggs followed her.

"Go back to the police station before someone sees you," she whispered back as she turned the corner and disappeared from view. Riggs took a deep breath and ran his fingers through his hair. Riggs trudged after her. Behind the last row of bookshelves was a plain door with a small generic label: 'Cataloging Manager.'

She had already forbidden him to go there. Twice. Riggs turned the handle and swung the door open. It was a small office with a single desk, several filing cabinets, and a decent window with a view of nothing in particular.

Victoria was sitting behind her desk. "Do you have any idea what my life was like?" she demanded. "The newspapers pestered me for months. The first articles weren't so bad, all things considered, but after the second case, the reporters started showing up at my doorstep, photographers started following me around town, and they even started harassing my husband at work."

"Your handling of those cases was damn clever," Riggs reminded her.

"My cleverness hardly made the headlines," she retorted. "The reporters took a different approach, and no one had to be clever to see what they were driving at."

"But I think you moved in with your husband," Riggs ventured, "and it seems you're wearing a ring, so maybe some good has come of it."

Victoria closed the door so they couldn't be overheard. "Look, Riggs, you were supposed to keep me out of the papers—"

"You barged into my investigation," Riggs said. "I never asked you to get involved."

"You thought *I* was the murderer!"

"Of course I did, but it wasn't personal."

"And you were giving me enough rope to hang myself!" she insisted.

"But that was just the first time," Riggs explained, "the last time, you definitely came to me. You wanted to get involved."

Victoria put her hands on her hips. "And what did I get for helping you solve it?"

"How about justice?" Riggs argued. "It's a fine thing to put a murderer behind bars!"

"It was your job, and I paid for helping you. I paid with my privacy and my reputation. Those newspapers had a field day at the expense of a "professional woman involved in crime." Innuendos, indecent accusations, and my sex life was alluded to so blatantly that the whole city was reading and discussing it. And those nicknames!" Victoria moaned. "It was horrendous."

Riggs sighed. The nicknames were terrible. The newspapers had seized the opportunity to sensationalize the attractive woman working with the police, and it didn't help that she was attractive, estranged from her husband, and had a high-profile job in the city government. Riggs had tried to keep a lid on it, but it hadn't worked. And the police chief—who loved a good scandal—had coined a few of the racier phrases himself.

"Do you have any idea how hard it is for a woman to be taken seriously, especially a woman who stands out?" Victoria demanded. "Another fiasco with the Seattle police could ruin my career and my marriage. Oh, those damned reporters!" She huffed and mimicked a male voice, "Do you use your sex appeal to manipulate men? Do you really think it's right for married women to work alongside men? How many policemen have you dated? If you become pregnant, will your husband be surprised?"

Riggs was starting to blush. "I get your point."

Victoria took a deep breath and sat down on the edge of her desk. "Do you know why my name isn't on the door?"

"Because you're hiding?"

She nodded. "I was sick of reporters following me around. Every time there was a crime, they wanted to know if I was heading to police headquarters. It's not just that I don't want the spotlight; all the publicity was really hard on Walter. So here I am. I gave up my wonderful job at City Hall just to prove that I'm not involved with police work. Don't you see that I can't just jump into another investigation?"

Riggs accepted defeat and walked over to the door. "I understand." He took out the can of smoked oysters and set them on her desk. They were very good oysters and had cost him nearly a dollar.

She raised an eyebrow. "Is that a peace offering?"

"I'm sorry to have bothered you," Riggs said. "The case is already closed, anyway. Fisher said it was suicide."

"Then why are you here?"

"Because Fisher said it was suicide."

Victoria laughed. Riggs moved his hat to his other hand, which caused the paper bag he was carrying to crinkle loudly. He shifted the bag again and dropped his hat so he would have to pick it up. "The funny thing is," he mused as he bent over. "She was so sure of herself...." He grabbed his hat.

Victoria opened a notebook and pulled a pencil out of her bun. "Who was so sure?"

"A woman who came to my office, Miss Baker. She kept insisting her friend was murdered. And she didn't have any proof, but then I found this dress." Riggs pulled the dress out of the bag.

"I'm a librarian, not a dress expert," she informed him. "There are some nice dress shops on Fifth Avenue. If you want to do research, the card catalog is downstairs. Fashion 391.009, tailoring and dressmaking, 646.433, materials and fabrics, I believe that's 746—" Victoria stopped talking as Riggs held up the dress.

He waited.

"The only recent suicide was that young woman who went off the bridge two weeks ago," Victoria said, "A woman by the name of Roberta Pike... but the newspapers said she was a stenographer."

Riggs nodded. "So, what can you tell me about this dress?"

"Only what most women could tell you." She looked at the label and felt the fabric. "The quality is excellent. And I'd say it was fitted by a decent tailor. Apart from that, I can only say it's the current fashion, and it's even this year's color. But any dress shop could have told you that. I'd like to know how a stenographer was able to afford it." She leaned back and frowned at it.

The inspector didn't answer the question. Instead, he pulled the photograph out of his pocket and handed it to her. "Pike is the blond woman on the right."

Victoria's gaze went from the photograph to the dress. "Impossible."

Riggs's eyes twinkled with excitement. "So, do I have a case?"

"I don't know about that, but you have a mystery," she said. "This dress didn't belong to Roberta Pike. The woman in this photograph has a figure like Marilyn Monroe, she's wearing a size 14 or 16, but this red dress is for a woman with slimmer proportions." Victoria tapped her pencil to her lips for a few moments before inserting it back into her hair.

Riggs suggested, "Maybe Miss Pike used to be thinner."

"But it's this year's color," Victoria reminded him. "No one was wearing that shade last year. No, this dress was purchased recently, and that means it belonged to another woman, a thinner woman." She tapped her fingers for a few minutes, then she gave Riggs a side glance. "But you already knew all this, which is why you brought the dress. So I don't suppose you would be here if Miss Pike had a thin roommate or a kid sister. What about the other woman in this photograph, or her friend who came to you, Miss Baker, is she thin enough to wear this dress?"

"Yes, I think so."

She handed him the photograph and sat down on her desk. "This is off the record."

"I promise."

She sighed and said, "Okay, who are the women in Miss Pike's circle?"

For the next fifteen minutes, Victoria listened as Riggs summarized everything that he had learned since Monday. She was especially interested in Ruby's cousin, Sadie, and in the boyfriend, Sylvester Finnegan. But it wasn't until he came to the point of the missing lemon-yellow dress with the full skirt that Victoria interrupted him.

"Wait, you're telling me that this dress," she said as she tapped the photograph, "isn't anywhere in her apartment? It's just gone?"

"That's right."

Victoria looked at the colorless photograph. "The skirt looks like it's chiffon. How do you know it's yellow?"

"Ann Marie told me," Riggs explained and rubbed his mustache. "But I don't want to stir up a hornet's nest on Margaret Baker's hunch. Technically, I don't really have anything to go on. After all, Roberta Pike was only twenty-two. She was tipsy and upset, possibly heartbroken, and she had money troubles; she could have jumped off that bridge."

Victoria stared at the photograph and again at the dress. "Okay, Riggs, you've asked me for my opinion, and against my better judgment, I'm going to give it to you. But then you're going to walk right out that door, right?"

The policeman nodded.

"Okay then, if I were you, I'd follow the key. It'll probably lead you to the marina where you said her uncle has a boat. If it does, then I'll give you ten to one, that you'll find your answers there. When you know what's on the boat, then you'll know whether or not you're investigating a wardrobe mix-up or a murder."

Riggs nodded. He stepped out the door and was about to shut it when he turned back and whispered, "By the way, Bell. How many children do I have?"

She grinned and asked, "Don't you know?"

Riggs pressed, "Come on, if you're so smart, how many?"

Victoria went back to her notebook. "Two plus three," she informed him. "Now, get lost, will you?"

Riggs gave a slow nod and shut the door. Not even Fisher knew that. All in all, it was a good idea to come to the library.

Chapter Eleven: The Banker, Bruce Steele

Michael Riggs left the library and started making his way up Third Avenue. The afternoon was getting on. Riggs was debating whether he should head out to the marina to look at Ruby's boat or if he should just call it a day. If there was any evidence on that boat, it had already been sitting there for two weeks. Besides, it was Friday, and the sooner he got home, the sooner he could take off his shoes and help Amy with the kids.

He had already rounded the corner of Fourth Avenue when he noticed the Puget National Bank. After a quick glance at his watch, he decided the boat could wait until morning. He turned into the bank's lobby. Riggs gave his name to an efficient-looking secretary. A few moments later, he was shown into a good-sized office with a respectable, if not an impressive, view. Standing up to greet him was a tall, handsome man with dark hair, blue eyes, and an easy smile. He was wearing a blue suit with thin stripes, and gold cuff links. The signet ring on his left pinky had a sparkling sapphire.

"Good afternoon. I'm Mr. Steele. What can I do for you, Mr. Riggs?"

"Inspector Riggs, of the Seattle Police."

Michael Riggs was used to people flinching or dropping their jaws when he explained who he was, but Bruce Steele simply shook his hand. "Nice to meet you, Inspector. Please take a seat." He indicated one of the large leather chairs.

They both sat down. The banker leaned forward and smiled casually. "You're the second police inspector I've met this month, Inspector Riggs. So, are you here to discuss something in my line of work or something in yours?"

"The latter, I'm afraid," Riggs said. "I'd like to ask you some questions about a late friend of yours, Miss Roberta Pike."

"Oh, yes, poor Ruby. I can hardly believe it." Bruce frowned and shook his head. "It was a terrible business. Of course, I'll tell you anything you'd like to know. But, before we get started, may I make a suggestion?"

Riggs nodded.

"The weather is still decent, and I was just about to pop around the corner for a cup of coffee. How about if you join me? I need to stretch my legs, and we can discuss Ruby just as well there as we can here. "

As they left the office, Bruce took a moment to inspect himself in a mirror by the hat stand. As soon as his fedora was properly skewed to highlight the broad ribbon, the two men left the bank and walked around the corner to a small cafe on the same block. Bruce Steele chose a table on the patio and arranged the chairs so both men could watch the pedestrians passing along the street. A curvaceous redhead unknowingly captured the young man's attention, and his gaze followed her until she was gone. When there was nothing more to look at, Bruce smiled, sat down, and took off his hat.

"This is a great spot for people-watching," he said. Riggs agreed.

When their coffees came, Bruce took a sip and asked, "So, Inspector, what would you like to know about Ruby?"

Riggs took the photograph out of his pocket and handed it to him.

"Ruby loved to have her picture taken," Bruce said with a smile. "She always wanted souvenirs. She must have had a pretty dull life before she came here." He frowned and scrutinized the photograph closely. "I don't know that I ever saw this one."

"Do you know when it was taken?"

Bruce shrugged. "It looks like it was taken a while back. Maybe it was last Saint Valentine's Day."

"Could it have been as recent as May?" Riggs suggested.

Bruce Steele snapped his fingers. "That's it! It was May, the Memorial Day art auction, or something. It was Ruby's idea. Her rich uncle donates to the art foundation. He would sponsor things, and Ruby would get tickets."

"Do you know the other people in this photograph?"

"Oh sure, the fellow with Ruby is a guy named Sylvester Finnegan. He's a clerk for the county. Works for one of those boring departments that do building codes or something like that. Between you and me, I was never very impressed with him. As far as I could tell, he lacked ambition and brains, but he was a cad, so Ruby thought he was wonderful. The other woman in the photograph is my fiancée, Ann Marie Lewis. She owns a little coffee shop on Eastlake."

"Your fiancée?" Riggs repeated.

"That's right. And believe me, this photograph doesn't even do her justice. Ann Marie's really got something…and the way she smiles at you!" He gave a soft whistle and handed the photograph back to the inspector. "It was Annie who introduced me to Ruby last year. Ruby lived just around the corner from Annie's coffee shop, and the two girls really hit it off. I think Annie was the first person Ruby met in Seattle, besides her uncle and that dowdy cousin of hers, of course."

"And her brother," Riggs added.

"Did Ruby have a brother?" Bruce asked. "I didn't know that."

"And I didn't realize that Miss Lewis was your fiancée."

"No?" Bruce Steele paused and then waved his hand dismissively. "Well, I suppose she probably wouldn't put it that way at the moment, but that doesn't matter. Inspector, there are two things you've got to know about Ann Marie. One is that she's got the devil's temper, and the second thing is that she's proud. We had a sort of falling out last month. I stepped on her pride, and it's going to take her some time to get over it."

"So you believe that you two will reconcile?"

"I know we will. Ann Marie just needs a little time, that's all. And I'm prepared to wait. Actually, the whole thing was Ruby's fault, and we were both furious with her. A woman should know better than to shoot off her mouth, especially to a man's fiancée!"

"What did Miss Pike do?"

"Well, it was the same night that photograph was taken," Bruce explained as he tapped the black-and-white image. "I remember that fantastic yellow

71

dress Ruby was wearing. She looked like a million bucks, and she knew it. Anyway, after the art show, we dropped Annie off at her apartment because she had to work in the morning. But the rest of us went out dancing at a little joint on the lake. After Sylvester went home, Ruby invited me down to her boat, and we shared a bottle of champagne." Bruce looked down at his cuff link and adjusted it. "We had a good time, but the truth is, I was so lit I can't remember much of what happened. A couple hours later, I went to take Ruby home, and she realized that she'd left her keys on the boat. By then, it was very late, so I took her over to Annie's place instead."

Riggs raised an eyebrow. "Your fiancée didn't mind being woken up in the middle of the night?"

"Annie's a sport. And she would've done anything for Ruby. But the next morning, I get a telephone call from Annie, and man, was she livid! Apparently, Ruby had woken up with a guilty conscience and had told Ann Marie all about what happened on the boat. Ann Marie told me our engagement was off, and she never wanted to see me again."

Riggs took a gulp of coffee. "You must have been upset."

"I was devastated! How the hell could Ruby do that to her friend?" Bruce asked. "If things went a little too far, sure, that's bad, but Ruby should have known it was just a stupid mistake. We were both drunk, after all. She had no reason to go and tell Annie like that!"

Bruce shook his head and went on emphatically, "Sure, Ruby was a bombshell. She could turn any man's head, and she knew it. It didn't mean anything to Ruby. But Annie is an entirely different kind of girl." He ran his hand through his hair and leaned forward on his elbows. "She's not only beautiful, she makes a man feel grounded. She's sweet and playful, and she's got a good head on her shoulders. Annie's the sort of girl who makes a fellow want to think about marriage. I'm sure she'll come around in time; deep down she knows that I'm the right man for her. I may not be perfect, and I admit that I made a mistake, but that doesn't change the fact that I'm absolutely crazy about her."

"Did you talk to Miss Pike after that night?"

"You bet I did. I gave her a piece of my mind, and I told her what I thought of her. You know what Ruby did? She just laughed at me and said that I should have listened to her idea."

Riggs smoothed his mustache. "What idea?"

"I don't know," Bruce admitted. "Ruby was talking about some business idea or something the night before, but I don't remember. God, how can a woman be so hurtful to her best friend? I knew as soon as I woke up the next day that I'd done wrong by Annie. I was an idiot, but that's no reason for Ruby to go and make a mess out of everything."

"Was that the end of your friendship with Miss Pike?"

"You bet it was," Bruce said. "In fact, I won't even say that I was sorry when I found out that she was dead. I was shocked, sure. It's a rotten thing for a girl to go and end it all like that. But I'll admit there was a part of me that felt relieved. I won't say Ruby had it coming, but at least I know she can never come between me and Annie again."

Chapter Twelve: A Late Night Fire

After three weeks of nearly perfect weather, a summer storm erupted. A cold front swept through the Strait of Juan de Fuca and filled Puget Sound with unseasonably cool air. As the winds blew through the city of Seattle, the temperature fell, and darkening clouds threatened lightning and thunder.

Jacob Greenleaf rested in his wheelchair by the fire. It wasn't raining heavily yet, but the radio predicted it would, so the old man was bundled up to protect himself from the imminent draft. The long summer sun had only just set. The last shades of dusk filled the room with shadows, and the flame's light danced on the walls as if they were celebrating the storm. Mr. Greenleaf rested peacefully, sometimes reading his book and sometimes pausing to listen to the approaching cracks of thunder. The small brass clock on the mantelpiece began to strike ten. Mr. Greenleaf pulled out his old-fashioned pocket watch and compared the time.

"Curious," he observed. "That clock is six minutes fast. I told Mrs. Lamar to have it fixed."

Sadie was sitting on the couch reading. Her feet were propped up under a blanket. She was wearing a dark blue hostess dress and a charcoal-colored wool cardigan. "What's that, Uncle?"

He looked over and frowned at the leather-bound book in her hands. In the dim lighting, he couldn't make out the title.

"The clock," he repeated, "it's fast again. I told Mrs. Lamar to have it fixed."

His niece nodded impatiently before going back to her book.

The old man lowered his eyebrows. "Sadie, what is that book you're reading?"

"Oh, it's nothing, Uncle. Just a little story that my friend wrote. Like a silly fool, I promised her I would read it and tell her what I thought." She went back to her book, and her uncle turned back to the clock. It was such an attractive timepiece; he'd bought it in Chicago not long after the war had ended. But he was sure that it had been advancing lately. Just a few minutes a day. That's all. But what is the point of a clock if it can't keep proper time? If it couldn't be repaired, it would need to be replaced. "Reliability, that's the thing," he told himself wisely. "If you can't trust a thing, you shouldn't have it around."

He frowned at Sadie before looking back at the dancing fire.

Jacob Greenleaf watched it for several minutes before saying, "Now, I've been thinking, Sadie, about what you told that policeman. And you know, I really think that you're mistaken about that night."

"What's that?" Sadie mumbled, not bothering to take her face out of the book.

"The night Roberta died," her uncle said, "I'm quite certain that you went out that night. Although, I'm sure it doesn't matter."

"No, Uncle," she insisted with a tone that should have been reserved for children. "I'm afraid you've mixed up the days. I was home that night."

The old man was about to object when the telephone rang and interrupted him.

"Who in the world would telephone at this time of night?" he asked.

Sadie put her book on the highest shelf of the bookcase before she answered the ancient telephone. She lifted the heavy receiver and held it to her head. "Hello, Queen Anne 254."

Her uncle waited while his niece listened.

Outside, a bolt of lightning shot across the sky. The crack was almost instant.

Sadie frowned.

"I'm sorry, who is this? Oh yes, of course. This is Miss Greenleaf...." She listened, her brow furrowed. Her uncle turned his chair so that he could face her. She shook her head slightly as she spoke. "What, you mean arson?

Are you positive? But, couldn't there be a mistake? Who? Well, did you see who did it? The police? Yes, I hope so, too. I'll tell him, of course... is there anything we can do? No, I don't suppose so... yes, I'll telephone you first thing in the morning. Thank you for letting us know."

Sadie Greenleaf hung up the receiver and turned to her uncle.

"That was the caretaker at the marina," she explained. "He says that there's been a fire. The police are on their way, and he'll know more in the morning. But he called to tell us that the fire destroyed your boat."

Chapter Thirteen: Inspector Riggs
Re-Opens the Case

Michael Riggs switched off the television. "Okay, kids, the Lone Ranger has saved the day again. And now it's time for everyone under the age of ten to go to bed." Amy Riggs began shooing the younger children into motion. "Yes. That means you, too, young lady. Up to bed, you three. And brush your teeth. I'll be up in ten minutes to tuck you in, so you'd better be in your pajamas and in bed. Oh, and don't forget to close the windows."

Deflated, the youngsters began their tiresome ascent.

Amy and Michael Riggs's house was always full, but tonight Riggs's niece and nephew were staying over, and the house felt like it might burst its seams. The young relatives were spending the night so that Michael's brother and sister-in-law could go to the movies.

With the younger children finally upstairs, the four older children decided to play a board game and listen to the radio. Outside, the wind was really starting to howl. The larger gusts pummeled rain against the windows.

Amy sat down in her chair and leaned toward her husband so she could continue the conversation they had started earlier. In a quiet voice, she asked, "So you finally asked her? What did she say?"

Michael focused on the tools in front of him. "I told you, darling, it was no good. Bell flat-out refused to help. She practically threw me out on my ear for even asking."

His wife sighed. "Well, that's disappointing, but I suppose I can't blame her."

"She could have at least heard me out," Riggs lied, shaking his head. "After all, I took a big risk trusting her in that case last year. The least she could do is repay the favor." He selected the appropriate screwdriver from his box and began to dismantle a broken toaster.

"*You* trusted *her*?" Amy repeated. "I suppose that's one way to say it. But personally, I think it rings slightly nearer to the truth to say: 'You thought she was a murderer'."

"Only the first time," Michael reminded her, "and what else could I think? She had the opportunity to kill the old lady and one heck of a motive, and she's smart enough to get away with it." He dropped the last screw into a cup and lifted off the toaster's metal underbelly. "Besides, I was just doing my job."

Amy shook her head and picked up a ball of bright green yarn. "She certainly helped you do that! And then she did it all over again. And the newspapers had a field day with her! Do you remember the article called 'The Delicious Detective'? On the surface, it may have seemed flattering, but it was fairly suggestive. They never would have treated a man that way! Not in a million years. For a man, they just write the story, but as soon as there's a woman involved, she practically becomes the story."

One of the children turned from the radio and whispered, "Please, Mom. We're trying to listen."

Amy whispered an apology, and Riggs untwisted a yellow wire with some needle-nose pliers. In a hushed voice, he admitted, "It was pretty uncomfortable for her."

"And for her husband," Amy reminded him, "especially when they started implying that there might be something between you two."

The pliers slipped from Michael's hand. "What's that?" he whispered.

Amy shook her head and teased, "And he's supposed to be a detective." She suppressed a smile and continued her knitting. "It wasn't that subtle, dear. First, the newspapers said things like 'the unconventional cooperation' between the police department and Ms. Bell. Then they started using phrases like, 'the friendly collaboration with the soon-to-be-divorced woman detective,' which must have sold a ton of papers because, sure enough, by the end of the month, it had become 'an intimate partnership between Sergeant Inspector Riggs and the beautiful, mysterious, divorcee'—"

Michael broke in, "Amy, you don't actually think...."

"Editors just want to sell newspapers, darling," Amy said, "and nothing sells newspapers like scandals and sex. I knew they were trying to be sensational, but that doesn't mean Victoria's husband saw it that way. Those reports may have been devastating. A story doesn't have to be true to ruin a marriage, and it isn't just Victoria's marriage she had to worry about; a scandalous story in the newspapers might cost the woman her job. It's really unfair. Personally, I can't really blame Victoria for refusing to help you, although it is disappointing. But if I were her, I probably wouldn't want the risk either."

Michael Riggs twisted the last screw into place as the rain beat against the windows. He had been so happy to have Victoria's help with those cases that he'd forgotten how the story would appear to her husband. Of course, he'd thought about Amy when he read the stories, but he'd managed to convince himself that she hadn't noticed. Stupid of him. Amy was right; Victoria could have lost her job and her marriage.

The telephone rang, interrupting his internal reproach. Michael was happy to answer it, but less so when he heard Inspector Fisher's voice. Two minutes later, Riggs knew about the fire at the marina. It was a damn shame if the boat was completely destroyed, but nobody commits arson without a reason. This could be just the break Riggs needed to re-open the case. Within three minutes, he was grabbing his hat to join Fisher at the Eastlake Marina. Before he hurried out the door, he ran back to Amy and kissed her. It wasn't just out of habit; he really meant it.

The summer storm had reached full proportions. Riggs had to drive so his windshield wipers could keep up with the downpour. The lightning had mostly passed, but the water was falling in sheets. As Riggs drove from his north Montlake house to the Eastlake Marina, he turned left at the University Bridge, and on a sudden hunch, he pulled into the parking lot beside the Blue Bay Tavern.

Fisher was already at the marina, so Riggs could spare a few minutes. It was nearly nine-thirty, Friday night, the bar was busy. Riggs could hear music and voices as he approached the door. He didn't bother looking for Sylvester Finnegan's car because Finnegan only lived a couple streets away.

The tavern where Roberta Pike had spent her final evening was no fancier than Riggs had expected. It was a simple corner establishment offering a short list of uninspired drinks and an even shorter list of uninspired food. The floors, walls, and ceiling were dingy. Exposed wooden beams crossed the ceiling in an obvious attempt to add charm, but it wasn't working. There were a dozen small tables and along two walls, a row of lead-paned windows, each boasting its own high-back wooden booth. The atmosphere was dim and smoky. The bar itself was on the back wall, with several old stools crowded around it.

Inspector Riggs walked up to the bar and sat down beside Sylvester Finnegan.

"Hello, Mr. Finnegan," he said, and then in response to the bartender, Riggs ordered a beer.

Sylvester looked at the newcomer and took a gulp of his beer. It seemed to Riggs that it was only the most recent gulp in a long line of them. Sylvester wiped his mouth with his sleeve and said, "Well, Inspector Rubbs, I'm not surprised to see you again."

"Riggs."

Sylvester shrugged and repeated indifferently, "Riggs."

When the barman came back with the beer, the inspector opened his jacket to show him his police badge. "Inspector Riggs of the Seattle Police."

The barman looked at him and lowered his voice, "Oh, I see. Good evening, Officer."

Riggs pointed to the drunken man with his thumb. "Can you tell me what timeMr. Finnegan arrived here this evening?"

Sylvester glared at Riggs and demanded, "Well, what the hell do you need to know that for? It's not as though Ruby could've jumped off another bridge," he punctuated this declaration with a hiccup.

The bartender looked back at Riggs. "Well, Inspector, I can't say exactly. You see, I've been so busy and all. But it seems to me that Sylvester arrived just about five o'clock, give or take a few." He turned to Mr. Finnegan, "Isn't that about right?"

Sylvester nodded disgruntledly and the bartender retreated back to the taps and his less intimidating patrons.

"That sounds just about right to me," Sylvester agreed. "I left work just a few minutes early, seeing as how it's Friday and all. And I came right straight here... for my dinner. Burger and French fries, and a little beer," he raised his glass. "To wash it all down."

"Well, that's fine," Riggs acknowledged. He reached back and touched the coat that was hanging on Finnegan's stool.

It was dry.

"So you didn't stop by the marina at all?"

"Not that it would be any of your business if I did, but as a matter of fact, I didn't. I left work, and I came here." He pressed his index finger down on the bar to emphasize the word 'here'.

"What is it exactly that you do, Mr. Finnegan?"

Sylvester grimaced as though he smelled something offensive. "Boy, you're sure full of questions tonight, aren't you, Inspector? Well, it doesn't really matter. I don't have anything to hide. As a matter of fact, I work for the County in the Department of Permitting, if you really want to know. We manage maps and zoning codes for the whole county. It's very complicated stuff you wouldn't understand." He suppressed a hiccup. "But if you want to build something in King County, you have to come to me first. Yours truly. And I, personally, spend most of my valuable time looking up lots of restrictions for important people who want to know. But they don't know where to look. You see, information sometimes has a way of hiding in the drawers. When people want to build stuff, I'm the guy who tells them whether or not they can get a permit," he paused to order another beer, then added, "Someone else grants the permits."

Riggs sipped his beer and asked, "And how long have you worked there?"

Sylvester ran his fingers through his hair and adjusted his tie so that it was even less straight than it had been originally. "Oh, a couple of years, I suppose, since I left good old Ohio."

"I didn't realize you came from Ohio."

"Yes sir, born and raised on a corn field. It was just me and my old man, and after he died, I decided it was time to get away from the cows and corn. There's so many cows and corn out there you can't even hide from them. So I looked at a map for a couple of weeks, then I bought a one-way train ticket, and I landed myself in Seattle: way out West. I thought maybe I could be a logger or a fisherman in the Great Northwest. There's lots of trees out here, you know. And fish. But as it turns out, I got a job working for King County in the Department of Permits."

Riggs waited while Mr. Finnegan finished his beer and ordered another. "One more thing, Mr. Finnegan, what do you know about Miss Pike's boat?"

"Ruby's boat? The *Bluebell*, or *Anna Belle*. or whatever it's called. What do ya' want to know about that old thing for? It wasn't hers, anyway. It was her uncle's boat. Her rich old uncle. You should go ask him about it."

"Did Miss Pike spend much time there?"

Sylvester shrugged. "I suppose so. She took me down there several times. It was a beautiful thing. We never took it sailing or nothin'. It was just kinda' fun to sit there and relax as it rocked a bit."

"And do you know if she kept any of her personal belongings there?"

Sylvester Finnegan frowned at the inspector and then back at his own glass. When he spoke, his breath was short and choppy. "Ruby's things?" he repeated, "You mean like ruffled curtains, and necklaces, and hatboxes? Ruby's hatboxes...."

"Well, Mr. Finnegan?

Sylvester gulped his beer, wiped his mouth on his sleeve, and mumbled sloppily, "I doubt it."

Five minutes later, Riggs pulled up to the Eastlake Marina and got out of his Plymouth. There was a commotion of activity on the little boardwalk by the boathouse. Despite the steady downpour, a small group of onlookers had gathered under hats and umbrellas to try to get a better look at nautical carnage. The firefighters were coming back up the dock, wet and miserable. Inspector Fisher was talking to the officer who had been the first one to arrive at the scene. The frazzled caretaker was trying to sort out the concerned boat owners from the casual onlookers, and a couple of reporters were taking down statements from anyone who was willing to open their mouth and gab.

Riggs used his umbrella to shield his face and skirted his way past the reporters. He came up to Fisher and the other officer.

Fisher turned to the lower-ranking police officer and said, "I assume you know Sergeant Inspector Riggs?"

The younger officer stood up taller and tried to assume an air of mature competence. "Officer Reilly, Sir," the young man said as he shook the Sergeant Inspector's hand. The three men passed beyond the gated entrance to the docks and stood well out of earshot from the crowd and the eager reporters.

"Well, boys, what can you tell me?"

The young officer, Reilly, began. "Well, Sergeant, I was patrolling at the south end of the lake. That's a great spot for folks to admire the view, you know. Last week we had a couple of incidents when the bars closed. Nothing too terrible, but there was one drunk guy who decided to climb a tree and get stuck, and there was a whole party of folks who were singing songs from the *Wizard of Oz* in the street after midnight—"

"Never mind," Fisher interrupted him, "the Sergeant is asking about this incident. Were you the first one to get here?"

"Besides the caretaker, yes. I was walking by Bruno's Italian Restaurant, you know, the one on the lake, and the next thing I know, Bruno himself is outside shouting at me and saying that a boat's burning. He points to the marina, and sure enough, I see the blaze. So, I hightail it over here just as the poor old caretaker is telephoning the fire department. I ran down to the boat with him, but there was nothing we could do." As Reilly was explaining, he led the two men along the dock, and pointed to the place where just an hour before, a sailboat had been docked.

"Was it still afloat?"

"What was left of it, but it was all in flames by then, and you could see there was no saving it. And just as we got here, it began to go down. Lucky for us, it was already half underwater when the flames got to its fuel tank. I hadn't even thought of that. It was like being in the army again! The caretaker said the tank must have been full to make such a large explosion, and my ears are still ringing."

"How many boats were destroyed?"

"Just that one, Sir. The caretaker said it was one of the nicest ones, too, called the *Isabelle*. He said it belonged to some old guy, and he paid the caretaker to do all the maintenance. Part of the dock got charred right here in the blast. And that other boat might have exploded too, but the caretaker managed to untie it and pull it to that empty boat spot there."

"Slip," Fisher corrected him.

Reilly's forehead wrinkled. "What?"

"It's called a 'boat slip'," Fisher explained.

Reilly raised his eyebrows in amazement. "What? But isn't a slip the thing a lady wears under her—"

The Sergeant cut him off. "So, we need to find out how someone managed to break into the marina?"

"Break in?" Fisher frowned. "Well, they'd have to come by water if they did. That big gate we just came through is the only dry access, and it's always locked. The caretaker lives in that little apartment above the boathouse."

Riggs looked up at the boathouse and the apartment above it. It was a small room on the second floor with no shortage of windows.

Fisher added, "And from there, he can see the gate, the docks, and all of the boats."

"So, did he actually see who started the fire?"

Fisher shook his head.

"No one started it, Riggs. It was a bolt of lightning."

Riggs's jaw dropped. "What? Are you sure?"

Both men nodded, and Fisher started to explain, but Inspector Riggs objected, "That can't be right. Listen, men, there are seven thousand boats in this city, half of them are on this lake, and this particular boat belonged to a woman who was murdered two weeks ago. That boat could have told us who killed her, and now you're telling me that a random bolt of lightning, an act of nature from an unseasonable storm, just happened to strike and burn the only boat in the entire city that could have led me to her murderer?"

The two men stood motionless until Reilly added, "Sir, the caretaker saw the lightning strike."

"It's too much of a coincidence," Riggs objected. "That fire was started by somebody who wants to destroy evidence. Someone who knows I've reopened the investigation of Roberta Pike's death."

"But the caretaker—"

"He must be mistaken," Riggs insisted. "You know as well as I do that witnesses make mistakes all the time. There was a lightning storm going on, for Pete's sake. The caretaker heard a crack of thunder, then he noticed the fire, and he just assumed—"

Reilly was frowning, and Fisher started shaking his head.

"I see where you're going, Sir, but it's no good," Fisher explained. "The caretaker wasn't the only one watching the storm."

Reilly cleared his throat. "We've got the two restaurants next door," he explained. "Bruno's Italian Place and the Silver Maple right next to it, and each restaurant has at least two dozen people who were eating their dinners and looking out at the lake when that bolt hit."

Riggs took a deep breath. "Did they see it? Did they actually see a bolt of lightning strike that boat?"

Reilly said, "Inspector Coleman is over there now, taking down their statements."

Michael Riggs turned back to the men and sighed, "Okay, if what you're saying is true, then this is the biggest coincidence I've ever encountered, and it's exactly between me and a murderer."

Fisher nodded. "Yes, Sir."

"Okay," Riggs said as he addressed both men, "I want you to check up on the caretaker, everything. Who he is, who he knows, and if he was familiar with the girl who used that boat. Ask a lot of questions. He could be lying, or crazy, or trying to pull an insurance fraud."

Reilly cleared his throat. "Sergeant, I don't think that's very likely—"

"I understand, but I want you to find out," Riggs instructed.

"Yes, sir," Reilly agreed.

"I want you to be absolutely sure that this fire couldn't have had anything to do with Miss Pike's boat in particular. And I want statements from those two dozen witnesses who saw the bolt hit. All of them. If there is a single hole in their stories, any discrepancy at all, I want to know about it. Do you understand?"

Both men nodded, and Riggs glared upward through his umbrella. The rain pummeled innocently. He reached in his coat pocket and took out his pipe and the key. The pipe went straight into his mouth, and he held it with teeth while he turned the key over in his fingers. Of course, there was such a thing as a coincidence. This boat may have held a clue to Pike's murderer, if there was a murderer. Then again, maybe it was all a wild goose chase. Maybe, Pike was just an unlucky kid who got drunk and fell off a bridge.

"Well, would you look at that," Reilly exclaimed. Riggs looked over to see the younger officer pointing at Pike's key.

"That's just like the caretaker's gate key," Reilly said. "How funny that you've got one, just like it!"

Chapter Fourteen: A Country Club Garden Party

Victoria stepped under the shade of the large white tent and tried to absorb the brilliant scene. The country club's Annual Flower Show was an explosion of colors, textures, and perfumes. She had never seen so many blossoms in one place, and their combined sweet aromas were heady. Even though she wasn't a gardener herself, Victoria found the collection inspiring. Beside her, Julia grabbed her arm and led her into the tent.

"Oh, Victoria, let's start over here. These roses won several prizes last year."

The two women headed over to a massive display of lemon-yellow roses. Julia was a passionate gardener, and she rambled as she ran over the strong points of the different floral varieties. To her, each variety held a unique beauty and quality. As they wandered through the tent, Victoria noticed a little calligraphy card beside each flower. It listed the flower's common names and its proper name, as well as the gardener who had grown and submitted it. As Julia chatted happily, Victoria read the card for each flower.

It was nearly an hour later, and they were almost finished when her gaze stopped on one of the elegantly hand-written cards. Beside a bouquet of pink roses was the name 'Mrs. Maxim Blackwell.' Victoria stopped. She re-read the name, Mrs. Maxim Blackwell. The Pike girl had worked at Blackwell Enterprises. Riggs had met the boss and his wife.

"You're being very patient with me," Julia was saying, "letting me drag you along like this. How about if we take a break and get something to drink?"

They stepped out into the sunshine and started making their way through the clusters of people who were admiring the displays. The most popular color for summer dresses was white, and the women's hats ranged from charming tea hats to lavish sun hats.

"This is almost as bad as the races," Julia whispered. "In my mind, a real gardening party would be one where we would all get to wear trousers and keep our sleeves rolled up."

Victoria grinned. "Well, apparently, your country club has different ideas."

As soon as they reached the clubhouse, Julia set her handbag on the bar. "I'll get you a drink," Julia announced as she ordered two cocktails, "and hopefully, you'll forgive me for dragging you here and boring you to death all morning."

"Oh, no. I'm very glad I came," Victoria said. It was true, and she was already regretting what she had decided to do. But it couldn't be helped. Mr. Blackwell's statement was suspicious. Besides, Riggs would never be able to approach Mrs. Blackwell like this. This was a golden opportunity.

"Julia, could you do a tiny favor for me, if the occasion arises?" Victoria asked.

Her friend smiled. "Anything you'd like."

The bartender gave them each a Singapore Sling. Victoria had a moment to reconsider. She had changed jobs, for goodness sake! Last time the reporters had harassed her for months. The Seattle police had trained officers to do this sort of thing, and yet, none of them could do this. It was a risk.

"Julia, do you know Mrs. Blackwell?"

"Celeste Blackwell? Yes, I've known her for years, but we're not especially close or anything. Why?"

"If you see her, I want you to point her out to me," Victoria explained.

Julia looked at Victoria and raised an eyebrow. "Why Victoria, if I didn't know you better, I might think you were up to something."

"Not at all. I've just been listening to gossip."

Julia shook her head. "No, you haven't."

"Okay, fine, I'm curious about things that I shouldn't be. I won't discuss it, but I'd just love to talk to Celeste Blackwell for ten minutes."

Victoria tried to smile, but it was hard when she was mentally kicking herself. It was bad enough that she'd spoken to Riggs. Now, she was jumping in with both feet.

Julia tapped her fingers on the table and lowered her voice, "Nothing to do with another investigation, is it? Don't worry. I won't say a word to Walter." Her suspicions mimicked Victoria's inner berating.

"After the hell they put me through?" Victoria demanded. "Not in a million years! No, I promised myself I'd never get mixed up in that sort of thing again."

Julia sipped her icy drink. "I'll help you, and then I'll forget all about it on one condition."

"What's that?"

"That someday you tell me all about some case you were involved in."

Victoria smiled. "Deal."

Julia nodded happily and leaned forward, "You know, I've suspected for years that Celeste doesn't really grow her own flowers. She has this brilliant old gardener who's deaf as a door nail. I think he's the genius, and she just takes the credit."

Victoria sipped her cocktail. "She's a fraud?"

Julia shrugged. "She's just always struck me as the sort of woman who's preoccupied with keeping up appearances. But, I don't think you're interested in her flowers," Julia suggested. "If I had to guess, I'd say you were wondering more about the gossip about her husband?"

"Something like that. Do you know anything?"

"Only the rumors," Julia admitted. "Some of the ladies have been talking, but they are the sort of women who like to talk, so I wouldn't put much stock in what they say."

"But what are they saying?"

"Some of them are wondering if Celeste's husband is carrying on with a younger woman."

"Do you know who?"

Julia shook her head. "I think it's just plain nastiness. Anyway, I doubt it's true."

"I'm not writing an article for the newspapers," Victoria reminded her, "I just want to know what people are saying."

Julia closed her eyes and tried to remember. "I think the girl was supposed to be a stenographer or something. You know, one of the pretty young girls who turns a lot of heads and gets a lot of jealousy."

"Is there anything else?"

"That's the worst of it," Julia said, "and the only evidence I've ever heard was just that Mr. Blackwell and this young woman were seen having lunch together. Which isn't terribly damning, if you ask me."

"Yes, but you have a devoted husband," Victoria reminded her, "so you don't have anything to worry about. But not all males are gentlemen. Tell me, exactly how did they describe the stenographer?"

"Oh, I don't have a memory like yours, Victoria," Julia reminded her. "I think they said she was very young and very beautiful. That part is probably true enough, or none of these old cats would be bothering to gossip."

"Do you think Mrs. Blackwell has heard the rumors?"

"If she hasn't, then she's the only woman at the country club who hasn't heard. It's been a hot topic for at least a couple of months."

Victoria frowned and took a sip of her drink. "You know Mr. Blackwell, and you don't think it could be true?"

"I suppose you never really know, but Maxim always seems so straight-laced. He's very focused on his business." She sipped her drink, then shook her head. "No, it's more than that; Maxim Blackwell always struck me as a boring old stuffed shirt who genuinely loved his wife."

Several minutes passed, and Victoria was just starting to talk herself into staying out of the whole thing when Julia leaned over and whispered, "Here she comes. That's Celeste Blackwell over there."

And without even looking at her companion, Julia stood up and walked over to Celeste. "Well, if it isn't Celeste Blackwell! I haven't seen you in months. How are you?"

Victoria turned to the bartender. "May I have another Singapore Sling?" And then she added in a softer voice, "And could you please make it a double?"

The bartender nodded, and Victoria hurried over to the other women. Celeste was saying something about the roses when Victoria interrupted, "I'm so sorry to intrude, but you wouldn't happen to be Mrs. Blackwell, would you? I was taken with one of the pink flowers, and the label said it was one of yours."

Celeste nodded gently. "Yes, I'm Mrs. Blackwell."

"Oh, I'm so glad I found you!" Victoria gushed. "My name is Mrs. Bell, by the way. And you see, there was this gorgeous pink rose variety in the large tent. It was absolutely lovely, but it only had four petals."

"Yes, that's right, four petals is typical for the *rosa sericea*," Celeste explained. "Do you enjoy roses?"

Just then, Julia interrupted, "Oh, I just spotted one of the judges, and I've got to have a word with her. Excuse me. I'll be right back." Julia left, and Victoria invited her new acquaintance to sit down.

"I've always been too intimidated to try roses," Victoria pretended to lament, "but I think they're absolutely gorgeous. Although, before today, I thought they always had five petals."

The waiter handed Victoria her double cocktail. She thanked him and passed it to Mrs. Blackwell. "Do you like Singapore Slings? Here, take this one, and I'll order another. No, I insist. I'm buttering you up so you'll tell me more about *rosa sericea*. Oh, how many sepals do they have?"

And before Mrs. Blackwell knew it, she was rambling on about her favorite variety of flowers and sipping a double cocktail with her new friend.

The two women discussed roses and garden pests for a good fifteen minutes. And Mrs. Blackwell was flattered at how much her new acquaintance appreciated her knowledge of gardening. Mrs. Bell listened as Mrs. Blackwell described pollination, fruit, and everything else that was worth knowing about a healthy rose garden. And as her second cocktail dwindled away, Mrs. Blackwell realized that her new acquaintance was a compassionate and trustworthy woman. By this time, Victoria should have been feeling properly ashamed of herself, but she was so busy working the conversation around to Ruby Pike she didn't have a chance to feel guilty.

It was about that time when a beautiful young woman with platinum blond hair happened to walk past their table; on a sudden impulse, Victoria turned to Mrs. Blackwell and said, "Oh, for a moment, I thought that woman was my husband's secretary, Miss Taylor, but it isn't her after all."

Mrs. Blackwell glared at the departing woman. Specifically, she glared at the woman's swaying hips. Celeste Blackwell took a breath that was so heavy her nostrils flared, and Victoria knew she was on to something.

"Of course, Miss Taylor is a very respectable young woman," Victoria added as though there was a doubt. "Not like most young working girls these days. It seems to me that half the girls nowadays are more interested in flirting with their bosses than in doing their jobs. It's completely shameful the way some of them behave."

"There was one like that at my husband's office," Mrs. Blackwell said with a scowl.

Victoria watched the other woman's face as she said, "And if a married man so much as notices them, these silly girls act like it means something."

"She thought she was terribly clever." Celeste frowned. "But she was just a little floozy."

Jackpot.

"That's exactly what I mean," Victoria insisted. "A man should be able to be friendly at work without everyone getting the wrong idea."

Celeste nodded. "But if a girl goes around looking for trouble instead of just doing her job, sooner or later, she's going to find it."

"You're absolutely right," Victoria agreed. "So, what happened to the girl at your husband's office?"

Celeste Blackwell shrugged sadly. "Oh, she found her trouble all right. I only read about it in the newspapers, but it was very sad. Apparently, she'd been out drinking at some bar with some man," Celeste took a large gulp of her cocktail, "And on the way home, she fell off the University Bridge."

Victoria shook her head sadly. "That's terrible, but it's like I said—girls today have no sense."

Celeste Blackwell raised her glass and gave a little smile. "Yes, and sometimes they get what they deserve."

Chapter Fifteen: Sunday Dinner and Double News

On Sunday evening, the entire Riggs family was gathered at Michael and Amy's home. They were having a traditional family dinner to celebrate an unexpected announcement. Harold Riggs, and his wife, Betty, were expecting their third child. Until three days ago, Betty had adamantly insisted that she was too old to have any more children. But apparently, her body felt differently.

The five adults were gathered around the dining table. The seven children were sitting around a makeshift table, which Michael had assembled by uniting three smaller tables. The whole ensemble was covered with two overlapping tablecloths. They started by making the appropriate toasts. The senior Mrs. Riggs always mentioned her late husband at these events, which inevitably made her teary-eyed. And as soon as that happened, she always brought up her oldest son and his wife, which inevitably made everyone else teary-eyed.

"They won't be joining us again on this side," she managed, "but they're watching from above, and I know they're celebrating with us tonight." She addressed her wet eyes with her napkin. Like most women of her generation, the older Mrs. Riggs didn't approve of excessive emotional displays, so she promptly instructed everyone to eat while it was hot.

The younger children jumped into the mashed potatoes while the adults served themselves more gracefully. The roast beef was astounding, the homemade bread was excellent, and even the buttery vegetables deserved a second portion. It was a festive celebration with food to spare. After the meal was consumed and the dishes were cleared, Amy brought out her decadent lemon cake with buttercream frosting. And by the time the adults were enjoying the second pot of coffee, the children were playing board games.

It was a little after eight o'clock when the telephone rang. Harold hurried to the kitchen to get it, and a moment later, he popped his head back into the room. "Michael, it's for you."

Riggs took his coffee and made his way into the kitchen. When he got there, Harold had the receiver pressed to his chest. He winked and whispered scandalously, "It's a woman, old boy."

Harold got a good punch in the arm, and Michael took the receiver. "Michael Riggs here."

"Riggs, it's Bell. I was at a garden party today."

Riggs cleared his throat and closed the kitchen door so that he wouldn't be overheard. "Garden parties aren't my thing," he explained, "unless this one had something to do with the Pike case. And the last I heard, you were strictly out of that."

"I've only got a minute before I change my mind," she informed him, "so you should close your mouth and listen."

"Mouth closed."

Without any unnecessary details, Victoria proceeded to relay the conversation she had with Celeste Blackwell. Riggs listened carefully, poured himself a second cup of coffee, and managed to shoo two incoming children back out of the kitchen.

By the time Victoria finished the story, Riggs was frowning and smoothing his mustache. "So, the respectable Mrs. Blackwell was more acquainted with the Pike girl than she let on," he mumbled.

"Yep. Not only did she know who Ruby was, but she knew her well enough to dislike her adamantly."

"Well, she played dumb to me," Riggs groaned, "and I was busy doubting her husband. I wonder if the charade was for my benefit or for his."

"There are only a few circumstances that could warrant such strong feelings on Mrs. Blackwell's part," Victoria pointed out.

"I agree. Mrs. Blackwell either knew something, or she suspected something. Now, I've just got to figure out if she was right." He paused to take a drink of coffee and then asked, "What's your instinct?"

"About Mrs. Blackwell?" Victoria asked. "I don't like her."

"But was there something going on between her husband and Ruby Pike?"

"That would be guesswork, not instinct," Victoria objected, "and my instincts are reminding me to stay out of this mess. So, you'll have to take it from—"

"Wait a minute," Riggs cut in, "you were right about the key; it goes to the marina gate."

"That's your lucky break."

"No, it isn't. The boat burnt before I had a chance to search it."

There was a pause on the other end of the line. "Was it arson?"

"It should have been, but it wasn't. The boat was struck by lightning on Friday night."

There was a long silence, and Riggs waited patiently.

"A lucky break for the murderer," she finally whispered. "Nature destroying the evidence. But that still doesn't change my position. I helped out because I could, but I'm not part of this investigation. My last tip is to have a look at Blackwell's bank account. If his wife is right, that's the first place to look. Especially his private account." And with that, the line went dead.

Riggs came out of the kitchen. Harold smirked at him, but Amy was too busy telling a story about the butcher to notice. For the next twenty minutes, Michael's mind kept falling back to the telephone call. Celeste Blackwell had lied to him. Maybe it was because her husband was there, maybe not. Of course, even if Blackwell was carrying on with Miss Pike, that didn't make him guilty of her murder.

Betty sat down to play the piano. Her musical talents were featured at most family gatherings. Riggs moved over to the far side of the room and sat down next to Amy. She had just started knitting a pair of baby booties and smiled at him.

Celeste Blackwell had lied. And she was nervous.

Amy leaned toward her husband and whispered, "What is it, Michael?"

He lowered his voice so he wouldn't disrupt the music. "I need help understanding human nature, specifically woman nature."

Amy kept knitting as her husband explained, "Let's say there's a girl who had lots of fancy dresses, and one has gone missing. I know she had it because there's a photograph taken of her in May, and she was wearing it then, but now the dress has disappeared. Do girls ever loan their dresses to their friends?"

Amy thought it over and whispered back, "That depends on the dress and on the girl. Did she look good in the photograph?"

He nodded.

Amy paused, then asked, "I guess what I mean to ask is: did the dress make her look good, or did the dress make her look absolutely fantastic?"

Riggs remembered the photograph of Ruby Pike with her friends, and Bruce Steele's description came back to him. "She looked like Marilyn Monroe in the dress."

"A bombshell." Amy put down her knitting. "Well, then I'd say it all comes down to the girl's character. I suppose she *may* have loaned a dress like that to her dearest, most beloved friend. But I doubt it. It's just too hard to find a fashionable dress that looks that good. It's not the sort of thing most girls would want to part with, even temporarily. I know that if I had a dress that made me look amazing, I wouldn't let it out of my sight."

Michael slipped his hand behind Amy's back and gave her a soft squeeze. "Okay, a quick review of the facts," he whispered. "First of all, you look amazing in everything. I know it, and you know it, so no playing games. Secondly, I get your point; we're long overdue for a nice evening out. How about if you start shopping for a new dress, and as soon as I finish this case, we'll go out for a proper evening."

Amy rested her head on his shoulder and sighed, "Without the kids?"

Michael kissed her cheek and whispered, "What kids?"

Chapter Sixteen: Sadie Gets Pensive

Sadie Greenleaf stepped out of her uncle's old Studebaker and instructed the housekeeper to wait. Freemont was a charming neighborhood, but Mother Nature seemed to have forgotten it was summertime. Sadie was wearing her most expensive gray dress and a black turban hat. She kept her black umbrella handy in case the clouds decided to burst. She closed the car door and scowled at her step-cousin's auto garage.

"Well, at least I don't have to live in a dump like this," she muttered to herself.

In the second garage bay, Eddie Pike was bent over the engine of the new 1956 Continental Mark II. A wrench was sticking out of the back pocket, and Sadie wrinkled her nose at his stained blue overalls. When she was near enough, she cleared her throat.

"Hello, Eddie. How's it going?"

He glanced up at her, but kept his hand submerged in the engine. "Oh, hello, Sadie. You're early, or I'm late. But don't worry; I'm almost done." He gave something a little adjustment and smiled. "This is a great machine Uncle Jacob got for you. I changed the oil and the filter, so it should run like a dream for another three months. One second...I'm nearly there."

Sadie turned back to the Studebaker and waved the housekeeper away. "It's all right, Mrs. Lamar. It's nearly finished. I'll see you this evening, and don't forget my uncle wants you to swing by the jewelers."

The older woman said something indiscernible and pulled away.

Eddie looked up. "Is Uncle Jacob's clock broken again?"

"I keep telling him to buy a new one, but you know how stingy he is," Sadie complained. While Eddie finished up his work, Sadie powdered her nose.

"It looks like you've been driving more than you did last spring," Eddie remarked as he stood up and pulled a rag out of his pocket. "The oil was lower and dirtier this time."

"Well, I hardly ever use the Studebaker anymore," Sadie informed him. She adjusted the delicate netting on her small gray hat. "I let Mrs. Lamar use it for the shopping and the errands. I think she likes to "be seen" in it. But I have to be home most of the time to look after Uncle Jacob."

Eddie raised an eyebrow. "You don't look like a woman who never gets out."

"Well, I have to go out today. I have things to do," Sadie insisted, "but normally, I just don't like to leave Uncle Jacob alone."

Eddie began wiping down the engine with his rag. "Yeah, I remember you saying that last year. But Uncle Jacob still looks pretty good to me. I know he's in the chair and all, but he's not really alone with Mrs. Lamar and her husband around."

Sadie looked down at her shiny black handbag and changed it to her other arm. "Well, you wouldn't know. Uncle Jacob never likes to let on how bad it is. He's terribly private about that sort of thing."

Eddie looked up at his distant relative and frowned. "Do you mean he's in pain?"

"He doesn't like me to talk about it," Sadie said in a sad, almost apologetic voice.

Eddie dropped the subject and turned back to the engine of the beautiful Continental. He understood engines. Sadie furrowed her forehead.

"Eddie, I wanted to ask you something. That man came by the house again yesterday."

"Yeah? What man?"

"Sylvester Finnegan," Sadie explained. "You know, Roberta's boyfriend."

Eddie glanced up for a second but went right back to his work. He rubbed the last smudge of dirty oil off of the modern machine. "I never met any of Roberta's friends."

Sadie fiddled with her gold earring and said, "Well, I only met him a couple times when he and Roberta stopped by the house. Uncle Jacob didn't care for him, of course. He thought Finnegan was a low-life. I never said anything to Roberta, naturally. I wouldn't want to upset her."

The engine was spotless, but Eddie kept cleaning it.

"He came by after Roberta died to pay his condolences, but this time he wanted to speak to me in particular." She leaned against the car and glanced down at Eddie. "I suppose he didn't want to disturb Uncle Jacob. He probably didn't want to cause him any more suffering than he already had, in his condition and everything."

"Probably not," Eddie agreed.

"Mr. Finnegan said he's been feeling depressed since Roberta died," she paused for a moment before continuing, "and he's hoping that I might give him something that belonged to Roberta, something sentimental that he could have as a remembrance of her."

Eddie tossed the dirty rag into a bucket. He lowered the heavy hood so that it settled in place with a short rumble. "I'll write up the invoice for the Continental." He took off his cap and headed towards the little office.

Sadie followed him and frowned. "How much does Uncle Jacob owe you for the oil change?"

Eddie shook his head and pulled out a notebook. "I don't charge family unless I have to buy expensive parts. But this is only a filter and some motor oil. That's nothing. But Uncle Jacob should have an invoice for his records."

Sadie seemed satisfied. As Eddie filled out the slip, she returned to the more delicate topic. "So, do you think it would be all right?"

He didn't look up. "What?"

"If I gave something of Roberta's to Sylvester Finnegan."

"A keepsake?" Eddie repeated. "I don't see why not. After all, he may have been in love with her."

Sadie shook her head. "I doubt it was that serious."

Eddie looked at her as he handed her the slip.

"And the police have already poked around," Sadie went on, "so they wouldn't care."

Eddie made a note in his records, and Sadie slipped the invoice in her handbag. "I don't suppose it matters what I do with her things. Uncle Jacob doesn't need it, and the police don't care. They never even knew about her yellow chiffon dress, but it doesn't matter. I'm just wondering what sort of memento a man would want from his dead girlfriend? At first, I thought of a book, but Roberta didn't have any books, and jewelry or makeup would be silly. Sylvester suggested her diary, but diaries usually have all sorts of personal details that aren't meant to be shared. But then, what should I give him?"

"Dunno," Eddie muttered, "but you might want to double-check with the police."

"Her dishes have a rose print, and no bachelor would like that. I suppose I'll have to give him some of Roberta's photographs. Did you know she had dozens and dozens of photographs of herself? It's a silly way to waste money, but I think it was like dope for her. A doctor would probably call her a narcissist, but I think it's nicer to just say that Roberta had a streak of vanity."

Eddie finished his notes and looked up. "Vanity? Yes, I suppose so," he acknowledged. A box of spark plugs was sitting on the floor. It had arrived that morning, and Eddie opened it up and began unpacking it.

Sadie watched him for a few minutes, and then she unlatched her black handbag and pulled out a small leather-bound book. While Eddie sorted the spark plugs into piles, Sadie opened the book and pulled out a photograph. Then she stuffed the book back into her handbag and held the photograph out to Eddie.

"I don't suppose you know who this is?" she asked significantly.

Eddie looked at the woman in the photograph. She was dark-haired, pretty, and she was wearing a pale dress with a dark sash tied around the waist like a belt.

"Her name is Ann Marie," Sadie explained before he'd had a chance to answer, "and she *used* to be Roberta's best friend."

Eddie frowned.

"I'm not sure why they were such good friends," Sadie went on, "because they didn't have much in common. Roberta's never even had to think about money, but Ann Marie is a working girl, and she's an orphan."

"So was Roberta," Eddie pointed out.

"Not really. Roberta always had Uncle Jacob to take care of her," Sadie objected. "But this friend of hers, Ann Marie, was poor. Now she has a little coffee shop over in Eastlake and one old aunt in a home somewhere, who she takes care of. Then, she got this rich banker to fall in love with her. Supposedly, Ann Marie was crazy about him."

Eddie handed the photograph back to Sadie, and she slipped it in her handbag.

"Well, that's nice for her," Eddie said.

"It was nice until Roberta messed it all up," Sadie announced.

"What are you talking about?"

Sadie shrugged. "Well, apparently, the banker had too much to drink one night. He and Roberta spent the night on Uncle Jacob's boat...."

Eddie frowned. "Is that true?"

Sadie shrugged apologetically, "It seems Roberta wasn't as perfect as everyone thought she was. It's just a shame that she had to ruin everything for her friend."

Eddie's face was hard as he pulled the keys out of the drawer and handed them to his cousin. "I'd better be getting back to work, Sadie."

They walked to the Continental, and Eddie opened the door for her.

"By the way," he asked, "how did you hear all that stuff about Roberta and the banker?"

Sadie Greenleaf smiled like a cat. She sat down and placed her handbag against her leg. She carefully adjusted the rear view mirror. "Actually, I learned it all from Roberta."

Chapter Seventeen: The Police Chief Puts on the Brakes

On Tuesday morning, the chief got wind of what Riggs was doing. Riggs had to stand in front of his boss's desk for twenty minutes, listening to an angry rant about wasting police resources, lousy judgment, and the fact that Riggs's reports were still unfinished. In short, the chief said that the Pike case was closed, and any inspectors who wanted to stay on the force should spend their time solving crimes, not inventing them.

Riggs wasn't convinced, but he knew who was in charge. Besides, he had no proof that Pike was murdered, just a key and a dress. He waited for the storm to pass, then he sat down and assured his boss that he would get his outstanding reports filed right away. He also promised to let the other investigators get back to their work. But Riggs didn't promise to stop the investigation. Instead, he changed the subject by making a joke about the mayor.

The chief laughed and finally relaxed. "Of course, you're not the first investigator to get distracted by an attractive woman," he added sympathetically, "but you can't let a pair of pretty legs overrule your better judgment."

Riggs wanted to explain that it was not Miss Baker's legs but her intelligence that had persuaded him, but he knew it wouldn't do any good.

"Speaking of which," his boss went on calmly, "while you were busy wasting time and blowing the department's budget, I don't suppose you managed to rope Mrs. Bell into your little fiasco, did you?" He paused hopefully. The chief loved a good story, especially a pretty one.

Riggs shook his head and said, "She's fed up with fiascos."

The chief huffed with childish disappointment. He was a big fan of the female sleuth. He thought she had been good for the department. He appreciated her brains. But he especially appreciated the way her hips moved when she walked in a pencil skirt. And he was sure everyone enjoyed all the amusing newspaper headlines Bell's presence generated.

Yes, the chief was a fan of Bell, but she certainly wasn't a fan of the chief.

That had been Riggs's morning. A couple hours later, he had finished most of his reports, so he ran out for an early lunch. His brain was going in circles, but he kept coming back to the ill-fated sailboat. He'd even sent some of the boys out on the lake with poles and hooks, but all they managed to recover was marine hardware and chunks of soggy charred wood. If the sailboat had held any clues to Roberta Pike's death, they were destroyed.

Riggs walked up to University Street and turned west to face the bay. He was just thinking how a brisk stroll along the waterfront might clear his head when he recognized the woman standing on the sidewalk. She was stopped in front of a display window, pointing at the mannequin and saying something to an older woman beside her. Michael Riggs walked up and touched the brim of his hat.

"Good morning, Miss Baker."

Margaret Baker looked at him in surprise. "Oh, good morning, Inspector Riggs."

"It's a nice day for shopping," he said.

"Normally, I don't have much time for shopping in the morning," Margaret admitted, "but now I have all the time in the world. You see, Mr. Blackwood fired me yesterday."

Riggs raised an eyebrow, but before he could say anything, the older woman chimed in, "Now, Margaret dear, you really shouldn't complain. I know it seems like a shock now, but I keep telling you it's all for the best."

"Oh, I'm so sorry," Miss Baker remembered. "This is my future mother-in-law, Mrs. Jenison. Mother, this is Inspector Riggs of the Seattle police. He's the man who I talked to about my friend."

The older woman did her best to hide her dismay at meeting a policeman. She gingerly shook his hand as if she might catch something unsavory. She produced a polite smile. "Well, um, how do you do, Inspector Riggs?"

"How do you do?" Riggs said, touching the brim of his hat. The older woman's perfume smelled like spice and roses. It filled Riggs's nostrils as he turned to Margaret. "Miss Baker, may I ask you what reason your boss gave for letting you go?"

"I wasn't 'let go,'" Margaret corrected him. "I was fired. Absolutely fired, and I've always done my job perfectly. Of course, 'officially' Mr. Blackwell said the firm is over-staffed, but that's a complete lie. We were already down a girl when we lost Ruby, and neither position has been filled yet."

"But Mr. Blackwell gave her an extra month's pay," Mrs. Jenison added helpfully.

"It wasn't right," Margaret insisted. "Mr. Blackwell was cross. He said he needed girls who would represent the company's 'best interests'. I'm sure the real reason he fired me is because I talked to the police about Ruby."

"But, Margaret, dear," Mrs. Jenison broke in, "you must remember it's a blessing in disguise. Why, just think how much time you'll have now to plan the wedding! I never like to see a bride getting herself all distressed, and there really is so much to do. And, after all, isn't that more important than your position as a stenographer?"

Margaret looked like she wasn't convinced, but she did her best to smile. Her fiancé's mother was trying to be helpful, after all. Mrs. Jenison turned to the Inspector. "My son, Otis, and I have been encouraging Margaret to quit her job for several months now," she explained. "It isn't necessary, and it's so much work for a young girl to go to an office every day, don't you think? And besides, since Otis was away in Europe, Margaret was so terribly depressed without him."

"Well, really, Mother," Margaret said, "I doubt the Inspector is interested—-"

"Oh, but it's true, dear," the woman interrupted pleasantly. "When Otis was away, you hardly ever came by the house for dinner, and your friends at the country club said they hadn't seen much of you either. Honestly, that job was taking so much out of you; I was beginning to get just a tiny bit worried. After all, when a girl is trying to plan a whole wedding without her bridegroom around, well, it's simply too much. Don't you think so, Inspector?"

But the inspector was spared from having to form an opinion because Miss Baker took a deep sigh and explained patiently, "Now, Mother, I already told you that I wasn't depressed. I was spending time with my friend Ruby while Otis was gone. I wasn't working too hard, and it may not matter anymore, but I actually enjoyed my job before I was fired."

But the future mother-in-law was far too sympathetic to concede. "Our sweet Margaret is very headstrong," she explained proudly. "My son, Otis, is on the board at my husband's company, and he's quite busy. He's lucky to have found a girl as sensible as Margaret. A man really needs a good woman if he's going to get anywhere in life. My brother is a Senator, you know, and one of these days, Otis may consider a career in politics, too. So it really was just a matter of time until our dear Margaret would have had to leave her position anyway."

She turned sympathetically to the young woman. "Oh, I know it shouldn't have happened this way, Margaret. You always worked very hard at Blackwell Enterprises, and Mr. Blackwell ought to have treated you better. It was very unfair of him." She sighed for sheer compassion and also so she could catch her breath. "But, dear, you must remember that I'm only thinking of what's best for you."

Margaret smiled and patted the older woman's arm. "Yes, I know you're thinking of me, and I appreciate it despite my complaining. I'm sure I'll get over it in a week or two, but, like you said, it doesn't really matter."

"That's the spirit," the older woman said encouragingly.

Riggs smoothed out his mustache. "Miss Baker, may I ask you a couple questions about Mr. Blackwell? It will only take a minute."

"Of course," Margaret said, then she turned to the older woman. "Mother, why don't you go in and try on that hat you were admiring, and I'll be right there."

"Well, all right, dear," the woman agreed, looking doubtful at the Inspector.

"But I'm not sure the silk bow will flatter a woman my age. Goodbye, Inspector Riggs, it was so nice to have met you." And after the appropriate response, Mrs. Jenison stepped into the shiny department store.

As soon as she was gone, Riggs came directly to the point. "Miss Baker, can you tell me if Roberta Pike was a particular favorite of Maxim Blackwell?"

Margaret raised her eyebrow suspiciously. "I think I know what you're getting at, Inspector," she ventured. "Office gossip is the bane of a working girl's life, especially a pretty working girl. And rumors don't have to be true to ruin her reputation."

Riggs waited, and Margaret took a deep breath and whispered, "About a month after Ruby started working at the company, Mr. Blackwell began to request her by name. Each office has a regular secretary, and when they need an extra stenographer, they just ring down. Whichever girl has the least amount of typing to do heads up for the dictation, and that's all. So, when Mr. Blackwell started requesting Ruby, of course, the other girls noticed."

Riggs frowned slightly. "What was your personal take on the situation?"

Margaret shook her head. "First, let me save you some time and give you the whole story. Any of the other stenographers would probably be happy enough to tell you that Mr. Blackwell requested Ruby personally. But they may forget to mention that Ruby was exceptionally fast with her shorthand, and Mr. Blackwell dictates so quickly that the other girls had a hard time keeping up with him. The fact that Ruby was probably the only one besides Mr. Blackwell's secretary who could keep up with him should have stopped the gossip, but it didn't. They even started calling her Miss Marilyn."

"Marilyn?"

"Because Ruby looked like Marilyn Monroe," Margaret explained. "And that may sound flattering, but they didn't mean it as a compliment. You see, all the girls have to dress nicely at work, but Ruby looked so good, some of the other girls may have felt intimidated by her."

"I see what you mean," Riggs agreed.

"One day, there was a rumor going around that Ruby and Mr. Blackwell had lunch together. I started asking all around because I knew how Ruby felt about Mr. Blackwell, but when it came down to it, none of the girls had actually seen anything. In fact, everyone was repeating the gossip, but no one seemed to know how it had started. As far as I can tell, office gossip has a magical way of replacing common sense with idle speculation. Of course, it could be true, but I doubt it. Ruby denied it. I think it's more likely that one of the girls was jealous of Ruby and made up the story. What I can tell you is that I don't believe Ruby had any personal interest in Mr. Blackwell."

"Did she say so?"

"She didn't have to. To put it bluntly, Mr. Blackwell wasn't Ruby's type. Ruby could have had almost any man she wanted. Mr. Blackwell was much older than she, and he's not particularly handsome or interesting. That kind of man wouldn't have appealed to Ruby."

"He's a wealthy man," Riggs suggested delicately.

Margaret shook her head. "That wouldn't have mattered to Ruby. She was all set to inherit a fortune from her uncle. In the meantime, she had enough money to get by. I don't blame you for asking that question, Inspector. Under the circumstances, I suppose it's only natural. But I'm quite sure Ruby never had any romantic interest in our boss."

Riggs nodded and was about to say more when Mrs. Jenison came bustling out of the shop. "I'm sorry to interrupt," she apologized breathlessly, "but I found a very sweet calot with flowers and ostrich plume, and just have to have a second opinion before I buy it."

"Yes, of course," Margaret said, and she glanced at her watch. "But don't forget, I only have until lunchtime, then I have an appointment at the florist." She turned to Riggs, "Goodbye, Inspector Riggs, and thank you for looking into it."

The policeman touched his hat and wished the ladies a good day. As he walked on, he could hear the older woman exclaiming loudly, "My goodness, was that today? I completely forgot about the florist, and I have a reservation at the Lounge. Well, that's all right, you can manage without me, can't you? Just remember, whatever you decide to get you must put it on my bill, and don't be frugal, my dear. I've always felt that a proper wedding should have lots and lots of beautiful flowers."

Chapter Eighteen: Maxim Blackwell's Secret

Nine blocks away, Mr. Maxim Blackwell was getting ready to leave his office. It was lunchtime. He was vexed and had started pacing back and forth almost twenty minutes ago. As lunchtime approached, he'd become so nervous that he looked as though he were struggling to catch his breath.

Behind his desk was a portrait of his late father. He slid it aside to access his personal safe. After spinning the dial three times, Mr. Blackwell swung it open and removed three bundles of cash. He didn't have to count them. He knew how much money was in his own safe. And since the police were almost certainly looking into his finances, this was the only money he could use without them knowing about it.

He leafed his thumb over the green bills, not tenderly but appreciatively. Then he slipped all three bundles into a large envelope.

This would be the last time.

He would have to deliver them himself, but this would be the last time. It had to be.

He thanked his good luck that Celeste had canceled their lunch date. He could have managed either way, but he didn't want any distractions—not today. It was better this way. And for the first time in almost a month, Maxim was beginning to believe that everything was going to be okay. Besides, he reminded himself for the hundredth time, they still don't have any proof.

He put on his overcoat and his hat before slipping the thick envelope into the deep inner pocket of his coat. The cash was surprisingly heavy. He would tell his secretary he was going for a walk. No, he would just say he was going to lunch. That was the best way to do it. He didn't have to tell her anything else.

Mr. Blackwell left his office and turned east up Spring Street. He had grabbed his umbrella out of habit, but even if it had been raining, he wouldn't have thought to use it. People passed around him, but he hardly noticed their faces.

It was a lot of money, but that didn't matter now. Everything comes with a cost. And this business deal would soon be closed.

Several hours later, Mr. Maxim Blackwell came home early. He greeted his wife with a controlled calmness that most women instinctively mistrust.

Chapter Nineteen: Former Lovers

Ann Marie Lewis walked down Yesler Way until she reached the oddly shaped triangle that everyone called a square. The irregular cobblestones in the oldest part of the city were difficult to walk on, especially for women in fashionable shoes. Ann Marie had to watch her steps so she wouldn't accidentally twist her ankle and look like a fool.

Bruce had asked her to meet him under the tall iron and glass pergola. And for some reason, she had agreed. Since the overhead glass covered several benches, it was an ideal meeting place when the weather was wet, but today everything was warm and bright. As soon as she looked up, Ann Marie spotted Bruce. He was standing a little way off beside the massive totem pole that dominated Pioneer Square.

Ann Marie paused for a moment and gently bit her lip, but when Bruce noticed her, she smiled. He strode over to her.

Bruce was wearing a quality brown suit, a new hat to match, and gold cuff links. As usual, he had chosen a blue tie to match his bright eyes and the sapphire in his signet ring. He smelled great, looked wonderful, and when he smiled at Ann Marie, he touched her arm gently.

"Annie," he said, "I'm so glad you came. I wasn't sure you would." He leaned down to kiss her, but she turned, so the kiss landed on her cheek.

"Neither was I," she admitted.

He grinned and winked. "But you did come, Annie. Now come on, let's go somewhere quiet so I can look at you."

Ann Marie didn't move. "Bruce, I told you I wouldn't have much time."

"Well, just a cup of coffee, then. You still like coffee, darling, don't you?" he flirted playfully. Ann Marie smiled, and Bruce placed her hand on his arm. They strolled together to a familiar place around the corner. "Of course, this won't be nearly as good as your coffee," Bruce flattered her, "except that I'll be able to enjoy it with you."

Bruce towered over her, but he led her gently by the arm. When they reached the shop, as always, Bruce held the door for her. They went to a table near the window that used to be their favorite. Bruce pulled out a chair for Ann Marie before taking off his hat and sitting down. She set her handbag beside her as Bruce leaned back and smiled.

"I can't deny it, Annie. I've missed you."

Ann Marie pulled off her white gloves. "Well, I'm sorry, Bruce, but I'm afraid you're going to have to go on missing me."

The waiter came by, and Bruce ordered two coffees, one with extra cream. And a piece of Ann Marie's favorite blackberry pie. After the waiter left, Bruce began talking about the weather. Ann Marie listened. Bruce always could make any topic sound charming. When their coffee arrived, Bruce asked Ann Marie about her shop.

When she told him about a new muffin recipe, he promised to stop by and try it. And when she mentioned that her refrigerator had broken again, Bruce offered to buy her a new one, but Ann Marie declined.

When she told him that a newly married couple was moving into the apartment next to hers, Bruce suggested that they invite the newcomers out to dinner. If anyone besides the waiter had been listening to them, he would have thought Ann Marie and Bruce were still engaged. But the waiter hadn't seen them in over a month, he knew better.

Finally, Bruce leaned forward and said, "It's great to be with you again, Annie. You know, it's been a long time."

Ann Marie nodded. "Yes, and a lot has happened."

"You mean Ruby?"

"Yes, I mean Ruby. It just doesn't seem real."

Bruce looked down and turned his cup on the saucer. "Have you seen Sylvester at all?"

Ann Marie shook her head. "No, but I met Ruby's brother, Eddie. He's nothing like what I expected."

"I'd forgotten she had a brother," Bruce admitted. "Is he anything like her?"

"No, I don't think so. He runs an auto repair garage in Fremont. He's sort of quiet, but he was probably still shaken up about Ruby."

"Do you remember Ruby's dowdy old cousin?" Bruce asked. "She was an unusual sort of woman. We only met her once or twice, but I always had the feeling she loathed Ruby. She had a funny way of looking at her. Of course, Ruby's uncle was the complete opposite."

Ann Marie sipped her coffee and looked out the window. A moment later, she took a deep breath and muttered, "What in the world am I doing?"

"Drinking coffee with me?" Bruce smirked. His smile was infectious.

She grinned but shook her head. "Not that. I mean, why am I here talking to you again? It must be because Ruby's dead. I guess I'm all shaken up too."

Bruce leaned forward to touch her hand. "This has nothing to do with Ruby. It never did. This has everything to do with you and me. That's why you're here."

Ann Marie pulled her hand away. "No, it doesn't have anything to do with me, Bruce. Not anymore."

But he reached out and took her hand. "Annie, I'm crazy about you. You know that, don't you?"

Ann Marie took a deep breath. "That's just not enough, Bruce."

"It's everything," he insisted. "Look, I love you, Annie, and I will always love you. Yes, I made a mistake, but you're here because you know, deep down, that we belong together. You have to give me another chance."

"Another chance?" she whispered and shook her head. "Bruce, I told you it was over."

"Annie, I miss the way you laugh and the way you walk. I miss the way you smile at me when I'm trying to show off, and you know I'm being a fool. You're the best thing that ever happened to me. Please give me a second chance; I'll prove to you how much I love you, Annie. I'll be the best husband any woman could ever want."

Ann Marie had to glance away because her eyes were wet. When she looked back at him, her voice was steady. "I'm sorry, Bruce, but I just can't…"

Bruce reached out and gently touched her cheek. He looked into her eyes. "Annie, you're the only woman for me."

"Then you wouldn't need to ask for another chance."

"I admit that I was drunk, and I was stupid. But we don't have to let one foolish moment, one mistake, ruin everything we have."

"Bruce, that may have been the first time with Ruby, but it wasn't your first foolish moment," she reminded him. "If I accept your proposal and give you another chance, how many more mistakes will I need to forgive over the years?"

"Annie, please listen. I know my behavior was pretty bad that night. After I took you home, I never should have gone down to Ruby's boat. I was drunk, and then I drank more, but that doesn't mean I did whatever Ruby told you."

Ann Marie looked at him, and her mouth opened in surprise. "Bruce, are you saying nothing happened? Because Ruby told me—"

"She was angry with me," Bruce objected. "You know what Ruby was like, how she liked to control people. It amused her, like some sort of a bizarre game. Ruby was trying to get me into a bad spot that night. I didn't know what was going on."

Ann Marie closed her eyes and put her hand on her forehead. "Bruce, are you saying that Ruby made the whole thing up?"

"It was always her word against mine," he explained. "Ruby was trying to punish me, and she was willing to hurt you in the process. But now that she's gone, she can't hurt either of us. Don't you see we can be together again? We can be happy. I've always loved you, Annie; you can believe that."

Ann Marie looked at Bruce's face, and her gaze fell down on his hand that was still holding hers. She was quiet for several moments, then she said quietly, "You have a new watch."

Bruce looked down at the shiny gold watch on his wrist. Ann Marie pulled her hand away from his. She took her gloves and her handbag and stood up.

"I'm sorry, Bruce," she said, and then she was gone.

Chapter Twenty: A Break-In

It had just started sprinkling when Michael Riggs sat down at his desk. It was only a light summer shower, and he hoped it would clear up before five o'clock. He usually didn't bother to bring an umbrella to work until the end of September, but he still didn't like the idea of getting wet on the way home. After running around all day, it felt great just to sit down. He hadn't even had a chance to look at the morning paper. But taking off his shoes and enjoying a hot cup of coffee might help him forget that the Pike case was still a dead end. Besides, the daily newspaper was a good excuse to catch up on events without having to track all over the city. Not that there was anything very interesting to be found in the city. No, it was just one large collection of humanity, all of whom seemed to agree that Roberta Pike's death had been anything but foul play. The inspector leaned back in his chair and put his socked feet up on his desk.

The telephone rang.

It would do that.

Riggs pulled down his feet so quickly that he bumped over his coffee cup, and before he could salvage the newspaper, the hot, black river had washed through one side of the pages and was making its way across the desk and to the floor. Riggs just managed to kick his shoes out of the way as the spill reached the edge and began dripping onto the floor.

He glared at the treacherous liquid, grabbed the offending telephone, and muttered, "Inspector Coffee, I mean, Inspector Riggs here."

"Hello, Inspector," a friendly voice responded. "This is Patricia Mooney."

Riggs tried to mop up the spill with the side of the newspaper that was still dry. He had to pinch the telephone receiver against his shoulder so his other hand could pull the wastebasket up to the desk. Perfectly good coffee in the trash.

"Hello, Mrs. Mooney. What can I do for you?"

"I just wanted to let you know that someone broke into Miss Pike's apartment."

Riggs forgot about the coffee disaster. He nearly dropped the wastebasket so he could properly hold the telephone.

"When?"

"Last night, I suppose," she explained. "I noticed this morning that the kitchen door of Apartment C was ajar."

"Her door was open?"

"Oh yes, the back door. Someone broke the lock. I reported it to the police. Well, I mean, you are the police, but I mean, I reported it to the regular police, but then I thought I ought to telephone you specifically since you were asking about Miss Pike. This might be important to your case."

Riggs dropped the dripping newspaper in the wastebasket. An actual crime. It was the first lucky break he'd had in a week. "Thank you, Mrs. Mooney. I'll be right over."

Riggs put his shoes back on, which his feet didn't appreciate in the least, but he hardly noticed. Riggs grabbed his hat and overcoat. It was still sprinkling, but that didn't matter. Umbrella or not, Riggs almost certainly had a case. Not just a clue. Not just someone's intuition, but an actual crime. And at Pike's home, too.

Even the chief couldn't call this a coincidence.

Riggs grabbed Pike's file and tucked it under his coat. Then he dialed the number for Mr. Jacob Greenleaf. He wanted to speak to Miss Sadie Greenleaf, but the old housekeeper told him that Sadie was out of the house. He'd try again later.

On his way to the elevator, Riggs managed to grab Inspector Fisher, who was always willing to abandon the office when he wasn't making headway with one of the secretaries, which was most of the time. At the moment, Fisher was feeling particularly neglected. As the two inspectors stepped out on the street, each man turned his collar up and his hat brim down against the drizzle.

Ten minutes later, Riggs stopped his Plymouth at 201 E Louisa.

Patricia Mooney had taken up a watchful post. She stood in the front yard under a large umbrella. When they arrived, she handed Riggs a large old-fashioned skeleton key and led them around towards the back yard of the apartments.

"Now, I haven't touched anything," she reassured them, "and I can't tell you if anything was taken; I've acted in enough plays at the amateur theater to know that you're never supposed to disturb a crime scene."

Each of the apartments had a back kitchen door that led out into a little grassy lawn that wrapped around the outer perimeter of the property. There were a few lines for drying laundry and most of the residents had set up little tables and chairs behind their apartments. As Mrs. Mooney had said, the back door to Miss Pike's kitchen was open. Riggs inspected the lock. It had been forced, probably with a screwdriver. That was usually the first thing a rookie crook thought of: a screwdriver. Riggs leaned in to examine the lock.

"Mrs. Mooney, are you sure this happened last night?"

"I'm sure that door was just fine last evening at five o'clock because I was back here trimming the rhododendron hedge," she explained as she pointed to the well-tended hedge for validation. "And then it started sprinkling about an hour ago, and I came back here to make sure nobody had left their laundry out. Which they could have done. You know how people are, and it didn't look like it was going to rain earlier. And that's when I saw it. Of course, it could have been done any time since I trimmed the rhododendrons, really. But I think it's most likely that it happened in the night."

Riggs nodded because it was easier than speaking. Mrs. Mooney went on, "Now, I don't know how long you gentlemen will need, but I have to get myself to the theater in forty minutes, and I want to get a locksmith here straight away to fix that door. Unlocked apartments are no good," she explained authoritatively. "Even in a good neighborhood like this, they can attract rodents, vagrants, and stray cats. And I can't abide stray cats." She shuddered.

Riggs thought about his own barely-domesticated cat, and he agreed with Mrs. Mooney.

"I understand," he said. "You can call your locksmith as soon as you want. I'm done with the door."

She thanked him and hurried off.

The two men stepped inside. At first glance, it didn't seem as though anything had even been disturbed, much less taken.

"I assume you checked out all the neighbors when you did your first report?" Riggs asked his partner as he looked around the stylish apartment.

"Yep, and they're squeaky clean," Fisher informed him. "Two pairs of single lady roommates; Mrs. Mooney, of course; and two older couples who've been here for decades. Nobody knew much about Miss Pike or her comings and goings. No one cared for her very much either. The general opinion was that she was a bit of a bad apple."

Fisher produced a small vial of powder, and the two policemen dusted for fingerprints, but whoever had broken into Ruby's apartment had been wearing gloves. There were patches on doorknobs and some of the surfaces that were smudged clean. After a general inspection, Fisher used his notes from Pike's file to begin comparing her recorded possessions against the apartment to see if anything was missing.

The drizzling stopped, and a few minutes later, the sun began to peek out through the clouds. Fisher was working systematically and quickly, combing through every inch of the apartment. He checked each item against his inventory. Riggs smiled to himself and thought, *Fisher may lack brains, but he sure makes up for it with his thoroughness.* He left the junior inspector alone and wandered around the little apartment. From the kitchen window, Riggs could see the sun's rays shining down on the lake below. It was a beautiful lake surrounded by buildings and dotted with boats clustered into marinas. He saw the marina where the *Isabelle* had resided before it was struck by lightning. One bolt of lightning had destroyed it within minutes. It was lousy luck, but things were turning around.

He walked over to the telephone, lifted the receiver to his ear, and was happy to hear that it was still connected. An idea nagged him, so he dialed a number at the library. A number he'd been told not to use.

Victoria answered.

"I'm glad you called me," she informed him.

That was unexpected.

She went on. "I've tried your office twice in the last twenty minutes. Of course, I couldn't leave my name."

Riggs lifted the heavy telephone and carried it into the little bathroom, shutting the door behind him. He lowered his voice. "What's happened?"

"I thought you should know Sadie Greenleaf is missing."

Riggs frowned and sat down on the edge of the bathtub. He looked at his wristwatch. "I called her house less than an hour ago, and the housekeeper said Miss Greenleaf was out shopping." His mustache felt like it was tingling, and he rubbed it. He didn't like the idea of Sadie Greenleaf's whereabouts being unknown. It didn't sound right. He could hear Fisher going through Ruby's drawers, so he quickly told Victoria where he was and why.

"A break-in," Victoria sighed. "That almost makes up for the fire, but I hope whoever did it isn't planning another murder."

Riggs looked out the window. Mrs. Mooney was approaching with a locksmith so he lowered his voice even more. "Just tell me one thing; how did you find out about Miss Greenleaf?"

"I called Miss Greenleaf to remind her that she has an overdue book. It didn't take much to get the housekeeper talking. You see, unlike your job title, *Inspector*, most people aren't afraid of a librarian."

"I disagree."

"Well, then, the whispering must be reassuring; it sounds confidential."

"Did the housekeeper say how long Sadie's been missing?"

"No, but they're worried. According to the housekeeper, Sadie *never* surprises them."

Riggs frowned at the bathroom floor. The break-in was a welcome development, but a missing person is never good. He finally had something to go on, but now he was running out of time. The locksmith started with the door.

"So what book does Sadie have that's overdue?"

"There is no book," Victoria explained. "Sadie Greenleaf hasn't checked out a library book since 1946, but I needed an excuse."

Chapter Twenty-One: Tracking Sylvester Finnegan

As soon as the telephone call with Victoria was over, Inspector Riggs flipped through his notepad. Then he asked the operator to connect him with the Department of Permitting. After a few minutes of dutiful bureaucracy and internal switchboards, he was connected to the department supervisor, who informed him that Sylvester Finnegan had left work at noon due to a headache. A third and fourth telephone call confirmed that he wasn't at the Blue Bay Tavern or his favorite diner, but if Sylvester Finnegan was at home with a headache, he wasn't answering his telephone.

The entire ordeal at 201 E Louisa took nearly an hour and fifteen minutes. In that time, the locksmith arrived and replaced the lock. He also expertly informed Riggs that the bolt had been forced with a metal object.

Michael Riggs, who had started his police career in burglaries, could have informed the locksmith that the metal object in question was a flat-blade screwdriver (probably a size 10), which had been wedged vertically and rocked in an upward motion until it popped the bolt spring. As a side note, Riggs could have added that this method was popular with amateurs. Besides the crude tool, professional burglars carry flashlights, and the good ones examine window putty. The putty around the door's window was chipping away so it would have been easier to remove the pane than to break the lock. But this burglar either didn't know that, or this was his first robbery, and he was working in the dark.

But Riggs was too busy thinking to explain any of this. He was nervous about Sadie Greenleaf, and he wanted to learn everything he could about this break-in as quickly as possible. Someone had grabbed the first tool they could find. They'd come at night because it was dark. They'd snuck around the building to this apartment, to Roberta's door, and forced an entry. Whoever it was, this amateur robber was connected with Roberta or her death.

So what had they taken?

It only took about ten minutes for the locksmith to replace the old lock with a bigger, meatier brass number that could hold up to a decent professional crook. And that was very good news for the new lock and bad news for the window's chipping putty.

Mrs. Mooney stopped by on her way to the theater to declare that after careful consideration, she had concluded that the break-in was not only the direct result of Roberta Pike's flagrant lifestyle, but it was undoubtedly the work of the shifty boyfriend, Sylvester Finnegan. Since her stolen heirlooms had still not been recovered, Mrs. Mooney felt that it was now squarely the duty of the Seattle Police to have Mr. Finnegan arrested and sent up the river, where he belonged.

As soon as Mrs. Mooney and the locksmith were gone, Inspector Fisher sighed and closed his inventory list. He turned to his partner and shook his head. "I just don't get it. I've searched everything in this apartment, and the only thing I can tell you for certain is that nothing is missing."

"It's all here?"

"Everything," Fisher said. "I was very thorough."

Riggs rubbed his mustache and took a deep breath. "Good. Then what we have now is an extensive list of everything that doesn't matter to Miss Pike's murderer."

"If only we knew what did matter."

"When we do, it will solve the case."

Fisher looked around the room. "Do you think he managed to search her boat before it burnt?"

"If he searched it, it's safe to say he didn't find what he was looking for. Maybe it still exists, or maybe it was destroyed in the fire. Whatever it is, it's important enough to make our murderer anxious."

Chapter Twenty-Two: The Disappearance of Sadie Greenleaf

The complete inspection of the break-in lasted until nearly five o'clock, and Riggs was anxious to go home. Like most days, he had promised himself he wasn't going to work late. He was tired of thinking, and he wanted to get home to enjoy a quiet evening with his family.

But the case wasn't a dead-end anymore. It was a real case, with a real murderer. And Sylvester Finnegan still wasn't answering his telephone. With one woman dead and a murderer who was desperate to find something, Riggs couldn't dismiss the fact that Sadie Greenleaf's whereabouts were unknown.

Riggs telephoned his wife and told her he'd be late. Then he put on his hat, scowled at Queen Anne Hill, and drove with Fisher around the south end of the lake. Mr. Greenleaf's house looked larger and emptier than it had before. Even the architecture seemed to be in a state of tension—or maybe that was the inspector's insides. And he wasn't reassured by how quickly the housekeeper led the two men into the library, nor by the worried creases on Mr. Greenleaf's face.

The old man was sitting by the fire, looking about ten years older than he had last week. As soon as they came in, he began talking. Riggs and Fisher learned the relevant facts. Miss Greenleaf usually took the Continental Mark II into town. She normally finished her shopping by eleven-thirty so she could be home in time for lunch. Sadie never failed to telephone if her plans changed, and she was always punctual.

Riggs glanced at his watch. It was an uncomfortable situation, but so far, Sadie had only been missing for five or six hours. If this weren't connected to a murder investigation, the police wouldn't even be here.

"The devil of it is," Mr. Greenleaf exclaimed irritably, "the more I think about it, I'm not even sure she was ever home."

"Excuse me?"

"Damn it," Mr. Greenleaf mumbled, resting his head in his hand. "I'm not myself at the moment. I'll try to explain it better. What I'm trying to say is that I'm not even sure that Sadie was home at all *last* night."

The hour count on Riggs's watch jumped from six hours to thirty.

Fisher's mouth fell open. Riggs sat down and looked at the old man. "Mr. Greenleaf, when was the last time you saw your niece?"

The old man ran his hand through his thin white hair. "Tuesday morning, about ten o'clock."

"Yesterday morning? Why didn't you file a missing person's report?"

"Because I didn't realize that she hadn't been here."

Riggs rubbed his face in his hands.

"Let me explain," Mr. Greenleaf said. "Sadie went out Tuesday morning to pick up my Continental from my step-nephew, Eddie. He had given it a tune-up at his garage. My housekeeper, Mrs. Lamar, drove Sadie to Eddie's garage. After picking up the car, Sadie called me about an hour later to tell me that she had decided to go to the cinema. She said she was going to meet a friend for dinner, so she wouldn't come home until later."

"Did you take that call yourself?"

"Yes, there's a telephone over there at my desk, and I happened to be sitting there when she telephoned."

"And you're saying that you don't know whether or not she came home at all last night?"

"That's right. Naturally, I just assumed that Sadie had come home late yesterday and left early this morning. She usually goes downtown on Wednesdays to do her shopping. So I didn't think anything of it. But when Mrs. Lamar went to Sadie's room an hour ago, she said the bed didn't look like it had been slept in at all."

"Did she say who the friend was?"

Mr. Greenleaf shook his head, "No, and I don't know any of her friends."

"What about the restaurant or the movie she was going to?"

The old man shook his head.

"I see," Riggs said. "I'm filing a missing person's report now, Mr. Greenleaf. I'll send out the alarm, and we'll do everything we can to find her. I'll want the numbers on your Continental Mark II. It's a brand new 1956, isn't it? Fisher, will you talk to Mrs. Lamar and her husband and take down the particulars?"

Fisher nodded and left the room.

Riggs was going to leave when he remembered what had been bothering him so much. "Mr. Greenleaf, can you tell me about your boat, the one that you let Roberta use?"

"Oh, the *Isabelle*? It burnt, you know, last Friday."

"Yes, I know. But Roberta used it, didn't she?"

"Oh, yes. I was going to give it to Roberta in my will, along with just about everything else. Roberta was terribly sentimental about that little boat, probably because it was named after her mother, my dear sister. Of course, she didn't know how to sail, but I knew how much she loved it, so I gave her the marina key so she could enjoy it."

"Do you know what she did on the boat?"

Jacob Greenleaf said, "I don't think she really *did* anything. Do you know how most little girls love dollhouses? Well, I think the *Isabelle* was like that for Roberta; it was just a quiet, dreamy little place where she could escape the world for a few hours. When she was little, Roberta always used to pretend that she was a queen, and everyone had to obey her."

He smiled.

"Do you know if she kept anything personal on the *Isabelle*?"

"Well, I don't really know. I haven't been down there in years. I think Sadie may have gone down there once or twice. And I know she went down there after Roberta died."

"Do you know why?"

Mr. Greenleaf shook his head.

Riggs rubbed his mustache. "Well, as soon as we find her, I'll be sure to ask."

Chapter Twenty-Three: Murder

Friday morning Michael Riggs was running late. Criminal had tipped the milk bottle off the counter during breakfast, and it had taken him ten minutes to clean it up. Amy probably wouldn't forgive Criminal for the wasted milk until he killed another mouse.

At the police station, Riggs snuck out of the elevator and managed to get himself a cup of coffee without being seen. He crept into his office, but he didn't turn on the light. As soon as his shoes were off, he saw Fisher approaching through the hall window. He was carrying two boxes, and he walked as though he'd been drinking coffee all morning.

He came straight to Riggs's office and opened the door without bothering to knock. "You're late, boss," the junior inspector announced. "You've been missing the excitement."

"I'm not sorry," Riggs informed him. "I was hoping there wouldn't be any excitement. I don't suppose it's good news?"

Fisher shook his head. "Nope, it's all the bad kind of excitement. They found a woman's body in a '56 Continental Mark II."

Riggs scowled. "Where?"

"Eastlake."

Riggs ran his hand through his hair and frowned. "I was afraid of that."

"This one was definitely murder. No doubt about it. Doc Hara says she was conked, good and hard, on the back of the head with a tire iron. They found it on the car floor."

"When did it happen?"

"Doc says Tuesday afternoon. Nobody noticed her 'cause there was a picnic blanket thrown over the body."

"Sadie Greenleaf?"

Fisher rubbed his neck. "Looks like it."

Riggs took a swig of his coffee. It was nowhere near strong enough, but it was better than nothing. "What do we know so far?"

"There are only two sets of fingerprints, one is hers. The other set probably belongs to her cousin, Eddie Pike. He'd just given the car a tune-up. They should be able to verify the fingerprints and her identity within the hour."

"Okay. Anything else?"

"We found this," Fisher said as he set something on the table. It was a round box, flat on top and bottom, and tall enough to hold a three-layer cake. "It's a hatbox," Fisher explained.

Riggs looked at it. The hatbox was about fourteen inches across, covered in a grass-green fabric, and trimmed with black lace. Riggs untied the black silk ribbon and removed the lid. Inside were eight or nine theater programs, mostly plays on the East Coast, one in London, and one in Paris. The only local program was from the Paramount Theater last spring. *The Lady my Love.* Beneath the programs were hairpins, hatpins, a pair of silk stockings, three brightly colored lipsticks, face powder, and two blushes. Riggs opened a small silk-lined box and whistled.

"This is interesting," Riggs said as he examined the contents. It was jewelry, and good quality jewelry, from the looks of it. Ten pieces; seven of them were contemporary and new, but three pieces looked like antiques.

"Too bad we didn't get a hold of this hatbox while Miss Greenleaf was still alive. I'd sure like to have known what she would have said about it."

"There's one more thing," Fisher said. "We finally heard back from the police in Ohio. They don't know any 'Sylvester Finnegan', but his age and description match the identity of one 'Keith Finnegan' who spent most of '51 and '52 in a state prison for fraud. He got out at the end of '52, but his father died a few weeks later, and then Mr. Finnegan skipped his parole. They haven't heard from him since. They're sending us his file and a photograph."

"That's promising." Riggs downed his coffee in one gulp and started putting on his shoes. There was work to be done quickly. It was a small consolation that the chief would have to eat his words about Riggs wasting police time; another woman was dead, and Riggs was worried. It wasn't until he stood up that he realized Fisher was still holding another box–a plain brown one.

"So, what's that?"

"Oh, this?" Fisher said happily, as he set the box down and lifted the lid. "This is something entirely different. I ordered this for my next plainclothes job," he explained as he carefully lifted up something hairy. He held it to his chin. "It's my new beard."

After the stress of the last couple days, Riggs appreciated a good laugh.

Chapter Twenty-Four: Roberta's Green Hatbox

On Friday morning, Riggs led Miss Baker into his office. "Do you two ladies know each other?" Riggs asked. Ann Marie was already sitting down. Both women shook their heads, and Riggs waited until Margaret was seated.

"Miss Baker worked with Ruby at Blackwell Enterprises," he explained, "and until six or seven weeks ago, Miss Lewis used to spend a fair amount of time with Ruby." Margaret's forehead furrowed for a moment, but she reached out her hand. "Ann Marie Lewis?" she asked. "Your name is familiar. I think Ruby mentioned you once or twice."

Riggs sat down behind his desk. "I've asked you both here because you two seem to have been Miss Pike's closest friends. Since I've started investigating this case, I've realized that not all of Miss Pike's personal possessions are accounted for." He took a deep breath and explained, "Unfortunately, the body of Ruby's cousin, Miss Greenleaf, was found this morning."

Margaret's brow furrowed. "When you say 'body,' do you mean she's dead?"

The inspector said, "Yes. I'm sorry to say that she was found in her car on the east side of Lake Union. It was parked on Yale Avenue, near the corner of Lynn."

"But that's right by me," Ann Marie exclaimed. "It's only a couple blocks from my apartment! And my coffee shop is just around the corner from Lynn Street."

Margaret glanced at Ann Marie, then she turned to Riggs and asked, "Inspector, are you saying she was murdered?"

The Inspector nodded. "I'm afraid there's no doubt about it. Now, I'm looking for her murderer."

Ann Marie rested back into her chair as if she might faint, but Margaret was sitting upright. "It must be the same person who killed Ruby."

Ann Marie leaned forward. She frowned for a moment and turned to Riggs, "Do you know when it happened, Inspector? I guess it must have been last night?"

"We'll know in a few hours," he lied.

Ann Marie nodded, but she looked like she was going to cry.

A seagull fluttered outside the window before settling itself on the ledge. Riggs took a paper bag from his drawer and opened the window. The fresh morning air rushed into the room. One by one, Riggs tossed four or five stale breadcrumbs at the bird, and one by one, the bird devoured them. Ann Marie regained her composure. When the crumbs were gone, the inspector sat back down at his desk, but the greedy bird waited impatiently for more.

Riggs brought out the green hatbox.

"Do either of you recognize this?" he asked. Both women shook their heads, and he set it down in the middle of his desk. "This box was found in the car with Miss Greenleaf. I have reason to believe it belonged to her cousin."

The two women exchanged uncomfortable glances as Riggs untied the silk ribbon. "I asked you both here because I'm hoping you can shed some light on this," he explained as he removed the lid. Margaret and Ann Marie stared as Riggs removed the items and laid them out on his desk. The neglected seagull boldly inched closer to the window and squawked his demands.

The inspector ignored the bird.

The women looked at the contents of the box.

"I gave Ruby that hat pin," Ann Marie said as she pointed to a simple hat pin with a blue-colored pearl. "It was for her birthday. And I think I've seen her wearing some of this other jewelry, except for these old-fashioned ones and this one with the rose."

Margaret nodded. "I think I recognize most of the jewelry," she agreed. "Ruby had some very nice pieces."

A few more items came out of the hatbox.

"That's Ruby's diamond necklace," Ann Marie said, "and those diamond earrings too. Ruby got them last Christmas from her uncle."

Margaret whispered, "And I remember that gold brooch with the rose made out of rubies. She only got it last month."

"Did she buy it herself?" Riggs asked.

Margaret picked up the gold brooch and turned it over in her hands. "No, I don't think so. She said it was a gift."

The seagull tapped his beak loudly on the glass, but his benefactor continued to ignore him.

"Did she say who gave it to her? Her uncle, maybe, or her boyfriend, Mr. Finnegan?"

But Margaret shook her head and set the brooch back down. "No. Actually, she wouldn't say. She was very silly about that sort of thing sometimes. I thought—" Margaret stopped and adjusted her own pearl necklace nervously.

"Yes?"

Margaret shook her head. "It's nothing. I'm sorry, I don't know about the brooch."

"But you have an idea?"

Margaret looked uncomfortable. "It was just an idea I had at the time. I can't imagine why it would pop in my head at all. I didn't have any reason to think about it."

Riggs sat down on top of his desk and looked down at her. "Miss Baker, I'm a Sergeant Inspector, and I've been doing this for a long time. You can trust me to know the difference between evidence and ideas. But sometimes, ideas are fueled by little facts we haven't fully noticed yet. An idea can be wrong, but it can sometimes lead us to the truth." He picked up the brooch and held it for her to see. "I would like to hear what you thought about this brooch."

Margaret hesitated and said, "Well, I thought—that is, I suppose I had the idea that Ruby might have had another boyfriend, someone besides

Sylvester. After all, if she'd gotten a brooch from her uncle or from Sylvester, she wouldn't have had any reason to be so secretive about it."

"And what would you have said if Ruby did have another boyfriend?"

Margaret looked surprised at the question. "Well, that's not a very nice thing to do, is it?"

"So, Ruby wouldn't have wanted to tell you," Riggs agreed. "Yes, it's possible Ruby was seeing someone besides Sylvester. But it's also possible that she had some other reason for not wanting to tell."

Ann Marie looked at the inspector. "Like what?"

Riggs didn't answer the question. Instead, he turned the golden piece of jewelry over in his hands and studied it closely. "It's a pretty brooch," he observed. "But jewelry comes in lots of different styles." He held the piece up at arm's length so he could see it from a distance. "Both of you knew Roberta Pike. Would you say this particular style suited her tastes?"

Ann Marie nodded, and Margaret said, "Yes, definitely. It's modern and a little gaudy, exactly the sort of thing Ruby liked. And she liked rubies especially because of her name."

"Then it's exactly the sort of thing that Miss Pike might have bought for herself?"

Margaret's mouth opened. "I hadn't thought of that."

Riggs set the brooch down on his desk. "If she admitted to having bought an expensive piece of jewelry herself, everyone would have wondered where she got the money."

"Oh, I see," said Ann Marie, "but if she said it was a gift—"

Margaret finished the idea, "Then everyone wonders about *the man,* and no one wonders about the expense."

Riggs rubbed his mustache. "Of course, there could have been a man involved, but in any event, we can say for certain that Miss Pike chose not to share the details about this brooch."

Margaret frowned and was about to say something when Ann Marie whispered, "Ruby's diary."

Margaret looked at the contents of the box.

But Ann Marie was looking at Riggs. "Inspector, did you find a diary with

Ruby's things?"

"Did she have a diary?" Riggs asked.

Ann Marie nodded, "Yes. You should check there, Inspector. She may have written something about the brooch."

Riggs's expression was simply curious, but his heart was racing. Pike had a diary.

"What did the diary look like?"

Ann Marie considered for a moment and shook her head. "I don't think I ever saw it."

"But you're sure she had one?"

"I'm positive. She used to call it her 'Confessional,' and she'd always joke about writing down other people's secrets. It was just a joke, but whenever somebody got drunk or started flirting, Ruby would laugh and say something like, 'Be careful, or your secrets will end in my Confessional.'"

Without a word, Riggs walked over to the window. He looked outside for several minutes while he rubbed his mustache. When he sat back down at his desk, he pulled his pipe out of his pocket. He studied it as he turned it over in his hands. The highly polished wood gleamed back at him, and he tapped it three or four times on his desk very gently as if the action might produce an answer. Ann Marie and Margaret tried not to exchange too many glances as they waited.

Finally, the inspector slipped the pipe back into his pocket and leaned all the way forward so that he could rest his elbows on the desk.

"Miss Lewis, I'd like to ask you a direct question, and I'd like you to think about it carefully before you answer me."

She nodded.

"Do you think it's possible that Ruby Pike ever used information about other people to encourage them to do what she wanted?"

Ann Marie's mouth fell open in dismay. "What? You—you mean like blackmail? Of course not! You don't really believe Ruby was a blackmailer? Why, she was just a kid!"

At first, Riggs didn't answer, but after several moments he said, "She may not have seen it as blackmail. But if she knew personal details about a person, she may have thought it was only fair to remind them of the fact when she wanted them to see things her way."

Ann Marie frowned, and she gently bit her lip. But as she considered the idea, her objection seemed to fade until it was all she could do to stare down at her lap. She took a deep breath and glanced at Margaret. Riggs waited patiently. In his experience, it was often the kindest people who had the most difficulty seeing the malice in others.

"I suppose," she said reluctantly, "well, when you put it like that, I suppose it's not impossible. Ruby did like thinking that she had power over other people. Oh, that's a terrible thing to say." She looked down and began to rub her gloves. For a moment, Riggs wondered if she was going to cry again.

After a while, Margaret shook her head and sighed, "I'm not sure you're right about that idea, Inspector. It's true Ruby liked to buy nice things. She spent a lot of money, and I know she wasn't an angel, but that doesn't make her a blackmailer."

"What would you say, Miss Baker, if I suggested that Ruby Pike not only occasionally used her information about people to induce them to go along with her, but I believe you were intended as her next resource?"

Margaret laughed in disbelief. "What? But I was her friend."

Ann Marie turned her head to look out the window as she whispered, "That wouldn't have mattered. Ruby didn't have a special standard for friendships."

Margaret looked at the other woman quizzically, but Ann Marie kept her attention fixed on the seagull until Margaret turned back to Riggs.

"Inspector, you're forgetting that it doesn't pay much to blackmail a stenographer. My salary wasn't high enough to justify blackmail."

"Things change," Riggs reminded her tactfully. "You were a stenographer last week, but in a few short months, you will be a comfortably married woman. Money will be less of an obstacle then."

Margaret shook her head in disbelief. "Ruby wasn't that good at planning ahead. And even if Ruby were willing to do that sort of thing, which I don't believe for a second, she would still need something to use as a threat."

"That's not necessarily true," Riggs explained. "Scandals are the best way to blackmail someone. But if a real scandal doesn't exist, a clever blackmailer can always create something that's convincing; something suggestive, even with weak evidence, can still damage a person's reputation."

From the corner of his eye, Riggs noticed Ann Marie's shoulders become rigid. The seagull flew away, but Ann Marie kept staring at the same empty ledge.

Chapter Twenty-Five: Sadie Greenleaf's Secrets

Before lunchtime, Riggs and Fisher searched Sadie Greenleaf's bedroom. It was a large room on the second story of her uncle's house. There was an old-fashioned wooden bed, a heavy Queen Anne dressing table, and a matching settee and desk. An elegant brass telescope stood on a tripod near the French doors. Riggs pulled back the heavy velvet drapes to expose a charming balcony with a view that stretched eastward over Lake Union. He unlatched the doors and stepped outside. In the far distance, he could see the Cascade Mountain range, but much closer was the lake beneath him and the marina.

He came back inside and looked through a telescope. He lined it up so he could view the dock where the *Isabelle* had been moored. "Miss Greenleaf's room has an exceptional view," he observed.

Mrs. Lamar nodded and wiped her eyes with her handkerchief. "You can say that again, Inspector," she agreed. "In my opinion, it's the best room in the house, although Mr. Greenleaf's is bigger. Miss Greenleaf may not have been her uncle's favorite niece, but he never treated her poorly, and that's a fact."

"I understand she was his brother's child," Riggs said.

"Yes, that was before my time, but I understand Tom Greenleaf was nothing like his brother. When Tom died, I don't think the brothers had spoken in years."

Inspector Fisher frowned. "That's unfortunate."

The woman cleared her throat. "Well, Tom never amounted to much. He gambled and drank and carried on with loose women. When he died, he left nothing except a daughter and a pile of debts."

"And his brother took care of both?"

Mrs. Lamar nodded. "For all his stubbornness, Mr. Jacob Greenleaf is a good man. He settled his brother's accounts and took Sadie right in."

"What about Sadie's mother?"

The housekeeper shrugged. "Mr. Greenleaf always assured Miss Sadie that her folks had been properly married in a church. But I don't think he knew the truth one way or another. I can tell you he certainly never tried to find out who the woman was, and I always say that actions speak louder than words."

"Then he was kind to his niece," Riggs agreed.

"Well, it's what I call Christian charity, if you know what I mean. He got a nanny to look after Sadie when she was young. And when she was grown, the nanny moved on, and Mr. Greenleaf gave his niece a decent allowance. Although I don't suppose I should be telling you any of this. It's none of my business."

"He must have been very fond of her," Riggs suggested, but the old woman shook her head.

"Mr. Greenleaf is a good man," she corrected him, "but everyone knew that he was just doing his duty for Sadie; it was the other niece he really adored."

"Roberta," Riggs acknowledged. "Did you like her?"

"I didn't know her well enough to like her or dislike her," Mrs. Lamar said. "I only saw her when she visited, but she was always very sweet and agreeable to her uncle."

Riggs nodded, and when it looked like the housekeeper had nothing more to say about Roberta, he changed the subject. "Mrs. Lamar, the last time you saw Miss Sadie, how was she?"

The old housekeeper leaned against the doorway, and her gaze focused on nothing in particular. "Oh, she was the same as always. Maybe there was something on her mind, and maybe there wasn't. She was a bit quiet, I suppose. But that wasn't unusual for her. Sadie was brooding by nature. She didn't have what anyone would call a cheerful disposition, and she never talked about her feelings. So, I couldn't say for sure. On Tuesday, I dropped her off at her cousin's garage, and she told me I could go. That was the last I saw of her. I went off to do the shopping."

"You assumed she would come home?"

"Of course, she always did. And Wednesday was her usual shopping day, so I wasn't surprised that the car was gone the next morning."

"Were you and Miss Greenleaf on good terms?"

"We were on perfectly civil terms," the older woman explained, "but we weren't close. Sadie was an unhappy sort of woman, and she liked to keep to herself. That was fine by me, and I stuck to my work. I can't imagine why anyone would be like that, but that was Sadie. She just had a negative outlook, I suppose. Maybe she inherited that from her mother…maybe she didn't, but either way, she kept to herself most of the time, and when she did talk, it was usually to mention something gloomy."

"What about her friends?"

"If she had any, there's not one that I can name. Anyway, she never brought anyone to the house."

"Had she been especially unhappy lately?"

"It's funny that you ask that," Mrs. Lamar said, "because these last few weeks, Sadie was almost the opposite. She wasn't happy, mind you. And it's nothing I can put my finger on, but somehow, it was as if a cloud had been lifted from her mind."

Inspector Riggs rubbed his mustache. "Did she say anything to give you an idea of what it was?"

The woman shrugged. "No, I don't even know why I thought it. She never confided in me."

"Was she fond of her uncle?"

"Not that I could see. I suppose she was grateful to him, but that's not the same thing as true affection. She did her duty by taking care of him and helping around the house, but I think she resented him." Mrs. Lamar stopped and shook her head. "I'm sorry, I shouldn't be saying any of this.

The poor woman is gone, and that's that. Besides, what do I know? I'm not family or anything. I just work here."

"I disagree," Riggs said. "Sadie didn't have many friends, and your honest opinions, kind or not, will help us to find her murderer."

Mrs. Lamar nodded and took a deep breath, "Sadie resented her uncle. She was indebted to him, and she resented him for it. But she was jealous, too. And she resented her cousin and everyone else who was happy. I think the bitterness ate away at her like a disease."

"She must have been miserable," Fisher said.

The housekeeper nodded. She was ready to go, but she stopped in the doorway and added, "Do you gentlemen remember the commandment about not coveting things? Well, in Sadie Greenleaf's case, they should have added a little bit about showing gratitude. A little gratitude would have done Sadie Greenleaf a world of good."

As soon as Mrs. Lamar left, the two policemen began searching the room properly. Sadie Greenleaf had a large built-in closet full of designer clothes. They were all modern, neatly organized, and all in dark, grayish colors. The top shelves were lined mostly with hats. The bottom two shelves were arranged with matching shoes and handbags. In most of the handbags, Fisher found bundles of paper money, usually in five and ten-dollar bills, but the bundles occasionally amounted to fifty dollars or more.

"She may have shared her cousin's obsession with beautiful clothes," Fisher observed, pulling out another wad of bills, "but it looks like Sadie Greenleaf was better at keeping her money." He flipped through the current stash. "That's three hundred and sixty-five bucks so far."

In the top drawer of the dresser, Riggs found a beautiful wooden box. He set it on the bed and began looking for the key.

"Hmm, well, I guess a girl never knows when she may need to buy another drab dress," he said. "And it's strange that she wore such dismal colors. My wife would only wear this stuff at a funeral."

Fisher agreed. "I think Sadie Greenleaf's life was a bit like a funeral. Although I'm not sure what she was mourning with all this money she had." He opened the drawer of the nightstand and pulled out a small key.

"How's this?" he asked before tossing the key to Riggs.

Riggs took the key to the wooden box. When he opened it, Fisher whistled so loudly that Riggs hit his arm.

"Hey, keep it down, or the housekeeper will come back."

"Wow," Fisher whispered, "you don't think it's all real, do you?"

Riggs picked up an amber necklace studded with several carats of diamonds. "I think it is," he said, holding it up to the light. He examined a few more pieces and kept his voice low. "Yes, it's real. My God, what a collection!"

Fisher picked up a strand of pearls. "I guess when a girl has a handsome allowance and no expenses, she's able to afford a few things over the years. Between this jewelry and the cash she's got tucked everywhere, I'd say Sadie Greenleaf was amassing quite a tidy little sum."

Riggs nodded. "And it looks as though she'd been at it for some time."

Chapter Twenty-Six: Sadie's Trail

The thorough inspection of Sadie Greenleaf's room produced no diary. When the work was finished, Riggs headed back downstairs. This time, Mr. Jacob Greenleaf was more composed, although he still looked terrible, and he kept repeating that he was in a state of complete shock.

"I'm at a total loss, Inspector. I just can't believe it," he said from his chair by the fire. "How could a thing like this happen?"

"I'm sorry for your loss, Mr. Greenleaf."

"First, you come in here and tell me that Roberta's death was no accident, and now someone murders Sadie?" The old man shook his head. "But why? Why would anyone do such horrible things? Those two were all I had."

"I realize this is a difficult time for you, Mr. Greenleaf, but I need to ask you some questions."

"Of course. Anything," the old man agreed. "I want this man brought to justice."

"I'm looking for Roberta's diary, Mr. Greenleaf. Do you know anything about it?"

Mr. Greenleaf shook his head. "No, I don't think anyone ever mentioned a diary to me. But I suppose it's not usually the sort of thing someone talks about. I mean, it's not very interesting."

"Did Miss Greenleaf read a lot of books?"

"No, she didn't really like to read, except for gossip and fashion magazines. And she did read the newspaper every now and then. She did the crossword puzzles."

"But no books?"

"No. Yes," he corrected himself. "Just the other day, I saw her with a little brown book."

"What was the title?"

"I don't think it had a title," the old man said. "I first noticed it about a month ago, and I saw her reading it a few times."

"Do you know where it is now?"

The old man frowned and looked at the bookshelves. "No, but you're welcome to look for it. I asked her about it once, and she said her friend had written it."

"Who were Miss Greenleaf's friends?"

"Well, really, I don't know," the old man admitted. "Sadie never had very many friends, not close ones anyway. She was a very solitary sort of girl. She was a member of the art museum, and she used to go to their luncheons, but that was several years ago. And I remember there were a couple of old school friends who Sadie sometimes met for shopping, but she hasn't mentioned them for a long time. I can't even remember their names."

"Did she ever bring friends to the house?"

"No, she wasn't social like Roberta," the old man explained. "Every now and then, Sadie mentioned people who she knew, but on the whole, I don't think she liked people very much."

"That's unfortunate."

Mr. Greenleaf shook his head. "Her father was the same way. Just wanted to be left alone to do as he pleased. Unless, of course, there was something he wanted. At least Sadie was good enough to be social when it was necessary. Until my health got bad, she used to go to social events and to church with me, but lately—"

There was a loud noise in the hallway, and Eddie Pike burst into the room. "Uncle Jac—" he began, but he stopped short when he saw Inspector Riggs standing there. He looked at the inspector, then went back to his uncle. "So, it is true," he whispered. "Ann Marie just told me, and I couldn't believe it. I thought there was a mistake, but it's true. Then Sadie is...Sadie is dead?"

His uncle nodded silently, and Eddie's face turned white. "But how..."

Riggs said, "I'm very sorry, Mr. Pike."

"No," Eddie interrupted him, "I have something to tell you." He fumbled a little as he realized he was wearing his plaid cap indoors. He pulled it off his head and tried to shove it into his back pocket. "I saw her on Tuesday—no—Wednesday. From what Ann Marie just told me, I may have been one of the last people to see Sadie alive."

"Yes, that's possible."

"Then I have to tell you what she said," Eddie hurried on. "It might be important. She came by my garage to pick up Uncle Jacob's Continental. I was finishing the tune-up, and Sadie was sort of rambling about stuff while I finished. She did that sometimes. Sadie said that Roberta's boyfriend had been by the house. She said that he asked her if he could have a remembrance of Roberta; specifically, he asked if he could have Roberta's diary."

"Did he?" Riggs asked, rubbing his mustache.

"That's what Sadie said," Eddie nodded, "but she wasn't sure if she should give it to him. She thought it might be too personal, and maybe she should give him some of Roberta's photographs instead."

"She had plenty of photographs," Mr. Greenleaf said.

But Riggs was still thinking. "You're sure Sadie was talking about Roberta's diary?"

"Yes, I'm sure. I thought at first Sadie meant that diaries themselves were too personal, but when I thought about it later, I realized she might have meant that *Roberta's diary* itself was too personal. I think Sadie may have read Roberta's diary, and she knew it said something about Finnegan; you'll have to see."

"We don't have Roberta's diary," Riggs informed him.

Eddie stared at the Inspector. "But Sadie must have read it because she seemed to know all about it. So it must be around here somewhere."

"We're anxious to find it too, Mr. Pike," Riggs assured him. "Policemen don't like things to disappear."

"That reminds me," Eddie added, "of something else Sadie said. But it wasn't about the diary; it was something else...."

He paused for a moment and looked up at the ceiling. "What was it?

Something that the police hadn't seen or didn't know…I was working, and Sadie was talking. She was sort of talking to herself, and I wasn't really paying that much attention. And she said something about the police and a dress. That was it! And she said the police didn't know, but it didn't matter."

"A dress we don't know about?" Riggs repeated.

Eddie nodded. "I think that's what she said. It was Roberta's dress." He snapped his fingers. "'A yellow dress,' that's what she said. But I can't remember the reason it didn't matter because I was only half listening."

Inspector Riggs rubbed his mustache and looked at Eddie intently. "Mr. Pike, what else did your cousin say?"

Eddie rubbed the back of his neck. "Well, Sadie showed me a photograph of Miss Lewis. Then she started to tell me her whole life story, all about how Miss Lewis had grown up poor and how she was an orphan. But when I asked her how she knew so much about Miss Lewis, Sadie said she'd learned it all from Roberta."

"And why did that stand out to you?"

Eddie raised his eyebrow. "I guess because I hadn't realized that they were on such friendly terms. I'd always thought that Sadie disliked Roberta."

Jacob Greenleaf frowned but didn't say anything.

"What else did she say?" Riggs asked.

"Not much. And just before she drove off, I said she should talk to the police before she gave anything to Mr. Finnegan."

"Did she agree to do that?"

Eddie shrugged. "I don't know what she decided to do. She was already in the car, and she just sort of smiled and drove off. And that was the last I saw of her."

"I see," Riggs sighed. "And by the way, Mr. Pike, you said you heard about your cousin's death from Miss Lewis?"

Eddie's face flushed. "Yes, she came to my garage right after she left your office this morning. She was pretty shaken up, poor kid. All of this has been pretty terrible for her."

Riggs said, "I hadn't realized you two were friends."

Eddie blushed. "We aren't really," he stammered, "I mean, we just met the other day, but she's a nice girl, and she used to be Roberta's best friend, and so we seem to have a lot to talk about, that's all."

"That's quite understandable," Riggs agreed, "and I'm sorry for prying. It's a matter of routine, you understand. But I'll need to know what you did on Wednesday after Miss Greenleaf left you."

"I was at my garage all day," Eddie said. "And after work, I went bowling with some friends."

"Can anyone vouch for that?"

"The two other mechanics can vouch for the time I was at work. Well, except between twelve o'clock and three o'clock, because I had to send them out on jobs. But they both came back just before three o'clock. And at five o'clock, we locked up, and I met a couple of friends at the bowling alley. I was there from about a quarter after five until midnight."

"Thank you, Mr. Pike. I'm sure we'll be able to verify that easily enough. Can anyone at all vouch for your whereabouts between noon and three?"

Eddie shook his head. "If I had known that I would need an alibi, I would have called someone."

Riggs smiled and put his hat on. "Oh, that's all right. It just would have been easier." Then the Inspector changed his tone and wondered out loud, "Now, I'll just have to see what Miss Lewis was up to on Wednesday."

"What, Ann Marie?" Eddie objected. "But, you can't possibly suspect her of anything. She's a sweet girl. She'd never get mixed up in a thing like this!"

Just as Riggs suspected.

The inspector slipped his notebook into his pocket. Now, all he had to do was tackle a boyfriend and track down a scandalous little confessional.

Chapter Twenty-Seven: The Boyfriend's Last Stand

At the Blue Bay Tavern, Sylvester Finnegan fidgeted on his bar stool. He turned his empty glass on the bar, re-positioned it on the coaster, and glanced again at the door. A man and woman he didn't know came into the bar. He watched them until they sat down, then he looked back at the door. Usually, the tavern felt comfortable and pleasant, but tonight, everything was wrong. He finally managed to pull his focus away from the door. He signaled the barman. The familiar graying man came over to him and swung his towel on his shoulder.

Sylvester tapped the bar nervously. "How 'bout another beer, Riggs?"

The barman frowned. "Riggs? The name's still Ralph, same as it's always been."

"Sorry, Ralph," Sylvester groaned, "I'm a little out of it."

The barman didn't have to be told. He poured the lager. "So, what's eating you?"

"Nothing, I guess," Sylvester shrugged. "Hey, I think I'll move over to a booth in the corner. Can you send my burger there when it's ready?"

"Sure thing," Ralph said.

Sylvester took his beer and moved to the farthest booth. Even in the middle of the day, it was the darkest part of the room. He sat with his back to the wall so he could watch the door. He didn't like being here, but he didn't want to go home. A beautiful woman came in and took the booth next to him. Good. Somehow he liked that better than the thought of it being available to just anyone. The waitress brought him his burger, and he took it without thanking her. He had just decided that he might be able to manage an appetite after all when he saw the two men come through the door.

Inspector Riggs found what he wanted in the corner. He and Fisher made their way over to him.

"May we join you, Mr. Finnegan?"

Sylvester put a French fry in his mouth and looked down. "I ain' got nothin' to say to you."

Riggs sat down first and scooted over to make room for his partner. "You remember Inspector Fisher."

"Not really. Why? Does it matter if I do?"

"He's the inspector who originally interviewed you about Ruby's murder."

Sylvester nearly choked on the fry. "*Murder?*" He swallowed hard. "What the hell are you talking about? Look, I already told you everything. Ruby was a pretty girl, that's all. I hung out with her 'cause she knew how to have a good time. But I wasn't the only fella she knew." He crammed another fry in his mouth. The two policemen let the silence become uncomfortable until Sylvester looked up. "She wasn't anything special to me. Ruby and Ann Marie liked to go out dancing. That's all. They knew a lot of fellas. If you think Ruby was murdered, it must have been one of the other guys in her life 'cause it sure as hell wasn't me!" Sylvester paused to gulp his beer. "Why don't you go hound that banker guy, Bud, no Bruce? Go ask him what happened to Ruby."

"No one's hounding you, Mr. Finnegan."

"Besides," Sylvester panted between bites. "I got an alibi!"

Riggs waited for a few minutes before leaning back in the seat. When he spoke, his voice was smooth and quiet. "Where were you on Tuesday afternoon?"

"At work."

"Your boss says you left work early on both Tuesday and Wednesday."

Sylvester looked up at them sharply. "Yeah, that's right. I didn't feel so good. So I went home early. If you wanna know, I sat in my apartment and watched the television until eleven that night." He took another bite of his lunch and looked down to chew it.

"Were you alone?"

"Yep."

"Mr. Finnegan, did you ever meet Ruby's cousin, Sadie Greenleaf?"

He took a gulp of his lager. "Nope."

Riggs took the photograph out of his pocket and handed it to Sylvester. "Sadie gave this to me. She said she knew you."

"Well, maybe I met her once or twice, and maybe I forgot. She isn't that good-looking, you know."

"She's dead."

Sylvester stopped chewing and forcibly swallowed. He looked back and forth at their faces. "And you think I did it?"

"We're not accusing you, Mr. Finnegan. This is just routine questioning. We're asking everyone who was involved with Roberta or her cousin to account for their movements on Tuesday."

Sylvester took his napkin and wiped his mouth. "Listen, bud, I don't have to answer your questions. I have an alibi for the night Ruby died. I was right here in this bar. And even if I had met her cousin, I didn't know her well enough to kill her." He stood up and tossed the napkin onto his unfinished lunch. He walked straight to the bar, handed Ralph a larger bill than was needed, and left without getting his change. He didn't even look back.

Riggs nodded at Fisher and muttered, "Keep it discreet."

Fisher grabbed his hat and followed the trail. The inspector sat for a few minutes and considered his options. He hadn't even gotten to the part where he asked Mr. Finnegan if his real name was Keith. No, it was better to save that part for later. He was conscious of the barman watching him, and after a few minutes, he stood up and moseyed over to the bar.

The barman came over and wiped down the bar. "What can I get you, Sir?"

"Do you remember me?" the policeman asked.

"Yep."

"You're Sylvester Finnegan's alibi," Riggs explained, "but the Pike girl was murdered, and now there's been a second murder. I've read your statement, but I'm going to ask you again. Are you absolutely positive that Mr. Finnegan never left the bar the night Miss Pike died?"

The barman wiped the bar for a few moments before he took a deep breath and leaned in, "I wouldn't like this to get out," he whispered. "I thought it was just a lovers' quarrel, you see. I figured if that dumb girl went and jumped off a bridge, it's hardly fair for Mr. Finnegan to take the heat for it. Everyone likes to blame a boyfriend, but she was tight."

"That's often the case," Riggs sympathized.

"So, I didn't like to say anything. But the fact of the matter is, when she stormed off that night, he followed her. But he was back here not ten minutes later. He said she'd have to sleep it off and stay until closing."

Riggs nodded. "I see. And I won't mention it unless it can't be helped."

"I appreciate it," the barman nodded.

"By the way," Riggs asked, "do you remember what she was so upset about that night?"

The barman shrugged and re-wiped the bar. "You know, after a few drinks, most folks sing the same song. A guy drinks too much and thinks his girl's got another guy, or she drinks too much, and it's the other way around. It happens a lot around here, especially after eleven o'clock. But Sylvester's girl was different. They argued at the table for a bit, just the two of them. And it looked like she was trying to convince him of something, and he wasn't having it. Finally, she yells, 'Damn you, Sylvester!' and then before she left, she shouted, "You bastard, I'll tell the whole world if I want to!' And that was the last I saw of her."

Riggs saw the barman looking past his shoulder, and he turned to see who was there. In the booth near the corner, the attractive woman was just sipping the last of her beer. She had brown hair and was wearing a peach-colored dress with a fitted bodice and a full skirt. Riggs turned back to the bartender and whispered, "Does she come here often?"

The bartender looked her up and down and shook his head. "Nope. First time. But I sure wouldn't mind if she started. That broad is easy on the eyes."

Riggs looked back at the barman. "Give me two beers, please."

The bartender winked, and a moment later, he handed Inspector Riggs two pint glasses and muttered, "Good luck."

Riggs gave a tiny smile and took the glasses over to the woman. The bartender watched the inspector approach the woman. He said something to her, and she looked surprised, but she seemed to agree because a moment later, Riggs was slipping into the seat across from her.

"What a smoothie," the bartender whispered to himself. "I wonder if he'll tell her that he's a cop?" And with that question, he went back to the work of refilling glasses.

Riggs sipped his beer while he made some small talk with his new companion. After a few minutes he asked, "So, has the bartender stopped watching us?"

"He's gone back to his work," Victoria confirmed, "but I swear, if anyone sees me talking to you—"

"Don't worry, Bell, they won't," Riggs assured her. Then he suppressed a smile and added, "And if they do, I can always cover it up by arresting you."

"That's not original or funny," she informed him, "but it may become necessary."

He came to the point. "So, were you able to overhear Finnegan?"

"Every word. And I agree with you. He's definitely guilty."

Riggs took a gulp of his beer. "Yes, but of what crime?"

"If you knew that, you wouldn't keep bothering me," Victoria said with a groan. "By the way, does your wife know I'm helping you?"

Riggs tried to shake his head, but it turned into an indifferent nodding motion. "I kept my word, only Fisher knows, but I think she may suspect something."

Victoria grinned at the inspector. "If you *think she suspects* then ten to one, she already knows. Amy is a clever woman." She wiped some condensation off her glass. "But she won't say anything to anybody, will she?"

Riggs shook his head decisively. "Not a chance; she has too much sympathy for what you and Walter went through last time."

"Well, that makes her the first," Victoria mumbled. "Now, you've got Fisher tailing Finnegan, but who else have you talked to?"

"I just came from the landlady, Patricia Mooney. She completely denies ever having met Sadie, and she doesn't know anything about her death. No alibi. She was home alone on Tuesday, memorizing her lines for her new play."

Victoria had just noticed the bartender was looking their way, so she tipped her head flirtatiously, put her hand on Riggs', and said, "Go on."

Riggs chuckled at her charade and tried to look like a determined womanizer. "I'm going to have another chat with Ann Marie. She and Eddie Pike are getting friendly, and I'm wondering if she has any motives besides the obvious one. Then, I think I need to pay a visit to Mr. and Mrs. Blackwell. Do you see any way they could have been involved with Sadie?"

"I only spoke to Mrs. Blackwell," Victoria reminded him, "but I'd say Celeste Blackwell is a very jealous woman. Whether she loves her husband or not, she's fiercely protective of him, and Roberta Pike had her green with envy. If Sadie were connected, it wouldn't have to be through her cousin. I don't know whether or not Mrs. Blackwell's fears were justified, but I'm quite sure that she hated Roberta Pike bitterly."

"Enough to kill her?"

"Possibly. I got the impression she was downright happy about Roberta's death."

Riggs nodded. Yes, he had to pay a visit to Celeste and Maxim Blackwell.

Chapter Twenty-Eight: Eastlake Coffee and Cakes

When Riggs left the Blue Bay Tavern, he passed the bridge and walked the eleven blocks southward through the Eastlake neighborhood. On a quiet side street, he found a quaint little shop known as Eastlake Coffee and Cakes. The name of the establishment was painted on the front window in pink and green letters. Beneath the red-striped awning were four little tables, each decorated with a simple cotton tablecloth. A brass bell above the door tinkled when he opened it, and Riggs could hear the faint sound of the music from the radio behind the counter. Lunchtime was over, but most of the chairs were still occupied. Riggs spotted Ann Marie Lewis.

She was working behind a case of cakes and pastries. When she saw him, she looked worried, but her tone was friendly. "Well, hello, Inspector Riggs. I haven't seen you for a few hours. Are you here to talk to me again, or would you like something to eat?"

Riggs looked at the irresistible desserts in the case and adjusted his plan. "Well, both, actually. Should I order here?"

"Not yet. My head's already full, and one more order would push me over. You go sit down, and I'll be there in half a second."

He walked back outside and sat down at the only available table. It had turned into a pleasant afternoon, but he hadn't had a chance to enjoy it. He had barely picked up the little paper menu when Ann Marie came out. She was wearing a lemon-yellow blouse and a pink apron with a ruffled white trim and large pockets. Her hair was pulled back with a sash. She smiled and asked, "So, Inspector Riggs, what would you like?"

"I'd like a coffee."

Ann Marie smiled. "And anything to eat? We have cakes, pies, and cookies..."

"What do you recommend?"

Ann Marie considered a moment. "It depends on what you're in the mood for. If you like chocolate, I've got brownies with filberts. If you like pie, I've got a fresh blackberry pie that just came out of the oven thirty minutes ago."

"What about cake?"

"I made a huckleberry cake with buttercream this morning. And I'm not one to brag, but folks have been raving about it all day."

"I'll go with that," Riggs decided. Ann Marie smiled and disappeared inside.

A few minutes later, she came back with the Inspector's order and an extra coffee for herself. She took off her apron and sat down across from him. "I'm due for my break anyway," she admitted. "Lunch was busy today. So, what do you want to ask me?"

Riggs tried a bite of the huckleberry cake and almost forgot what his question was. "Wow," he nodded appreciatively. "This is delicious!"

Ann Marie smiled but didn't say anything. Riggs savored his bite. The sweet purple berries seemed to compensate for everything that had happened in his day. He took a deep breath and sipped his coffee before he realized that he hadn't answered Ann Marie.

"It's only routine, Miss Lewis. But I need to ask you what you were doing on Tuesday afternoon."

Her brow furrowed slightly. "So that's when it happened?"

Riggs nodded, and Ann Marie sipped her coffee. "I didn't really know Sadie Greenleaf," Ann Marie said. "I met her a couple times, but I'm not even sure I would have recognized her if I passed her on the street. But it's strange to think that now she's gone, too."

"I understand." Riggs sighed. He waited a few minutes and asked again, "And what about Tuesday?"

She looked back at him. "Oh right, I was here on Tuesday. I came in early in the morning and worked here until the shop closed at five, then it took me another half hour to clean up.

"Can anyone vouch for you during that time?"

Ann Marie reached up and gently rubbed her ear. "No, I don't really think so," she admitted. "The girls who work for me can tell you that I was here all day. But the truth is that I could have slipped out for ten minutes, and they probably wouldn't have noticed."

"Did you slip out?"

Ann Marie looked at him and shook her head. "No, I was here. But since Sadie was murdered only a couple blocks away, I don't think I can claim to have a real alibi. Besides, both my girls left at five o'clock, and then I was alone until five-thirty."

"And what did you do?"

"I walked over to that little Chinese restaurant on Thirty-fourth and Lynn," Ann Marie sighed and looked away.

"Did you dine alone?"

"I had dinner with a friend," Ann Marie looked down at her coffee. "Just after nine o'clock, he walked me home. I went straight to bed. I usually go to bed early, especially when I have a lot of baking to do the next morning."

Riggs cut another bite of the delicious cake. "And who was the friend?"

"Hello, Annie!" a deep voice interrupted. They both looked up and saw Bruce Steele. "Isn't the weather great today?"

Annie shielded her eyes from the sunshine so she could look up. "Hello, Bruce."

He leaned over and kissed her cheek gently. He was about to say something when Ann Marie quickly added, "Oh, I'm sorry. Bruce, this is Inspector Riggs of the Seattle police."

"Yes, I've already had the pleasure," Bruce said, shaking Riggs's hand. "How are you doing, Inspector? Still sorting through this sordid mess?"

"I'm afraid so," Riggs said.

"Well, do me a favor and leave this beautiful girl out of it. My Annie is busy enough without having to worry about old acquaintances and their unfortunate tragedies."

Ann Marie's attention turned to something inside the shop. "Oh dear, I think Suzy is having problems with the till again." She stood up so she would have a better view of her young employee.

Bruce turned to the policeman. "I'll just get a cup of coffee, and then if you two don't mind, I'll join you."

Riggs nodded, and Bruce held the door for Ann Marie, then he followed her inside. From his position, Riggs had to turn his chair so that he could watch them discreetly. Riggs wondered if Bruce had been right when he said Ann Marie would eventually forgive him. Miss Lewis had been polite to her ex-fiancé. Then again, being polite isn't the same as wearing an engagement ring.

After helping young Suzy with the till, Ann Marie poured Bruce a cup of coffee, and the two of them stood talking. At one point, Bruce rested his hand on her lower back. But Riggs still wasn't prepared to declare that they were lovers. He was, however, convinced that Bruce Steele knew how to charm women. Ann Marie explained something, and Bruce nodded reassuringly. When she turned to help her employee, Bruce came back outside. He sat down next to the policeman, leaned back, and crossed his legs.

"That girl is absolutely fantastic," Bruce sighed. "I told you there's not another one like her. She works as hard as any man I've ever known, but somehow she always manages to look amazing, and she never loses her cool." He lowered his voice and added with a guilty wink, "Unless, of course, I've been really terrible."

"Patience is an admirable quality," Riggs agreed, and he thought, *within limits, of course.*

"Hey, look at this," Bruce said, reaching into his jacket pocket. He glanced over his shoulder to make sure that Ann Marie was still occupied as he pulled out a tiny velvet-covered box. "It's a new engagement ring. She hasn't seen it yet." And he opened the box to reveal an elegant golden ring bearing what must have been a full-carat diamond.

"It's beautiful," the inspector agreed.

"Yeah, she deserves it. She gave the old one back to me," he shook his head, "but this is a fresh ring for a fresh start. It's bigger than the old one, too. I need Annie to know how things are going to be from now on. She'll be able to look at this ring and know how much I love her."

Riggs said, "Well, I wish you the best of luck."

"It's not luck," Bruce corrected him. "It's like I told you, Annie needs some time to come around. I was a cad, but you can't judge a man by his worst moments."

As Bruce sipped his coffee, Riggs noticed his gaze was following someone who was walking by. Riggs glanced over and saw an old man in a plaid jacket and a beautiful brunette in a lime green dress. He ate the last bite of his cake and wondered which one of them had caught the banker's attention.

"I suppose," he said after a few minutes, "Miss Lewis told you that Sadie Greenleaf was murdered."

"Sadie Greenleaf?" Bruce repeated with a frown.

"Roberta Pike's cousin," the policeman explained. "Didn't you know her?"

"Oh, right. Annie mentioned something like that. No, I didn't know Sadie Greenleaf. I knew Ruby had a rich uncle, of course. I met him once or twice, but I don't think I ever met her cousin." He gazed out at the sidewalk, but this time there wasn't anyone worth noticing.

"That's funny," Riggs said, "because Sadie said she knew you."

Bruce laughed. "Well, you know how people are. They like to act like they're more knowledgeable than they really are. Ruby probably mentioned me. I was in quite a few photographs with Ruby and Annie. Besides, I think they went to the same hairdresser."

"The same hairdresser?"

"Yeah, I think that's a good place for gossiping. It takes hours for them to get their hair washed, trimmed, dyed, curled, and whatever other girlie things they have done to it. Ruby must have gone there at least twice a week. I'm sure her hair was bleached, but it was always flawless. And her cousin must have gone all the time too since she was a redhead and that must take extra work. Annie's not vain like that, of course, because she leaves her color natural, and she usually styles it herself."

"And you never met Ruby's cousin?"

He shrugged. "Not that I can remember."

"But you knew she was a redhead."

Bruce looked down at his cup and swirled the last bit of coffee around. "Yeah, well, I must have read it in the newspaper."

For a brief moment, Riggs thought about Inspector Fisher. He tried to think why, but he couldn't put his finger on it. "As a matter of routine," he asked, "I wonder if you could tell me what you did on Tuesday afternoon."

"Tuesday afternoon? Well, I was at work, naturally. I had a late lunch, but I was back in the office by two-thirty at the latest."

"Did you eat lunch alone?"

"Yep. Why? Do I need an alibi?"

"I just need to look at everyone's movements."

Bruce noticed another person walking past. And Riggs realized why he'd thought of Inspector Fisher. Fisher was continuously distracted by pedestrians too, but only if they were beautiful, moderately curvaceous, and had slim ankles. Apparently, Bruce Steele had the same preoccupation, and based on the woman who was walking by at the moment, he was susceptible to brunettes.

As soon as Riggs left the coffee shop, he ducked into a telephone booth. It was well past three, but she might still be in the library.

"Hello, Bell," he said when she answered the telephone. "Listen, things are heating up, and I might need you later."

"That's nice, but I'm not available. And I don't want you calling me at work either."

"You said you didn't want me coming in there."

"That, too. I'm not part of this investigation, remember?"

Riggs tapped the telephone box irritably. "Listen, can you tell me if any of the newspapers mentioned anything about Sadie Greenleaf being a redhead?"

There was a sigh, and Bell said, "Don't you read the newspapers anymore?"

"Of course I do, but I'm not in my office. There's a murderer on the loose. Two women are already dead, and I'm running out of time. Come on, with a memory like yours, I know you know."

There was a pause and a short huff. "Fine. None of the articles so far have mentioned Miss Greenleaf's hair color."

Chapter Twenty-Nine: The Blackwell Estate

A short while later, Riggs pulled his brown Plymouth into the Blackwell's estate. It was an imposing property firmly established in the middle of Highland Drive. The house itself was a large modern cube. It was absolutely symmetrical and thoroughly devoid of charm.

It was so superior that Riggs didn't bother to lock his decrepit car. A robber in this neighborhood would only have laughed at it anyway. Riggs put on his hat, ascended the hard marble steps, and rang the shiny steel button. A shrill tone announced him by echoing obediently. An elderly butler opened the door so quickly that Riggs wondered if he'd been standing just behind the door, waiting.

The butler led Riggs into a massive white room with elegant black furniture, elaborately embossed wallpaper, and several vases full of blood-red roses. An ornate brass and crystal chandelier hung overhead. The butler left, and a few minutes later, Mr. Blackwell strode into the room. He was fastening a diamond cuff link onto his pristine dinner shirt and looking thoroughly annoyed.

"Inspector Riggs," he observed, "my wife and I were just getting ready for our dinner engagement. Was there something you wanted?"

Riggs thought the answer was obvious, but he refrained from pointing that out. "I'd just like to ask you a couple questions. It won't take a minute. It's about your spending."

Mr. Blackwell stopped short, and the cuff link slipped from his hand. "My spending? That's rather impertinent of you, isn't it?"

"I'd like to know if you've had any large expenses lately."

"What the devil—"

He turned to close the doors behind him, but an echoing slam stopped him. A moment later, Mrs. Blackwell walked in carrying an open-flowered handbag and studying its contents. In her hand was a bottle of tablets. "Maxim dear, have you seen my mother-of-pearl brooch? I just can't—"

She stopped short when she saw the policeman. Her husband stooped down to pick up his cuff link. As he inserted it into his sleeve, he said, "Darling, I suppose you remember Inspector Riggs, of the Seattle Police?'

She glared at the inspector, and her nose flared slightly before she regained herself. "Yes, of course. What brings you here, Inspector?"

"I just stopped by to ask your husband about his expenses."

Celeste Blackwell frowned. She looked down at her hands and slipped the bottle into her handbag.

"My expenses," Mr. Blackwell snapped angrily, "are entirely my own affair."

Celeste's gaze shot to her husband and back at the policeman. "What sort of 'expenses' are you referring to, Inspector?"

"It's just a routine investigation," Riggs explained. "I'm sure your accounts are entirely above board, but it would save everyone a lot of time if you could tell me about any particularly large expenditures that you've had lately. Anything over, say, five hundred dollars that you've spent in the last three months."

Mr. Blackwell looked back toward the policeman. "I can't imagine what reason you could possibly have for asking me this, Inspector. I spend the typical amount of money for a man of my resources."

Riggs nodded in agreement but waited expectantly.

Mr. Blackwell frowned. His wife glanced at him, and he straightened his tie.

"However, as I have nothing to hide, I may as well inform you that I have withdrawn a little bit more lately in order to purchase some gifts for my wife. I'm sure you agree that's hardly a police matter. If you still insist on meddling in my personal affairs, you'll have to talk to my banker, but I doubt he'll appreciate your impertinence any more than I do."

"Thank you, Mr. Blackwell," Riggs said politely, "Having your permission will save me the trouble of a warrant."

Blackwell huffed indignantly, but before he could object, the inspector asked, "Now, what were you doing last Tuesday afternoon?"

"This is absolute nonsense!" Maxim Blackwell snapped, "And as far as permission goes, let me say that—" Blackwell stopped himself.

"Tuesday afternoon," Riggs gently reminded him.

"I resent the question!"

"But will you answer it?" Riggs asked, "After all, since you have nothing to hide."

"Of course, I have nothing to hide! Last Tuesday, I was in my office all day. I ordered a sandwich for lunch and worked from my desk. I left at six o'clock, and you can write that down in your police report and send it to the newspapers if you think anyone needs to know!"

Riggs did write it down.

"And how about you, Mrs. Blackwell? Where were you last Tuesday?"

Her husband cut in angrily. "Inspector, this is intolerable! I won't have you harassing my wife! What the devil is this Tuesday rubbish about anyway?"

But Celeste Blackwell answered firmly, "No dear, I don't mind answering the Inspector's questions. Whatever he's investigating must be terribly important." She turned to Riggs. "If you really must know, Inspector, on Tuesday, I was at my club from noon until five o'clock. I lunched with some of my friends, and then we stayed for the gardening committee meeting. I'm the chairwoman this year."

"Thank you," Riggs said. "Do either of you know a woman named Sadie Greenleaf?"

"Wasn't she that unfortunate woman whose body was found in her car?" Celeste wondered. "I read about it in the newspaper."

"No, of course, we didn't know her!" Blackwell shouted, and he glared at his wife.

She shrugged and held up her hands. "Well, I certainly never met her."

"One last question, Mr. Blackwell. Could you please tell me why you fired Miss Margaret Baker?"

"I'm a businessman, and this is America," Blackwell stated. "I don't need a license to fire my employees. If I decide some girl ought to go, then that's that, and it's no police matter. I've got a business to run, and I won't tolerate employees who make more trouble than they're worth."

"Was it because Miss Baker told me that Roberta Pike was murdered?"

Celeste gasped and turned pale. For a moment, Riggs wondered if she was going to faint. But her husband hurried over and gently lowered his wife onto the sofa. He opened her handbag, took one of the tablets, and put it in her hand. Then he strode briskly to the cocktail table and poured her a small glass of amber liquid. "Here, Celeste. Drink this. It will help."

Mrs. Blackwell slipped the tablet in her mouth and feebly sipped the liquid. After a few minutes, she whispered, "Oh, Maxim dear, I suddenly felt so faint. Thank you."

Her husband used his handkerchief to pat her forehead. When it seemed as though the lady might recover, Maxim stood up and glared at Riggs. "As you can see, Inspector, my wife has a very delicate constitution. And since the unfortunate events you're investigating do not concern either of us, I won't have you upsetting her. Good day, Sir!"

Chapter Thirty: Sylvester's Unlucky Shadow

Saturday morning dawned warm and sunny. Inspector Fisher was wearing a new Stetson with a red plaid ribbon. It was loud. He was also disguised, with a false beard and a pair of dark glasses. He had just relieved the night undercover man. Now it was Fisher's turn to sit in the unmarked black car across the street from Sylvester Finnegan's apartment.

The apartment building was a simple two-story brick structure with white windows and a heavy white door in the middle. Fortunately, Sylvester's apartment was on the second floor, so the stakeout only required a man at the front. Sylvester had been home since ten o'clock the night before. So far this morning, he had yet to make an appearance.

His movements on Friday had been suspicious. Namely, Finnegan had emptied his bank account. While that's never a good sign for a murder suspect, it still wasn't enough to justify an arrest, so all they could do was watch and wait. Riggs had five bucks that Finnegan would try to skip town over the weekend, but Fisher's fiver said Finnegan would stay put until Monday.

"He knows we don't have anything on him," Fisher had argued. "He'll stick it out if he can."

But Riggs saw it differently. "If he's guilty, he'll be too nervous to act rationally, and if he's innocent, why the hell is he acting so guilty?"

When the small diner opened for breakfast, Fisher saw his opportunity and moved inside. There was a counter along the window, a perfect place to sit and watch the apartment building while drinking a cup of joe. Plus, he'd be able to watch the pedestrians at the same time. Sunny weather meant pretty sundresses, short sleeves, and feminine hats. It was a wonderful time of year, and Fisher wanted to enjoy it.

The waitress smiled at him, and it occurred to him for the first time in his life that women might find beards attractive. After all, the fake beard he was wearing might make him look more intellectual. She was a pretty girl, about twenty-two or twenty-three years old. Her hair was short and curly, and her fingernails were polished red. Fisher smiled back and tried to look intriguing. Fisher had intended to watch the apartment building while he ate, but the way the waitress walked around the diner made it difficult for Fisher to focus on a plain white door across the street.

Later, his only consolation would be that even if he had been properly watching the apartment at eleven o'clock, he still wouldn't have seen anything.

At eleven o'clock, Sylvester Finnegan opened his kitchen window. The window was on the backside of the apartment, and it overlooked a narrow alley and the windowless wall of the adjacent building. The only real view was a small gravel parking area where the alley joined a crossing alley. Directly beneath Finnegan's kitchen window was a collection of garbage cans, a couple of old chairs, and a couple of decrepit-looking bicycles. Sylvester looked around to make sure that no one was watching. Then he dropped a worn leather overnight bag into the alley. It landed with a thud beside the garbage cans. Perfect.

Fisher had just managed to start a friendly conversation with the waitress when he saw Sylvester exiting the white front door. The timing was unlucky, and the young inspector was obliged to grab his hat. He threw some change on the counter as he dashed out.

Sylvester headed north, and since he was on foot, Fisher left the car on the street and followed him on foot. Sylvester kept his hands in his pockets as he strolled along at an inconspicuous pace. He slowed down periodically to look at a shop window, and he even stopped at a newsstand to grab the morning paper. Most notable to a cop on a tailing job, Mr. Finnegan never looked around to see if he was being followed.

Thirteen minutes and seven blocks later, Sylvester reached the Blue Bay Tavern. It was just opening for lunch. Sylvester settled in at the bar. He greeted the bartender, ordered a lager and a BLT, and began reading his newspaper. Fisher slipped in about three minutes later. The tavern was practically empty, and it felt like a dark cave after the brightness of the late-morning sunshine. The policeman sat down at a booth near the back where he could watch Finnegan from a distance. Even with his convincing beard and glasses, Fisher couldn't be positive that Sylvester wouldn't recognize him, especially if he happened to be facing him.

The waitress came over, and Fisher ordered a root beer and a sandwich. A few more people arrived for lunch, and Sylvester was on his second beer before he reached the sports section. Thirty minutes later, he was halfway through his third beer, so Fisher wasn't surprised when Sylvester left his jacket at the bar and headed to the back. As soon as Sylvester was out of sight, Fisher hurried after him, but the bathroom was located at the end of a dead-end corridor.

Satisfied, Fisher went back to his booth and focused on his lunch. For a cheap tavern, the Blue Bay made a decent fish sandwich. Fisher hadn't properly finished his breakfast because the beard complicated matters. The dim booth made eating easier. As Fisher savored his early lunch, his mind drifted back to the pretty waitress he'd met that morning. There was something about her smile, or maybe it was the way she wore her curly hair so short. Fisher periodically touched his jawline to make sure his beard was still glued in place. And the waitress had a charming laugh too. All in all, it took a full eleven minutes and thirty-four seconds before Fisher realized that Sylvester Finnegan had climbed out the bathroom window.

Chapter Thirty-One: Patricia Mooney's Hard Work

Mrs. Patricia Mooney was pleased with herself. The roses looked fantastic this year. Over the last ten years, she had accumulated twenty-five rose bushes around the apartments of 201 E Louisa Street. Each bush was a different variety, and this year they were all doing exceptionally well.

Patricia looked down and mumbled to herself, "But who invited you, Dandelions?" The thought of dandelions reminded her of childhood when her grandmother would drink dandelion tea. "Humph, it always tasted like dirty rainwater," Patricia said out loud. "It smelled awful, too." But it may have been healthy. After all, her grandmother had lived to be ninety. Maybe it was the dandelion tea that did it. Patricia Mooney frowned. Was there anything more miserable than losing the ones we love? Of course not. She shook her head and sighed, rather dramatically, to herself. "Death is a cruel price to pay for the pleasure of living."

Maybe she would give dandelion tea a try after all. The weeds had to go anyway. She dropped down to her knees and began tackling the largest and most offensive of them. Big, nasty-looking plants. When she focused on them, she realized how prevalent they'd become. And some of them seemed to believe that they were meant to be ferns. They had begun cropping up all around the pink rhododendron bush in front of Apartment C.

Apartment C.

Patricia looked at the front door. This was where Roberta Pike had lived.

It had been her last home. Patricia remembered her stolen heirlooms—gone forever. There was no doubt that Roberta Pike was to blame. Patricia knew that she could never forgive that brat of a girl. She had tried to settle the matter in her heart, but the rage was too deep. Patricia remembered how furious she'd been when she accused Miss Pike of robbing her; the arrogant girl just tossed her pretty hair to the side and grinned. "I'm so sorry, Mrs. Mooney," she cooed heartlessly, "but I really don't know what you're talking about. If you've lost something, I suppose you ought to go to the police rather than accusing your tenants."

Stupid girl. Conceited, vain, stupid girl. Patricia could spot a liar when she saw one, and Roberta's thinly masked denial was infuriating. Patricia was so angry she could have smacked Miss Pike on the spot. Lord knows the little thief deserved it, and worse. It was the only hope of getting her heirlooms back that had forced Patricia to remain civil.

That was when Patricia had come up with a plan.

A simple plan. Not legal, but wholly justified.

One night while Roberta was out, Patricia put on her gloves, and with her spare key, she snuck around to the back door of Roberta's apartment. She didn't want any of the neighbors to see her. And with an electric flashlight, she searched Apartment C: every drawer, every cupboard, every place where that vain thief might have hidden Patricia's heirlooms. In the end, she hadn't found anything. And the next morning, the police came to tell her that Miss Pike was dead. The wheels of justice weren't always slow. The police believed it was suicide. Of course, Patricia couldn't tell them what she'd seen without revealing that she'd been in Roberta's apartment.

It was a pity, too, because Patricia still had a nagging feeling about it. It bothered her because it was strange, and the timing was odd.

It happened just after Patricia searched the apartment. She was slipping out the back door when she heard it. At first, it made her heart jump because she thought Miss Pike was home. But the landlady realized almost right away that it couldn't be Roberta Pike at the door.

A silhouetted shadow approached the front door quietly. It looked like a man's shadow. He used a key to let himself in.

Mrs. Mooney hadn't waited to see who it was. As he was turning the key in the lock, she was slipping out the back door. Once she was safely inside her own apartment, she peeked out of her window. But all she could see was a dim light behind Miss Pike's curtains. She waited for over an hour, but she never saw anyone leave. Even now, she didn't particularly care who it was, but her mind kept drifting back to the puzzle. And she sometimes wondered if whoever it was may have known something about her stolen heirlooms.

She would never know.

Mrs. Mooney thought about her grandmother's beautiful amethyst ring, and the brooch, and the necklace with the roughly cut antique diamonds. These sentimental treasures connected her to a family and a history that was long over. And now, they were gone too.

"Oh, dear," Patricia mumbled, almost loud enough to be audible to the dandelions. "There's simply no justice in the world, except of course, that the lying little thief is dead. But even that doesn't give me back my treasures."

Patricia had just plucked the last shabby green leaf out of the earth and tossed it into her bucket when a shadow moved over her. Looking around, she could only see a man's massive form blocking the radiant sunlight. He towered over her, and she had to shade her eyes so that she could make out the man's face. He was a tall man, about twenty years younger than her, well dressed, and handsome. Despite the fact that she was old enough to be his mother, his good looks were enough to make her catch her breath.

He took off his hat. "Excuse me, Ma'am. Are you the landlady here?"

Patricia nodded. "Mrs. Mooney is my name."

"I'm sorry to disturb you, Mrs. Mooney," the attractive man explained, "but I was hoping I could ask you for a favor. You see, the late Miss Pike was a friend of mine, and I once loaned her something. If you could be so kind as to let me into her apartment, I won't have to bother her family."

Chapter Thirty-Two: Eddie and Ann Marie

E ddie Pike strolled along the street until he came to Eastlake Coffee and Cakes. When he saw the shop, he stopped and stood there for several moments. It was Saturday, and instead of the overalls and sneakers he usually wore at the garage, Eddie was wearing slacks, a pressed plaid shirt, and a light brown fedora. It was well after lunchtime, and the coffee shop was practically empty. Eddie took a deep breath, opened the door, and stepped into the shop.

The inside was pink and tidy, and Perry Como was playing on the radio. Ann Marie Lewis was standing behind the dessert counter, decorating cookies with bits of candied oranges. She glanced up at the newcomer, went back to her cookies, did a double take, and smiled. "Why hello, Mr. Pike, I didn't recognize you."

Eddie came up to the counter and took off his hat. "Good afternoon, Miss Lewis." He cleared his throat. "I suppose I look like a different man when I get cleaned up."

"No," she said. "I think you look like the same man. I just didn't expect to see you."

Eddie smiled awkwardly. "This is your place, isn't it? It's nice."

"Thanks. I'm proud of it," she beamed. "Coffee, tea, cakes, and that sort of thing. I've always loved baking." Ann Marie wiped her hands on her apron and waited. For several moments neither of them said anything. When the silence became too awkward, she began, "So, Mr. Pike, would you like something to eat, or did you come to see me?"

Eddie's gaze darted to the dessert case. "No. I don't know, exactly. I mean, yes. Um…" he pointed quickly. "Is that cherry pie?"

"Fresh cherries," Ann Marie confirmed. "I made it last night."

"I'd like some of that, please. And a cup of coffee."

"Would you like it with whipped cream or a scoop of vanilla ice cream?"

"Yes, please," Eddie stammered. "I mean both. May I have both?"

"Sure thing." The young woman nodded and reached for a plate. "You go sit down, and I'll bring it right over."

There were only two other customers in the shop. Two old ladies were sitting together, discussing the marvels of modern washing machines. Eddie sat down on the other side of the shop. He pretended to listen to the radio until Ann Marie came over with a huge slice of red sticky pie and a mug of hot coffee. Eddie thanked her, and she went back to the counter and the candied orange pieces. Eddie ate. His gaze kept wandering in Ann Marie's direction, but whenever she caught him looking her way he quickly went back to his pie. Fifteen minutes later, Ann Marie finished her decorating and slid the platter of cookies into the display case. Then she took off her apron, poured herself a glass of water, and went over to where Eddie was sitting.

"So, how was the pie?"

"Best pie I've ever had," Eddie said. "Cherry always was one of my favorites. I used to get it sometimes in school, but it was never half as good as this."

"You're flattering me," Ann Marie said. "And I was just beginning to think that the pie was just an excuse."

"An excuse for what?"

Ann Marie shrugged. "Maybe to talk to someone who knew your sister. You look like you've got something on your mind."

Eddie sighed and shook his head. "Is it that obvious?"

Ann Marie nodded. "I've got a few minutes if you want to talk."

Eddie stood up and pulled out a chair for her. Ann Marie sat down and waited.

"I've been walking around the neighborhood for two hours," Eddie began.

He rubbed the back of his neck. Ann Marie waited. She sipped her water before asking softly, "Why were you walking around?"

"I'm not exactly sure," he admitted. "I'm sorry that Roberta's dead, but the truth is that I barely knew her. I know that's a crazy thing to say about my half-sister, but we were never close. After my father died, they sent me to boarding school in California. I was just a kid, and Roberta was practically a baby."

"Didn't you ever see each other?"

"We saw each other during the holidays for the first few years, but after a while, I just stayed at school. Then I joined the army. I wrote to her a few times, but she never wrote back. When she moved out here last year, it was the first time I'd talked to her in three years."

"And now you feel guilty?"

"And embarrassed," Eddie nodded. "I wasn't much of a brother to her."

"And she wasn't much of a sister to you," Ann Marie reminded him, "but it's still okay to miss her."

Eddie sighed deeply and leaned back in his chair.

"I heard about Sadie," Ann Marie ventured.

"That's almost unbelievable. I really don't know what to make of it."

"Were you close to her?"

Eddie shook his head. "I was never close to any of them. I was away at school before Sadie moved in with Uncle Jacob. I didn't meet her until after the war. She was always civil to me, but our only connection was Uncle Jacob."

"It's terrible that someone did that to her."

"I hope they catch him," Eddie agreed.

Ann Marie leaned forward and asked, "Do you think her death is related to Ruby's?"

"I don't know," Eddie shook his head. "I'm sure that policeman is considering the possibility. The thing is, if Roberta's death wasn't an accident…." Eddie stopped short and exhaled with defeat. "You see the problem?" he asked. "I didn't even know her well enough to have an opinion about whether or not she jumped off that bridge. Roberta was my only blood relative, and I don't even know what she thought of me."

Ann Marie leaned forward and touched his hand. "Mr. Pike, may I call you Eddie?"

He raised his eyebrows, but he managed to nod.

"Look, Eddie, I don't have much by way of family, either, but I don't think Ruby would have wanted you to beat yourself up like this. Her death was a tragedy, and you have a right to be upset whether or not you two were close."

Eddie sat, and Ann Marie took his mug and refilled it. When she sat back down, he smiled and said, "Thank you, Miss Lewis. And I don't just mean for the coffee."

"Ann Marie," she corrected him.

"Thanks, Ann Marie."

"You know, Ruby mentioned you once or twice," she said after a couple minutes. "She was immature, but she wasn't indifferent to you."

"Let me guess," Eddie ventured wearily. "Based on what little she said to me, she probably complained that I work in a dirty garage, I don't know any interesting people, and I spend my Saturday nights bowling."

"Nothing as bad as that," Ann Marie insisted, "but she complained that her brother didn't own a tuxedo."

"Guilty as charged," Eddie shrugged. "I always had the impression that I bored her silly."

"Most of the world bored her silly," Ann Marie explained. "Ruby was like that. She couldn't enjoy herself unless she was wearing something fashionable and drinking cocktails with fascinating people."

"And you are one of those fascinating people."

"Ruby and I fell out," Ann Marie reminded him. "I wasn't a good match for her circles. But she did like you, in her own way. And her complaint about the tuxedo was because she thought you'd look great in one." Anne Marie smiled carefully and added, "And now that I've met her brother, I'd have to agree with her."

Eddie flushed, and Ann Marie politely turned away to refill her water glass.

"You're not the only one who listens to gossip," Eddie said as soon as he'd recovered. "Sadie told me a few things about you."

Ann Marie sat back down. "Sadie? Really?" she asked suspiciously. "She must have heard it from Ruby. I'm curious what she said about me."

"Nothing bad," Eddie said quickly. "Just the normal stuff, that you have an aunt and your own bakery."

"Guilty as charged," Ann Marie said. "My aunt's name is Martha. She lives in a small retirement home on Lake Washington. She loves lilacs and baking, and before she lost her eyesight, she came down here to help me pick out all the colors for my shop. I visit her every Sunday morning."

Eddie took a deep breath and said, "I enjoy your company, Ann Marie. I don't suppose you'd want to have dinner with me tomorrow night?"

Ann Marie's mouth opened in surprise. "Well, I don't know…"

"If you'd rather not," Eddie began quickly, but Ann Marie cut him off. "It's not that. Eddie. I'm just wondering, did Sadie tell you why Ruby and I fell out?"

"More or less," he admitted reluctantly. "But I had the impression it was all over with… him."

Ann Marie paused for a moment, and then she smiled. "Okay, Eddie. I'll see you tomorrow night."

Chapter Thirty-Three: One Flies Away and Another One Crumbles

O n Monday morning, Riggs marched his way back down the stairs from the Chief's office. Sylvester Finnegan was still missing, and the full-blown manhunt was taking every man the department could spare. Worse still, the fact that there hadn't been enough evidence to arrest Finnegan didn't quell the boss's rage. Never mind that you can't arrest a guy just because he doesn't have an alibi. Apart from being a convenient suspect, there was no indication that Sylvester Finnegan killed Sadie Greenleaf, and his motive, if it existed, was pure speculation. All of that was, of course, before Fisher had lost Finnegan at the Blue Bay. Now that the top suspect was missing, the fat had hit the fire.

That was almost forty-eight hours ago, and Mr. Finnegan was still gone without a trace.

When Riggs stepped out onto his floor, Fisher interrupted his brooding. "Hey, Riggs," he said, rushing over, "I wanna tell ya—"

But Riggs just shook his head and kept walking. "Not now, Fisher, I still have Chief's bite marks in my hide, and I need a chance to think."

In truth, he wanted to lock himself up in his office with a cup of coffee. He could take his shoes off, relax, and put his brain to work. Something told him that if he could only get some peace and quiet, he might just come up with something good.

"But listen," Fisher persisted, following him down the hall, "I just wanted to say—"

"Forget it," Riggs said as he patted the younger man's shoulder, "you're a good officer, Fisher. It happens to all of us sometimes." He gently but firmly pushed Fisher aside and stepped into his office.

A woman was there.

Damn it.

Her elegant hat was so large she could have blended in at the Kentucky Derby. She turned to look at him.

Mrs. Blackwell's lavender dress matched her grand hat, but it was her pearls that looked the most out of place in Riggs's office. Celeste Blackwell lifted a tear-dampened handkerchief to her eyes, and it occurred to Riggs that she might be the one person he actually wanted to see.

"Fisher, could you please get a couple cups of coffee?"

Fisher nodded. "Sure thing, Boss Man."

Riggs contemplated his tactic as he hung up his hat, but he had barely turned around before Mrs. Blackwell burst into tears. "Oh, Inspector," she managed between sobs. "I just don't know what to do! This is terrible. I can't even discuss it with my therapist because they golf together."

"Who?"

"My therapist and my husband, and I couldn't bear for him to know. I'm afraid it's driving me mad. When you left on Friday, I couldn't take it anymore. I confronted Maxim about everything. I thought I might have a nervous breakdown, but I just couldn't go on living, day after day, without knowing the truth."

Riggs sat down at his desk. He wasn't going to need a strategy for this one. "Mrs. Blackwell, the truth about what?"

Her face contorted. "The truth about Maxim and that cheap floozy!" she shouted.

Riggs nodded. Of course, it would be that. The simplest explanation often was the right one.

Mrs. Blackwell went on passionately. "I confronted Maxim and demanded that he tell me everything!"

"Of course," Riggs nodded sympathetically.

"And there was the money, too," Celeste added angrily. "I knew about that already. One thousand dollars twice last month, and last week it was another twenty-five hundred." She tucked her damp handkerchief into her handbag and pulled out a fresh one. Riggs could see her initials embroidered on it. "And I know because he didn't take it out of the business account. He took it out of our personal account. I suppose he thought I wouldn't notice, but what am I supposed to think?" she demanded, but she didn't wait for a response. "My mother always said that a good wife should stand by her husband, but I'm not just a wife...I'm a woman, after all!"

Riggs rubbed his mustache. "And what did your husband say, Mrs. Blackwell?"

"Oh, he told me there had never been any *impropriety* with Miss Pike. According to him, stenographers like to start those kinds of rumors because they get bored. Maybe that's true, but I say Miss Pike must have earned her terrible reputation one way or another. Still, it had nothing to do with my husband. And as for the money, that part was a little complicated. Maxim said that he had taken it from his work account in the first place for tax reasons, and he's just been putting it back from our personal account, so the feds don't know. I don't know anything about taxes, but Maxim says it saves a great deal of expense if you move your money around at the right time."

Riggs prayed that his coffee would arrive soon. Apparently, Mrs. Blackwell's moral compass was fixed firmly on monogamy and didn't venture into other directions like tax evasion or fraudulent business practices.

He took a deep breath. "So, what brings you here?"

"Well, at first, I felt so relieved to know that there had never been anything wrong, but this morning I went to Maxim's office, and while I was waiting, his secretary said something about the long lunch he'd taken last Tuesday. Well, of course, I told her that she was mistaken. We had a lunch date on Tuesday, but I canceled it so I could attend the ladies' luncheon at my club. And Maxim had distinctly told you and me that he had stayed in the office and ordered a sandwich. You remember him saying that, don't you?"

Riggs nodded.

Celeste Blackwell furrowed her brow. "But his secretary insisted that on Tuesday, Maxim had left the office to meet someone. She said he was away for nearly two hours. Why would Max lie to me?" She breathed deeply and opened her handbag. She removed a little bottle and took a tablet. Riggs was about to offer to get her a glass of water when she swallowed it dry. "Don't you see, Inspector? Miss Pike is gone. There can't be any impropriety with her because she's dead. That should have solved everything. So why did my husband lie to me unless he was with another woman?"

Riggs leaned back in his chair.

"Mrs. Blackwell, exactly how well did you know Miss Pike?"

She looked at him doubtfully. "I didn't know her, but I knew about her. I was suspicious. Maybe it was my feminine intuition, but I worried there might be something between her and my husband. A few weeks after she started working there, Maxim began acting funny. I didn't like Miss Pike. When she died, I just wanted everything to go back to normal."

Mrs. Blackwell rested her face in her hands. Riggs thought about his own wife. His own beautiful, headstrong Amy. If Amy Riggs ever suspected her husband of doing the things that Mrs. Blackwell suspected her husband of doing, she wouldn't waste time crying into a handkerchief.

"Oh, Inspector Riggs," Mrs. Blackwell cried desperately, "what am I going to do?"

Riggs was about to suggest that she find a new therapist, but there was a brief knock, and Inspector Fisher entered. To Riggs's annoyance, Fisher didn't have any coffee. Instead, he was wearing his hat and carrying a couple small sheets of paper.

"I'm sorry to interrupt you, Inspector, but the Chief wants an immediate reply to this," he said, handing Riggs the notes.

Riggs read the top one and stuffed them all into his pocket. "Mrs. Blackwell, I want you to come back here at four o'clock this afternoon. And I want you to bring your husband."

The miserable woman sighed gratefully, "Oh, Inspector Riggs, do you really think you can help me?"

"Just come back at four o'clock," he repeated as he stood up. "And I'll sort it all out."

"Oh, I'm so relieved!" Mrs. Blackwell said, touching her handkerchief to her eyes. "I thought you'd be able to fix things. We'll be here, Inspector. Thank you."

Riggs guided the distressed woman to the door. As soon as she was gone, he turned to Fisher and demanded, "In an alleyway?"

"Yep. Behind his own apartment. Apparently, he was dumped behind some trash cans."

Riggs abandoned the idea of coffee and grabbed his hat. "Does the Chief know?"

"Not yet; this just came in from Wiberg."

"Good ol' Wiberg. Let's get out of here."

Chapter Thirty-Four: The Consultation That Never Happened

As the two inspectors hurried out of the station, Riggs came up with a plan. They had only walked about a hundred feet when he ducked into a telephone booth and dropped a dime in the machine. He spent the next five minutes arguing with someone. When he finally came out, his face was red, but he looked satisfied.

"Okay, Fisher, I think it's time for some lunch," Riggs announced. "Let's go to Pier 54." They started heading west, down the hill to the waterfront.

Fisher looked at his watch. "It's a little early for lunch, isn't it?"

"I don't care if you eat, but you'll need to order something," Riggs instructed. "We need an excuse to hang out at the pier. She agreed to meet with us, but it has to be a discreet place where we can't be overheard."

Fisher didn't say anything else. The two men proceeded until they reached the dingy seafood shack along the sidewalk at the pier. Riggs ordered a portion of battered cod, fried potatoes, and a cup of salty clam broth. Fisher stuck with the fish and an ample dose of malted vinegar. When they had their food, the two men meandered out onto the pier.

They strolled out over the water until they found an isolated place to sit down. Crates and wooden pallets were stacked against the building. Massive heaps of salt-soaked lines were coiled up on the pier. The only boat was an old tug that looked abandoned. Fisher leaned against a stack of pallets and started eating his cod. A few minutes later, a woman came strolling down the pier. Under the bright mid-morning sun, her face was in the shadow of her green hat, but Riggs knew who she was. She was casually eating chips from a paper bowl, and she occasionally paused to look at the view or watch the seagulls on the rocks below.

When she was close enough, Riggs asked, "So, how did you know the pier would be isolated?"

Victoria checked over her shoulder just to make sure that no one else was coming before she answered simply, "It's low tide." Then she turned to Fisher, "This is in the strictest confidence, you understand? If anyone ever asks you, this never happened."

Fisher nodded obediently. "You got it, Bell."

"We won't say anything," Riggs promised, and then he turned to the woman. "Look, something else has happened."

Fisher's mouth fell open. "What, do you mean she's already in on this?"

Victoria turned to Fisher. "Absolutely not. I don't help the Seattle police, and I'm not a sleuth. And if you tell anyone that you've spoken to me, you'll be sorry."

"I didn't know ladies could swear," Fisher smirked.

"Ladies do a lot of things," Bell explained sweetly. "And not all of them are very pleasant."

Fisher stopped smiling and said, "Seriously, Bell. Don't worry; no one's going to learn anything from me. I know you don't want this to get to the newspapers."

"And you don't want any more dead bodies," Victoria reminded him as she took a bite of fried oyster.

Riggs looked at her. "You know?"

"I guessed," she corrected him. "It's been a couple days, and Sylvester Finnegan still hasn't been arrested because...?"

"Because he's dead," Riggs confirmed. "We were tailing him, but he got away. At first, we thought he'd skipped town, but his body was found in the alleyway behind his house. He'd been dead about forty-eight hours. That puts it on Saturday."

"How?"

"Just like Sadie Greenleaf, someone hit him. We found a brick by his body."

"Did he have a bag?"

"He had a small suitcase. As far as we can tell, Finnegan dropped the bag out of his kitchen window. He must have known we were following him, because he deliberately shook his tail before going back for the bag."

"Except someone was waiting for him."

"Exactly."

Riggs filled in the details while Victoria ate her oysters and chips. She was particularly interested in the money that Maxim had been withdrawing, and she agreed it pointed to either blackmail or an affair.

"But that last withdrawal, the $2,500, was taken out *after* Roberta Pike was already dead," Fisher reminded them.

"So, we focus on blackmail," Riggs decided. Then he added, "Also, I'm not sure this was the first time someone broke into Roberta's apartment."

Fisher leaned against a stack of coiled lines. "How do you figure?"

"Well, we know about the break-in last Wednesday, or very late on Tuesday. But I think someone else broke in before that."

"You're thinking of the yellow dress that's missing," Fisher said. "It could have been destroyed on her boat."

Victoria nodded. "Yes, but what about the red satin dress? It was hanging in her closet, but it never belonged to Roberta Pike."

Fisher pushed his hat back on his head. "So you think that's what our murderer is looking for?"

Victoria shrugged and took another bite of oyster. "You can't ignore the dresses. And what about the money? Roberta was supposed to inherit her uncle's money, but what would have happened after she died? Would it have gone to Sadie? And, now that Sadie's dead...."

Fisher perked up. "You're right! With both Ruby and Sadie gone, Eddie Pike is the old man's last living relative!"

Bell nodded. "Eddie Pike could have killed his half-sister and his cousin to get his uncle's inheritance."

Fisher frowned. "But why would Eddie Pike kill Sylvester Finnegan?"

"Maybe Sylvester knew the truth," Riggs said. "Or he suspected it. Either way, Eddie may have had to kill him." Riggs reached into his pocket for his little notebook, and he remembered that he'd never read the second note Fisher had given him earlier. He unfolded it. It was a telephone message.

"Hey, listen to this message," Riggs said. *"From Miss Margaret Baker: I found what must be Ruby's diary. It was behind a plant pot on my porch. Out this morning, but I'll bring it to the station this afternoon."*

Fisher frowned. "She's going to ruin the fingerprints."

"I doubt it," Riggs said, "the murderer would have wiped it before hiding it on Baker's porch."

But Victoria shook her head and whispered, *"Aber warum jetzt?"* She dumped the last crumbs of her lunch over the railing of the pier. The seagulls squawked greedily and gathered around the scraps. There was a man walking along the pier, and Victoria kept her back to him until he had passed. Then she lowered her voice and said, "I don't like the diary suddenly turning up like that, and I think you need to hurry. First, you have to find out about Mr. Greenleaf's will. Second, you need to make sure the jewelry from the hatbox belongs to the landlady."

"That'll be easy enough," Riggs said. "Should we arrest Eddie Pike?"

But Victoria wasn't listening. "I haven't met Ann Marie," she said to herself, "but you said she was in the photographs?"

"Several of them," Riggs confirmed.

"Good; I'd like to see every photograph you have of Ann Marie Lewis."

Fisher nodded. "Sure thing, I can send them by messenger today."

"There may not be enough time," Victoria said. "Bring them yourself. Just make sure you're not followed. Now tell me about Sadie Greenleaf's closet."

The two men looked at each other uncertainly, and Riggs began, "Well, it was a big closet with the usual sorts of things: dresses, skirts, blouses. Oh, and there was quite a bit of cash, too."

"Aber, Naturlich," Victoria said with a grin. "That's because Sadie was a thief. We already know that she stole her cousin's diary, so we can also assume she was in the habit of stealing from her uncle. But that doesn't matter; tell me about her clothes."

"We didn't have time to go through everything," Fisher explained. "She had a huge closet full of clothes, hats, shoes, handbags, everything!"

"But she was a redhead," Victoria explained, "so what colors did she like to wear?"

"Colors?" Riggs frowned and closed his eyes to help him remember. "Well, I'd say they were all sort of darker colors, you know. There was a lot of dark brown and greens and blues and…." He strained to remember. "You know, the sort of colors you see in autumn."

"Wasn't there anything bright or cheerful?" Victoria pressed. "Please, try to remember. All the colors in her closet were dark and autumny. Did anything stand out at all?"

"Oh, yes," Riggs remembered, and he opened his eyes. "I noticed something folded up with the scarves on the top shelf."

"Aber welche Farbe war das?" Victoria demanded. "Sorry. The color; was it yellow?"

Riggs stared at her, and his mouth fell open. "Are you saying that was Roberta's yellow dress?"

"If it is," Bell said with a grin, "things are finally beginning to make sense."

Chapter Thirty-Five: The Last Will and Testament

F isher set about getting the photographs to Victoria, and by one o'clock, Michael Riggs was back at Mr. Greenleaf's house. So much had happened in the last week that the old monstrosity was beginning to feel like a familiar old monstrosity. Riggs rang the bell, and the faithful Mrs. Lamar took him back up to Sadie's bedroom. This time, Riggs went directly to the closet and pulled down the yellow fabric from the top shelf. It rustled as he laid it out on the bed.

A lemon-yellow evening dress with a full chiffon shirt.

Riggs pulled out the photograph he'd been carrying around for the last week. The smiling faces of Ruby, Sylvester, Ann Marie, and Bruce. But he didn't need to look again to know that this was Ruby's dress. This was the dress that Ruby had worn the night she took Bruce Steel down to her boat. The dress she had worn on the night that ended with a ruined engagement and two friendships.

But why was it here? This dress didn't match Sadie Greenleaf's figure or her style. Mrs. Lamar couldn't help him so Riggs bagged the dress and went to have a word with Mr. Greenleaf. The old man was sitting in his wheelchair near the window. He looked exhausted. The fireplace was dark, and the room smelled of stale ash.

"Inspector Riggs," the old man said. "I am at a complete loss, but I expect that the Seattle Police Department isn't. It is my job to mourn, but it's your job to find the bastard who did this. Tell me, why would anyone do such a thing?"

"I don't know, but I'll find out," Riggs promised.

The old man looked at him. "I expect you to, Inspector. But I want to make myself perfectly clear: this man may be insane, and then again, he may not. I don't give a damn either way; I want him caught."

"I assure you, Mr. Greenleaf, we're doing our best."

The old man frowned. "All the same, I am considering hiring a private investigator. I don't question your skills, but I'm determined to have justice."

In his years as an investigator, it wasn't the first time Riggs had been threatened with private competition. So far, Riggs had always come out on top.

"I remember there was a nasty case last year," the old man said. "It was all through the newspapers, and it was solved by a private investigator, a woman, as I remember. You probably remember her."

"That's right," Riggs said, "but she's not a detective."

"You resent her because she's a woman," the old man said. "They are encroaching on our jobs, and it's not comfortable. I understand. Of course, it was one thing during the war, but that's all over now. And that particular woman had a lot of sex appeal, as I remember. She must have caused quite a stir for you boys. But I don't care if she is a woman." He pointed at Riggs. "Inspector, if you don't solve this case today, I'm going to hire this woman to solve it for you!"

"I understand," Riggs said truthfully, "but right now, I need to ask you a couple of questions about your nephew, Eddie Pike."

Mr. Greenleaf shrugged and huffed at the same time. "There's not much to know about Eddie."

"Then tell me what there is."

Mr. Greenleaf frowned and said, "That boy always has been a little strange. After his father died, we sent him to a boys' school in San Francisco. It was a good school, and there wasn't much culture here for a young boy at the time. Eddie received a proper education. And Isabelle had the time to care for poor little Roberta. After all, the girl was only four or five years old when her father died. Sweet Roberta, she was devastated, poor thing."

"How old was Eddie?"

"Oh, he was about twelve years old, I think. He wrote us a couple letters to say he was happy. His teachers reported that he was an average student and that he had friends."

"And how often did he come home?"

"At first, he came home for Christmas and summer, but after a couple years, he decided he'd rather stay near his friends. When he got older, I expected him to work at my firm, but he joined the army instead. They trained him to be a mechanic. When he was twenty-one, he received a small inheritance from my sister. Eddie was in the army at the time, but he didn't blow it. He saved it, and he must have saved a lot more besides, because after the war was over, he was able to buy his own automobile garage."

"You were surprised?"

"I never understood why he didn't just ask me for a nice desk job. I could have given him something respectable where he could keep his hands clean. He could have really worked his way up in my company. But I guess Eddie would rather wear dirty coveralls than be on a board of directors."

"Did he say why he did it?"

"I never asked him. He's a nice enough young man. He helps out around the house when I need a handyman, and of course, he services my cars. I invite him here for Thanksgiving and Christmas dinner every year, but apart from that, I don't see too much of him."

"Do you like him?"

"I just don't understand a man without ambition," Mr. Greenleaf shook his head. "He's a nice young man, but what is he doing with his life?"

"When was the last time you saw him?"

"He came by on Saturday," Mr. Greenleaf said. "Actually, I sent him to you."

"Me?"

"Well, Eddie was asking about Roberta's things," the old man explained. "I think he said something about a hatbox where Roberta kept something. He wanted to know where it was, and I told him he should go talk to you about that sort of thing."

"Did he think the hatbox was here?" Riggs asked.

"I don't think so," the old man furrowed his forehead, "but it reminds me of something…oh my goodness, what is it?" Mr. Jacob Greenleaf rubbed his chin, scowled, and tried to remember. "I just can't remember what it was."

After several minutes, Riggs cleared his throat and asked, "Mr. Greenleaf, can you tell me about your will?"

The old man looked up with a mixture of surprise and annoyance. "My what?"

"Your will."

"Oh yes, of course," he said, "I figured you'd want to know about that sooner or later. I am a very wealthy man, after all. Here," he said, wheeling himself over to a heavily polished desk and opening the drawer. "Here it is. I had Mrs. Lamar bring me a copy."

He handed an envelope to the inspector and added, "You can keep that if you'd like to. My lawyer has the original. In plain English, it says that Sadie gets an allowance, but the bulk of my money would go to Roberta. I also left a retirement income for Mr. and Mrs. Lamar and the sum of ten thousand dollars to Eddie Pike."

"And if Miss Pike died before you?"

The old man took a deep breath. "Then the estate would go to Sadie." He reached over to the sofa and grabbed his wool blanket. He frowned as he laid it over his lap. "Now that both Roberta and Sadie are gone, it all goes to Eddie. But I may as well tell you that I've already made an appointment with my lawyer to change that."

Riggs looked up. "Oh, really."

The old man shook his head. "Inspector, no man likes to admit his weaknesses, but at my age, I don't know what else to do. The truth is that someone has been stealing from me. I don't know who, but it's been going on for some time. Of course, Mrs. Lamar and her husband are above suspicion. I trust them more than I trust my own eyes. But Eddie comes here to repair things around the house for me. He has a key."

"You suspect that Eddie has been stealing from you?"

"I don't have any proof," the old man grumbled, "so I don't intend to prosecute. But I have noticed that money tends to disappear. Of course, I'm old, and I could be wrong. Sadie always said I had an overly active imagination. I won't cut him out completely, but I think I'll leave him just ten thousand dollars, and the rest should go to charity."

Riggs thought it over and suggested, "Mr. Greenleaf, have you ever considered that Miss Greenleaf could have been responsible?"

"Sadie?" the old man repeated in surprise. "Of course not! She'd never do a thing like that. Besides, I provided her with a handsome allowance, so she always had enough money. But I don't know Eddie well enough to know if I can really trust him. Oh, but that reminds me—there are some flowers there." He pointed to a vase of yellow tulips. "Sadie told Mrs. Lamar that they're from a man, a friend of Roberta's."

Riggs pulled his pipe out of his pocket and looked at the flowers.

Mr. Greenleaf watched him. "Do you think it's important, Inspector Riggs?"

"I'm not sure," the inspector admitted, "but I have a feeling this case is about to bust wide open."

Chapter Thirty-Six: Ann Marie's Quandary

At three o'clock on Friday afternoon, Ann Marie Lewis was stepping out of her apartment. The day was warm, and she had changed into a light blue summer dress with short sleeves. She had to shift the paper-wrapped parcel she was carrying so that she could lock the door. She had barely turned the key when a voice behind her startled her.

"Hello, Ann Marie."

She turned around so quickly that she dropped the parcel. Eddie Pike was standing on the pathway behind her.

"Eddie," she said, "what on earth are you doing here?'

"I'm sorry," he said, picking up the parcel and handing it to her. "I didn't mean to startle you."

Ann Marie frowned uncertainly. "Is something wrong, Eddie? You look all flushed and nervous."

Eddie held up a folded newspaper, "I think Roberta's boyfriend is dead."

Ann Marie stared at the newspaper and back up at Eddie. "What, Sylvester? Dead? Are you sure?"

"I think it's him," Eddie explained, "but the newspaper doesn't give a name, and they mention that his girlfriend died unexpectedly last month. They must mean Roberta."

Ann Marie shook her head. "I just can't believe it. Sylvester? Was he… does it say how it happened?"

Eddie glanced at Ann Marie, then looked away and nodded.

She took a deep breath and whispered, "I see."

"I thought he was the murderer," Eddie stammered. "I told the police he'd been talking to Sadie. I felt so sure. I thought they would arrest him, but now someone has killed him, too."

Ann Marie turned pale. "That means the real murderer is still out there."

Eddie looked down at his shoes and took a deep breath. "First it was Roberta, then her cousin, now her boyfriend. I feel sick about it. It's as though someone wants to destroy Roberta and everyone who knew her." He rubbed his hair and looked up at Ann Marie. "And I started to worry that, that…."

Ann Marie stared at him. "Eddie, are you saying you think I'm the murderer?"

"Of course not!" he objected. "I'm worried *for* you. Whoever hurt Sadie and Sylvester might come after you, too."

Ann Marie sighed with relief and leaned back against the door. "Oh, I see," she said. "Well, that's much nicer than being accused of murder. But Roberta and I weren't friends anymore, so I don't think I have anything to worry about."

"No, but I do," Eddie said.

Ann Marie looked at him, and he took a step toward her and said, "Listen, this might sound funny because I haven't known you very long. But I don't have much family left in this world, and the truth is, I never did much for them when I did have them. I regret that more than anything. What I mean is, you're a nice girl, and I don't think I'd ever forgive myself if something happened to you."

It was several moments before she spoke. "Eddie, are you saying—"

"Please don't ask me what I'm saying," Eddie interrupted with a grin. "It'll only make me blush again." He looked away and blushed anyway.

Ann Marie smiled. "Listen, Eddie, why don't you come inside. I'll make you some tea."

"I don't want to trouble you," he said.

"You're no trouble," she said. "Besides, I'm pretty shaken up, too. It would be nice to have someone to talk to."

Eddie pointed to the package. "But, aren't you on your way out?"

"Oh, this?" she said, tucking the package under her arm. "It can wait. Come inside. If you don't want tea, I can make coffee." She unlocked the front door, and Eddie followed her into the hallway. He was about to shut the door when a voice called out.

"Annie, Annie!"

Bruce Steele hurried up the walkway toward them.

"Bruce!" Ann Marie exclaimed. "Bruce, why are you here?"

Bruce reached out and touched Ann Marie's arm. She was warm. He leaned in to kiss her, but he paused when he noticed the other man. Bruce straightened up.

"Annie, I'm afraid I've got bad news: Sylvester is dead. It was in the paper. Someone killed him in the alley behind his apartment."

"I just heard about it," Ann Marie said. Then she turned toward Eddie and asked, "Did you say the newspaper didn't mention his name?"

Bruce squared his shoulders and stepped forward so that his body blocked the doorway. "Who the hell are you?" he demanded.

Annie put her hand on Bruce's chest. He looked down at her. "Annie, do you know this man?"

"Yes, Bruce. Of course, I know him."

Bruce turned back to Eddie. "So, who are you?"

"Bruce, stop it!" Ann Marie objected, "You have no right to speak to him that way."

"On, no?" Bruce asked, still glaring at Eddie. "There's a murderer running around. Ruby's dead, and someone is picking off her friends, one by one."

"I'm not the murderer," Eddie said. "Sadie Greenleaf was my cousin, and Roberta was my half-sister."

"You're Eddie Pike?" Bruce realized.

Eddie turned to Ann Marie and handed her his newspaper. His voice was calm. "There are two newspapers in this town, Ann Marie. I read the Post, and it didn't mention Sylvester's name."

Bruce turned back to Ann Marie as if something had occurred to him for the very first time. His gaze moved between the two of them before he asked

Eddie, "Did Annie invite you here?"

"Whether I did or not," Ann Marie interrupted hotly, "is my own business."

Bruce smiled at Ann Marie, "Of course, dear." Then he turned to Eddie. "I appreciate your concern, Mr. Pike, but you won't be needed now."

Ann Marie scowled at Bruce. "As a matter of fact, Bruce, I just invited Eddie up for a cup of tea."

Bruce took a deep breath and turned to Ann Marie. "Annie, you know I always respect your wishes, but please don't do this. You hardly know this guy, and there's a murderer on the loose. Even if you weren't my fiancée, I couldn't just walk away and leave you alone with a possible killer."

"I'm not the murderer," Eddie said, "but for all I know, you could be."

"Me?" Bruce shouted. "Are you an idiot or just plain old crazy?"

"You knew my half-sister, Mr. Steele. You also knew Finnegan and my cousin, Sadie. I'm not saying you did it, but what I am saying is that until the murderer is caught, I intend to make sure Ann Marie is safe."

Bruce's face became red. "You mean she can't be alone with anyone but you!" He moved forward so that the two men were face to face and lowered his voice, "Listen, Buddy, Ruby had a rich uncle. I think you're the one who wanted to see that tramp dead."

That was when Eddie swung. His fist flew through the air, hitting Bruce squarely on the jaw. It didn't knock him down, but he was stunned. Eddie wiped his hands together and turned to go, but Bruce grabbed him by the shoulder, swung him around, and hit him on the chin. Bruce swung again, but this time Eddie ducked, and Bruce's fist crashed into the door. Then Eddie plunged himself into Bruce's stomach, denting the door and ramming Bruce's body long backwards into the yard. Bruce jumped up and grabbed Eddie's shoulders, but Eddie spun around and surprised Bruce with two more hits.

That was when Ann Marie turned on the garden hose.

She doused them both until the brawl subsided. With a few shoves and glares, the two battered men got to their feet. Bruce's jaw was swelling, and Eddie's jacket was torn. They were both dripping.

Ann Marie glared. "I'm going to the police station," she announced angrily.

"So, if you hoodlums are still hell-bent on protecting me, you'll have to quit acting like a pair of childish, drunken idiots!"

Chapter Thirty-Seven: The Boiling Point

"The amethyst ring belonged to my grandmother," Patricia Mooney lamented. "She brought it over from England. Then there was a golden necklace with some roughly cut diamonds. It wasn't worth much, but to me, it was priceless. And the last piece was—"

A quick knock interrupted her description. Inspector Fisher stuck his head in. "Sorry, Inspector Riggs, but Miss Baker is here. Do you want to talk to her, or should I just take the thing?

Riggs nodded. "No, please bring her in. I've got some questions for her. I'm sorry, Mrs. Mooney, this shouldn't take long."

Margaret Baker came in. Beside her was a well-dressed man in his late thirties. "Inspector Riggs, this is my fiancé, Mr. Jenison." The two men shook hands, and Riggs introduced Mrs. Mooney.

Mr. Otis Jenison surveyed the policeman cautiously. "It's very unsettling to have one's fiancé mixed up in this sort of thing," Mr. Jenison said. "I never met this friend of hers, but I'm proud of Margaret for alerting the authorities. A person ought to do their civic duty."

"Well, I appreciate that," Riggs said. "Miss Baker has been extremely helpful to my investigation.'

Mr. Jenison nodded. "Margaret was right to come to you. I just hope that her name doesn't wind up in the newspapers. We're going to San Francisco for the weekend, and I hope you have this matter settled before we get back. I really don't feel comfortable with a madman on the loose."

"Otis, dear," Margaret said and patted his arm. "I'm sure there's nothing to worry about."

While Otis tried to appear reassured, Margaret handed Riggs a paper bag. "Here you are, Inspector. I found it on my porch this morning behind a flower pot."

Riggs opened the bag and found a small leather-bound book and a man's gold watch. A quick inspection of the book told him that it was about two-thirds full of handwritten entries. The penmanship was simple, messy, and probably feminine. It appeared to be more of a scheduling calendar than a private diary. All the pages seemed to be present. The gold watch was another matter. It was fairly new, with only the slightest wear. The back was engraved, '*to B.S. With love from A.L. Happy Birthday.*'

Riggs frowned at the items. "You say you found these behind a flower pot?"

"Yes, I was picking up the milk bottle this morning, and the corner of the book just happened to catch my eye. I probably shouldn't have touched it, but that didn't occur to me until I'd already looked at it."

Otis Jenison glanced at his watch and cleared his throat gently. "We really should get going, my dear. We still need to eat before we catch our airplane." He turned to Riggs and explained, "This weekend, my family is celebrating my grandmother's eightieth birthday."

There was a commotion in the hallway, and Mr. Blackwell burst into the room with his wife and Inspector Fisher behind him.

"I demand an explanation for this!" Mr. Blackwell shouted. "First, you invade my home with your questions and insinuations, and now, my own wife tells me that she's had a private meeting with you. I am a highly respected citizen in this town, and I find your methods improper. My lawyer should have been consulted, and under these circumstances, I don't believe that my wife is responsible for her actions. But as you have succeeded in coercing or threatening her, I demand that you tell me exactly what was said!"

"We'll get to that," Fisher growled. Then he turned to Riggs and added, "And if you're not busy, Inspector, Miss Lewis, Mr. Pike, and Mr. Steele are all in the lobby wanting to talk to you."

Riggs raised his eyebrows and smoothed out his mustache. "This could get interesting," he said with a grin. "Bring them up and get some more chairs, will you? I guess it's time we got all of these people in the same room together. Mrs. Blackwell, would you care to have a seat? Mr. Blackwell, sit down."

Instead of sitting, Mr. Blackwell huffed like a bird that was trying to double its size. But Mrs. Blackwell murmured something and sat down without looking at anyone.

A minute later, Ann Marie came into the room. Riggs saw Eddie and Bruce, both looking as though they'd just lost a bar fight. Bruce glared around the room, but Eddie just followed Ann Marie. As Fisher brought in more chairs, Mrs. Mooney and Margaret Baker looked around the room with interest, but most of the others kept their gazes down.

When Fisher brought more chairs, Riggs asked him, "About our lunch meeting today, were you able to deliver those files?"

Fisher nodded. Every photograph they had of Ann Marie had been given to Victoria.

Riggs looked around and said, "Everyone in this room was connected in some way to Roberta Pike. In fact, I believe that one of you has the clue that can solve her murder. But since you are not all acquainted with each other, I'll introduce each of you. He started on his left and worked around the room as if he were dealing cards. "Mrs. Patricia Mooney was Roberta's landlady. Bruce Steele, you were Roberta's friend. Miss Ann Marie Lewis used to be her friend until they had a falling out two months ago. Mr. Eddie Pike was Roberta's half-brother. Mr. Blackwell was her employer. Mrs. Blackwell claims that she never met Roberta Pike, but the only person who had absolutely nothing to do with Roberta Pike is Mr. Otis Jenison. I've been able to verify absolutely that he was in England when Miss Pike was murdered." Otis Jenison looked shocked, but Riggs went on. "And finally, we come to his fiancée, Miss Margaret Baker. This entire investigation started with Miss Baker's insistence that her friend Roberta Pike was murdered."

"Unfortunately, that got me fired," Margaret added.

Mr. Blackwell tightened his jaw. "You were let go because we were overstaffed with stenographers."

"You hadn't even filled Ruby's position yet," Margaret objected.

Mrs. Blackwell spoke up angrily. "Miss Baker, please don't forget that my husband's company has treated you very well. You hadn't been with them very long, but he still promoted you because Mrs. Jenison is a good friend of mine."

Margaret blushed and turned to her fiancé. "I'd like to go now, Otis. Unless, of course, you need me for anything else, Inspector Riggs?"

"No, no, thank you for bringing this by," the inspector said. "I hope you enjoy your week—l"

The door opened, and Victoria strode into the room. The netting of her hat was pulled down over her eyes, and she folded it up as she took off her hat. Fisher's jaw nearly dropped as she sauntered through the crowd of murder suspects and right up to Riggs's desk. Victoria hadn't set foot into the police headquarters in nearly a year. And here she was, chewing gum and acting like she owned the place.

Riggs tried not to stare as Victoria opened up her handbag and handed him the envelope with Roberta's photographs.

In a charming and slightly southern accent, Victoria cooed, "Well, I did what you asked, and as far as I'm concerned, I think we're just about finished with this little project."

Now Riggs stared.

Fortunately, everyone was looking at Victoria, so no one noticed the shock on the inspector's face. Riggs rubbed his face and looked at Fisher. It was a good thing the younger inspector was in the back of the room, because his mouth was hanging open.

Riggs looked back at Victoria and cleared his throat. "Um, you say it's finished?"

"Just about," she drawled and handed him a note. "As soon as you review these points, we'll be able to call it a week."

"Right," Riggs frowned. "You're sure about that?"

She waved her hand dismissively. "Oh for heaven's sake, you've already done all the hard work. This is just a little piece of cake."

Riggs glanced down at the list and realized that it was a short list of evidence that Victoria wanted him to go over. He looked at her, and she winked. Then he glanced around at the expectant faces and realized that an explanation was in order.

"Well, everyone, this is Miss—"

"Miss Judith Glocke," Victoria announced happily. "But I'm not really Riggs's secretary," she confessed as she flipped some hair behind her shoulder. "He's actually my second cousin on my mother's side. But I promised I'd help out for a couple days while his secretary is out of town." Victoria finished her lying and turned back to Riggs. "Now, Michael, oops, I mean '*Inspector Riggs*,' where's that letter you wanted me to proofread?"

Riggs could hardly speak, for that matter, he could hardly think, but he somehow managed to put his hands on Jacob Greenleaf's will and get it into Victoria's general direction.

"All righty, then," she said with a wink. "I'll just read this while you and these nice folks have your little meeting." As soon as she'd moved to the back of the room, Victoria signaled Fisher to close his mouth.

Riggs stuffed Victoria's note in his pocket and continued, "In fact, Miss Pike's death would have gone on record as a suicide had it not been for her friend Margaret Baker. Unfortunately, we now have not one but three murders."

An absolute silence fell over the room, and Riggs said, "The interesting thing, in this case, is the character of Miss Pike herself. First of all, let's consider her name. Her family called her Roberta. Her devoted uncle believed that Roberta was in every way a well-behaved young lady."

Mrs. Mooney interrupted with a short laugh.

The inspector continued. "That was Roberta Pike, beloved favorite of her wealthy uncle and destined to inherit his fortune when he died. But there was another side to Miss Pike, a side that she carefully hid from her uncle. To her friends, Roberta Pike was known as Ruby, a modern and perhaps somewhat self-serving young woman who enjoyed socializing and nightclubs. Ruby's only real problem was funding her extravagant lifestyle while keeping it a secret from her conservative uncle. It's worth noting that her cousin, Sadie, was jealous, and unlike their uncle, she didn't believe Roberta was a virtuous saint." Riggs turned to Eddie. "Does that sound right to you, Mr. Pike?"

Eddie nodded. "Yes, Roberta's attitude was always different around Uncle Jacob."

"And did Sadie resent her?" Riggs asked.

Bruce butted in, "I think sooner or later, everyone resented Ruby."

Eddie turned towards him sternly. "Like some people, Roberta had a knack for getting what she wanted. Isn't that right, Mr. Steele?"

Riggs nodded. "Sadie was our top suspect until she was murdered. For years, she had been stealing cash from her uncle. And when Ruby started using her uncle's boat, Sadie used her uncle's key to sneak into the marina and snoop on her cousin. At one point, Sadie stole a green hatbox of Ruby's personal things. Sadie wanted evidence that would force her uncle to see Roberta for who she truly was."

"But now, she's dead, too," Mrs. Mooney said. "She's the one you asked me about, right? She was murdered just a few blocks from my house in Eastlake."

"That's right," Riggs said. "Sadie's body was found in her uncle's black Continental. And the hatbox was there, too." Riggs looked back at Victoria and saw that she was done with the will. "And that brings us to Ruby's boyfriend and our second suspect, Sylvester Finnegan. Until recently, Mr. Finnegan worked in the county's office of the Department of Permitting. His supervisor is going over his work now, but it appears that Mr. Finnegan may have doctored some of the city's zoning lines on certain maps. Curiously enough, the dates of those errors coincide with large deposits in Finnegan's bank account."

Mr. Blackwell cleared his throat. "Do you mean he was incompetent?"

"No, I mean that he was being compensated to alter those maps. Land developers are very happy when a city zoning code changes in their favor. In this case, two pieces of relatively cheap residential land near Lake Washington were rezoned. Those lots have now tripled in value."

"Oh, my God!" Ann Marie gasped. "So that was their game! I knew Ruby was getting extra cash from somewhere, but I assumed she got it from her uncle."

Mrs. Mooney huffed. "I knew it! That Mr. Finnegan was a crook. I knew he was up to no good. His eyes were very shifty."

Riggs continued, "Sylvester claimed that on the night Ruby died, he stayed at the Blue Bay Tavern until closing. Even though the tavern is right by the University Bridge, it was a watertight alibi until a witness came forward with the truth."

Margaret looked up. "And what's that?"

"On the night Ruby died, Sylvester Finnegan followed her out of the tavern. He came back ten minutes later."

"But that's incredible," Eddie said. "They had been arguing. If Finnegan followed her, he could have pushed her off the bridge."

Riggs went on. "A careful investigation revealed that his real name was Keith Finnegan, and he had served time in an Ohio prison for fraud. After Finnegan got out of jail, he skipped his parole and moved out here. He and Ruby had been working together. When she died, he was desperate to get her diary in case she'd written something incriminating about him. First, he may have broken into Ruby's apartment to look for it. Then he tried to get it from Sadie."

Margaret furrowed her brow. "But, if he murdered Sadie to get the diary, how did it end up on my porch?"

Riggs looked around the room. "Because the murderer got it first."

Chapter Thirty-Eight: A Confession

M r. Blackwell burst out, "My God! There's no point, is there? I'm the one you're after."

Mrs. Blackwell turned so abruptly she nearly fell off of her chair. "Maxim! What in the world are you talking about?"

"I could sell them for a fortune," Mr. Blackwell rambled miserably, "but only if the zoning was right for building a fish cannery. Those lots were just outside the commercial zone. Miss Pike realized my predicament and arranged it with her friend. He had access to the zoning maps. For twenty-five hundred dollars, he would rewrite the lines, and no one would ever know."

"But things went wrong," Riggs said.

"I got a note: someone demanding money to keep quiet. I thought it was Ruby, so I was glad when she died. But then Mr. Finnegan contacted me. He said he needed money to run. He said if I paid him, he would disappear. I wasn't sure if I was paying blackmail or if I was helping my blackmailer's murderer to escape. But I was so desperate that I gave him the money."

Margaret glared at him. "So you were willing to help Ruby's murderer escape just to save yourself."

"But I didn't kill her!" Maxim objected. "Didn't you hear the inspector? Finnegan's the murderer...he's the one they're after!"

"Apparently, you don't read the Post," Riggs said. "If you did, you would know that Sylvester Finnegan is dead."

Blackwell turned white. "How?"

"He was trying to skip town when someone hit him on the head." Riggs turned to Bruce. "Mr. Steele, I'm going to ask you a direct question, and I'd like a straight answer. Did Ruby ever try to blackmail you?"

Bruce frowned. "Well, I don't know that I'd call it 'blackmail,' but she said…." He paused and glanced over at Ann Marie before continuing, "Ruby said that she could tell a story that would ruin my engagement."

Eddie Pike glared. "Sounds like you had a good motive yourself."

"You're a rat!" Bruce jumped to his feet, and Eddie joined him. The two men would have come to blows if Riggs hadn't moved between them.

"Sit down," he instructed. "Both of you."

The men sat back down. The shouting stopped, but the air was full of heavy breathing and bitter resentment. Celeste Blackwell leaned over to Victoria and asked, "Miss Glocke, haven't we met somewhere?"

Victoria smiled sweetly and said, "Yes, it was at the garden party last weekend. Aren't you the lady with the pretty roses?"

The older woman raised her eyebrows for a moment then her face became hard. Victoria went on loudly enough for everyone to hear. "You know, the more I learn about Miss Pike, the more surprised I am that she never tried to blackmail anyone else. For instance, Mrs. Blackwell would have been a prime target."

Everyone's attention to Mrs. Blackwell as Victoria went on in her sweet southern voice. "I imagine that an unscrupulous girl who was looking for cash could have invented all sorts of things to upset her boss's wife."

Celeste glanced around uncomfortably. "Well, as a matter of fact, she did."

"What are you talking about, Celeste?" her husband demanded.

"I hated that girl," Mrs. Blackwell burst out. "She said we had to talk. I met her for lunch, and she suggested, that is, she implied that, well, she said…."

There was a painful silence until Victoria asked, "Mrs. Blackwell, did Miss Pike imply that unless you gave her money, she would pursue a romantic relationship with your husband?"

Celeste Blackwell opened her mouth to speak, but she stopped. She buried her face in her hands.

Maxim Blackwell burst out, "Well, of all the nerve! As if Miss Pike or any other woman could…." He left the sentence unfinished and leaned toward his wife. "You should have known that was nonsense, Celeste. You should have told her to go to the devil." His wife was quivering and Mr. Blackwell provided her with a fresh handkerchief.

Riggs cleared his throat. "And it wasn't just the Blackwells and Mr. Steele. Anyone who had money was vulnerable. In fact, I believe Roberta Pike befriended Margaret Baker with the idea of someday extracting money from her."

Otis Jenison gasped audibly. "What, Margaret? How?"

Margaret turned to her fiancé. "Inspector Riggs thinks that Ruby may have been looking for a way to damage my reputation."

"Well, of all the audacious ideas!" Mr. Jenison huffed. "I wish I'd had the opportunity to meet that woman. I'd give her a piece of my mind."

"Mr. and Mrs. Blackwell and Mr. Steele each had a motive for murdering Roberta Pike," Riggs explained, "and they each had the opportunity. For that matter, each of you had the opportunity to murder Sadie Greenleaf as well."

The room fell silent.

Bruce started to object, but Riggs stopped him and went on.

"Miss Ann Marie Lewis, Ruby had an affair with your fiancé. You have no alibi for her murder. And although you were working on the afternoon Sadie was murdered, your shop is so close that you could easily have slipped away long enough to have met Miss Greenleaf and hit her on the head."

Ann Marie held her head up. "I've already admitted as much."

"True. But that doesn't make you innocent." Riggs turned to the landlady. "Mrs. Mooney, you hated Roberta because you believed she robbed you."

"I still believe it," the landlady declared, "and I won't forgive her just because she's dead. But there's something else I'd like to say." Patricia Mooney took a deep breath, "On the night that Miss Pike was murdered, somebody snuck into her apartment."

"How do you know that?" Ann Marie asked.

"Because I'd been drinking sherry, and I was there myself," Mrs. Mooney explained. Everyone stared at her. Even Mrs. Blackwell managed to stop crying and raise her head. Patricia Mooney took a breath and began again, "I mean, on that night, I'd gotten all worked up. I just kept thinking about my jewelry and how that girl had stolen it. She was very rude to me. I kept thinking that my jewelry was probably right over there, sitting in her apartment, waiting to be sold. And all my anger just sort of welled up inside me. I decided I would go right on over there myself and reclaim my rightful property. Her lights were off, and I went the back way so the other neighbors wouldn't see me. I let myself into her apartment, and I searched everywhere. And just as I turned off my flashlight to leave, I heard someone coming in the front door."

Bruce leaned forward. "Who was it?"

Mrs. Mooney shrugged. "I don't know, but it wasn't Roberta. I left as fast as I could. Of course, at the time, I didn't know that she'd been murdered. And when I found out she was dead, I was too shocked to say anything."

"Are you sure that you didn't kill Ruby?" Bruce suggested. "If she caught you searching her apartment, you could have hit her with your flashlight and dumped her off the bridge."

Mrs. Mooney turned in her chair to face him. "Miss Pike was a wicked person, and she had it coming, but I am not the one who did it."

Ann Marie frowned and looked at the landlady. "Mrs. Mooney, I don't quite understand. If you didn't see who it was, how can you be sure it wasn't Ruby?"

"Because whoever it was knocked softly before they used the key, and you don't knock on your own door, do you?"

Mr. Otis Jenison piped up. "Look here, Inspector, I don't like to tell a man how to do his job, but it seems obvious to me that two of the victims are from the same family. Have you considered who is going to inherit the money?"

Riggs glanced at Victoria, and when she nodded, he said, "With both women gone, their uncle's sizable fortune will now go to Mr. Eddie Pike."

Everyone looked at Eddie.

Mr. Blackwell looked at the young man and raised his chin. "Well, Mr. Pike, what do you have to say about that?"

"First I've heard of it," Eddie said. "Uncle Jacob was my stepmother's brother, so I never expected to inherit anything."

"But the inspector says you will inherit," Mr. Jenison insisted.

Eddie glared at him. "That doesn't make me a murderer."

"So you deny murdering your half-sister?" Bruce asked.

"I haven't murdered anyone," Eddie said. "But there's more evidence, isn't there, Inspector? What about Roberta's dress?"

"There are two evening dresses in this case," Riggs explained. "One was a yellow dress. There are several photographs with Roberta wearing it, but it wasn't anywhere in her apartment." He turned to Bruce and said, "I suppose you remember that dress?"

Bruce shifted in his chair. "Why would I? I wasn't familiar with Ruby's wardrobe."

"Because it was the dress," Ann Marie said, "that Ruby wore to the Art Show on Memorial Day weekend."

Riggs went on. "The strange thing is that we found that yellow dress in Sadie's closet."

"You forget, Inspector," Bruce added, "I wasn't acquainted with Miss Greenleaf."

"Oh, you knew Sadie Greenleaf, all right," Riggs contradicted. "That's how you knew she was a redhead. That detail wasn't mentioned in the newspapers, but you knew it because you paid her a visit the morning before she died."

"You don't have any proof of that," Bruce said.

"You brought flowers, but that was just an excuse to see Sadie. What were you really after, Mr. Steele? Was it Ruby's diary?

Bruce said nothing.

"I know what he wants," Mrs. Mooney interrupted, "because he asked me for it, too. He's looking for his gold watch. He was by my place the other day, wanting to search Ruby's apartment. Of course, I didn't understand why Miss Pike would have this man's watch since he's supposed to be engaged to this other lady." Mrs. Mooney indicated Ann Marie, but her glare was in Bruce Steele's direction.

Mr. Blackwell cleared his throat and explained, "I think we can assume that this man forgot his watch after a rendezvous with Miss Pike. She exposed the affair, and he killed her. But naturally, he still had to recover his watch. He probably left the yellow dress with Miss Greenleaf in order to incriminate her before he murdered her."

Bruce stared open-mouthed for a moment. "You're setting me up!"

"The dress was my doing," Ann Marie admitted. Everyone except Victoria turned to look at Ann Marie. While they all stared the other way, Victoria scribbled a note and passed it to Riggs.

"I had Ruby's yellow dress," Ann Marie explained, "because she left it at my house that night. The next morning, I loaned her a pair of trousers and a blouse to wear home. That's when she told me…well, she told me about the affair. We argued, and I told her I never wanted to see her again. I was too upset to think about the dress. I just shoved it into the back of my closet. Later, when I found out that she was dead, I knew I had to do something with it, but I didn't know what. Over the weekend, I finally got up my courage to take the dress to Sadie. I didn't want to explain why I had it, but Sadie never even asked."

Ann Marie's hands were clenched together, and as soon as she was done explaining, she looked down into her lap. Bruce reached over and held her hand. He leaned close to her and whispered, "I'm sorry, Annie."

Mr. Blackwell burst out, "Well, that's very touching, but there's still a murderer on the loose!"

Riggs reread Victoria's note and stroked his mustache. "There's no need to get upset," Riggs announced, "I know who the murderer is."

Everyone stared as the inspector took his wooden pipe out of his pocket and rubbed it with his thumb. "Inspector Fisher and I sorted it all out this afternoon. But since I don't have my notes in front of me, perhaps my cousin, Miss Glocke, would be good enough to go over the main details. She has an excellent memory."

Chapter Thirty-Nine: Dresses and Murders Explained

Eddie looked shocked. "You *know* who murdered Roberta and Sadie?"

"And Sylvester Finnegan," Riggs said. He turned to Miss Glocke. "I suppose you should start with the dress."

Victoria nodded and took out her chewing gum. She wrapped it theatrically into a scrap of paper and tossed it into the wastepaper basket. "If I'm remembering correctly," she said to Riggs, "you always say a case is solved when all the pieces are explained. Since this young lady just explained the yellow dress, I'll explain the red dress."

Riggs opened his desk drawer and pulled out the paper parcel. He unwrapped it and held it up for everyone to see: an expensive spaghetti-strapped evening dress made of satin with a form-fitting torso.

"This dress is very interesting," Miss Glocke explained. "Because while the yellow dress had disappeared, this dress was in Miss Pike's closet even though it didn't belong to her."

"It looks like her sort of dress," Ann Marie said.

"Well, it's fashionable and very modern," Miss Glocke agreed, "and I never met Miss Pike myself, but I understand she had quite a figure—like a pin-up girl. So we have to wonder, could a woman with an hourglass figure really fit into a dress this slim?"

Ann Marie frowned. "I see your point. No, it's too small."

"So what was it doing in her closet?" Miss Glocke asked.

No one answered, and Victoria went on. "The obvious reason is that someone wanted to give the appearance that Miss Pike owned this dress. But why? We've searched through Roberta's collection of souvenir photographs, and there isn't a single one with a woman wearing this dress."

"But that doesn't prove anything," Bruce objected. "If that photograph does exist, anyone could have it."

"And let's not forget that Roberta Pike was in the habit of blackmailing people," Miss Glocke added. "So, the next question might be: *What happened to the photograph of a woman wearing this red dress?*"

"What about Sadie?" Eddie pointed out. "She was about the right size for that dress."

"But Sadie was a redhead," Miss Glocke pointed out, "and she only wore deep earthy colors."

"That's right," Mrs. Blackwell confirmed. "That shade of red would make a redheaded woman look dead."

It was an unfortunate choice of words, and she turned to Ann Marie and blurted, "But it would fit you, wouldn't it?"

"That doesn't mean it's hers," Bruce objected. "I can positively swear that I have never seen Ann Marie in that dress."

"The dress doesn't belong to Miss Lewis," Miss Glocke confirmed.

Bruce Steele looked at her and asked, "How do you know that?"

"Because Miss Lewis never shows her upper arm."

Ann Marie blushed, and Bruce turned to her. "Is that true? Why not?"

Ann Marie sighed and began rolling up her left sleeve to show her upper arm. "I got it in the car accident that killed my parents," she explained as she exposed a large scar just shy of her shoulder. "I'm not embarrassed by it, but I'd rather not have people looking."

"Well, it's not my dress," Mrs. Blackwell burst out. "I may be slender enough to wear it, but it doesn't suit my age or my class."

"We seem to have run out of women," Miss Glocke said. "Miss Baker is above suspicion. After all, she's the one who came to Inspector Riggs insisting that her friend had been murdered."

"Well, I certainly agree with that," Otis Jenison said. "Margaret has done everything she can to help the police find the murderer."

"And a person who'd gotten away with murder would never go to the police," Bruce said.

Riggs sat down on his desk and took his pipe out of his pocket.

"That's entirely true," Miss Glocke agreed. "Unless, of course, the murderer still felt vulnerable to blackmail. For instance, what if the murderer still hadn't managed to destroy an incriminating photograph?"

The room fell silent, and for a moment, no one dared to speak.

"You know it's a funny thing," Riggs speculated as he rubbed the wooden pipe in his hand, "but Sylvester Finnegan was always talking about how Ruby used to get in trouble with a girlfriend of hers. He talked about Ruby and her friend going out with men to parties and nightclubs."

"What friend? Bruce demanded.

"Finnegan mentioned Ann Marie by name," Riggs said. "But he was the kind of man who was always mixing up names. He mixed up several names, including mine, before it occurred to me that when he talked about Ruby's friend, he might have been talking about Margaret Baker."

Otis Jenison frowned.

Margaret cleared her throat and said, "Inspector, if you are suggesting that I was being blackmailed, I can promise you that I wasn't. Besides, there are no photographs of me that I would have any reason to be ashamed of."

Nicht mehr, Miss Glocke muttered under her breath. Margaret Baker looked at her, and Miss Glocke resumed her southern accent and explained, "That's because the indelicate photograph, the one that was taken while you were wearing your beautiful red dress, that photograph was destroyed the night Mr. Greenleaf's boat burnt."

Riggs rubbed the pipe on his sleeve. "No one could have anticipated that bolt of lightning," he explained, "including the murderer. In fact, if it had happened even a few days earlier, you never would have had to come to me."

"I came to help you find my friend's murderer!" Margaret declared.

"You came here for one purpose: to expose your friend as a blackmailer," Riggs corrected her. "While your fiancé was away in Europe, you were enjoying a wider social circle. You and Ruby frequented bars and nightclubs, and you kept less-reputable company. Mr. Jenison comes from a conservative family, and he has political ambitions. He isn't likely to marry a woman with a questionable past. But you didn't count on Ruby being a blackmailer. When she realized how wealthy your fiancé was, she knew she had you. However true her stories may have been, you couldn't afford letting her keep a suggestive photograph as evidence. You had to come to me because that photograph was still missing. And before it was discovered, you had to expose Ruby as a blackmailer and yourself as an innocent victim."

"That's a lie!" Margaret said.

Riggs shook his head. "No, it's not a lie. Ruby did try to blackmail you. She could have ruined your reputation and your engagement with Mr. Jenison. You had to silence Ruby before Mr. Jenison got back, and you had to destroy the photograph."

Margaret gripped her handbag.

"You knew Ruby frequented the Blue Bay," Riggs explained, "and after Sylvester went back to the tavern that night, you hit Ruby on the head, took her apartment key, and pushed her off the bridge."

"So it was you?" Mrs. Mooney said. "I heard you coming into her apartment that night."

Riggs put his pipe back into his pocket. "You couldn't find the photograph in her apartment, but you left your dress to lead us to Ruby's blackmail attempt. You even went to Sadie in hopes that she might have the photograph, and that's when you learned about the boat. If the photograph was on the boat, then sooner or later, it would be found, and you might be recognized. Your best shot was to expose Ruby as a blackmailer before the photograph was found."

Margaret shook her head. "If any of that were true, Sadie and Sylvester would still be alive."

"But Sadie Greenleaf was so eager to expose her cousin's character that she trusted the wrong woman," Riggs explained. "After I met you last Tuesday, you didn't go to the florist with your mother-in-law. You met Sadie Greenleaf. She told you Ruby had an affair with Bruce Steele, and she showed you the hatbox with Bruce's watch and Ruby's diary."

"This is ridiculous," Margaret said. She laughed angrily. "I'm the one who gave you the diary and the watch! I found them."

"You took them from Sadie after you hit her with the tire iron. You had to get the diary to ensure it didn't expose you. After you looked it over, you pretended to discover the diary and the watch to throw suspicion on Ann Marie Lewis and Bruce Steele."

"But why would she kill Sylvester?" Ann Marie asked.

"Because Sylvester was also looking for the diary. He was worried about himself, but Margaret thought he wanted to blackmail her, too. She watched his apartment from the back parking lot. When she saw him drop his bag into the alley, all she had to do was wait for him to come back."

Margaret gave a terse smile and took her gloves out of her handbag. "Well, this is rather ludicrous," she said as she pulled on her gloves. "You may be enjoying this little fantasy, Inspector Riggs, but I don't think it's amusing. I'm going to San Francisco for the weekend, and I sincerely hope you manage to solve this case soon. I still want to know who killed my friend."

She turned to go, but Otis reached out and grabbed her arm. "I don't think so, Margaret."

She stared for a moment in shock.

"Otis, darling, don't tell me you're actually listening to this nonsense?" she demanded. "Why, the whole thing is ridiculous! *I'm* the one who went to the police. They weren't even competent enough to realize that Ruby had been murdered. They thought it was suicide. I came here to do my civic duty. I've told them everything I know, and I've given them evidence, and now they're trying to pin it on me! No, I've had quite enough of this. With or without you, Otis, I'm leaving." Margaret turned around and saw Inspector Fisher standing behind her.

"I'm sorry," Otis said, "but this is the first thing that has made any sense."

"You can't prove it!" Margaret shouted. "You bastards can't prove a damn thing! You may have managed to convince these people and my stupid fiancé, but you'll never convince a judge!" She turned to Otis; her voice was low and steady, "All right, Otis. Have it your way. Go find yourself some dry, straight-laced girl who's willing to put up with your dull life and your overbearing mother. I'm not sorry. In fact, I'm actually glad to have escaped that weary existence. I'm far too adventurous to have settled for a man like you anyway."

Fisher took Miss Baker's arm and led her from the room. As soon as she was gone, Otis Jenison sank down into his seat. He shook his head. "I'd like to say that I'm shocked," he said, "but I feel like this is the first time in months that everything has made sense. A hundred pieces have just fallen into place for me. When I was away, my family and friends hardly saw Margaret. She was never home when I telephoned in the evenings. And the florist called this morning to say that she hadn't ordered the flowers yet. I guess a part of me has been doubting Margaret for a while, and now I finally understand why."

Riggs said, "Both she and Roberta were very resourceful women."

"And unscrupulous," Otis said. "I may be a straight-laced man from a boring family, but at least I'm smart enough to realize how lucky I am."

"Lucky?" Mrs. Mooney blurted out. "To have been engaged to a murderer?"

"Lucky that I'm not going to marry one. My mother will be simply devastated." He grinned at the thought. "She was very fond of Margaret. I guess the next time I want to get married, I won't have to ask for Mother's approval. Now, if you don't need me anymore, I have a few telephone calls to make and a plane to catch."

Chapter Forty: The Calm After the Storm

They all watched Otis Jenison leave. "That young man's taking it very well," Mrs. Blackwell said. "He has good character, but his poor mother will be positively mortified when she finds out."

Mr. Blackwell put on his hat and squared it. "Personally, I've never felt so justified in firing someone in all my life. She was a cold-blooded murderer, even if she was a good stenographer. Oh, well, we don't have to think about it anymore. Celeste, dear, we have a dinner engagement this evening, and I need time to change. Inspector Riggs, Miss Glocke, thank you." He opened the door for his wife before adding, "Oh, Inspector, about that other matter. I assume that someone will want to speak to me?"

"You mean about the bribery and the fraud?" Riggs asked flatly. "That's not my department, Mr. Blackwell. But I expect there may be a couple months of jail time in your near future."

"Oh, Maxim!" his wife sighed miserably. "They wouldn't really, would they? Couldn't you just pay a fine or something?"

"Now, don't worry about it, dear," Maxim said. He turned back to the inspector. "Please tell your people that they may contact my lawyer directly. That's really the best way to handle these legal things. Randolph is his name; you'll find him in the directory."

"I'll do that," Riggs said, and with a civil farewell, Mr. and Mrs. Blackwell departed.

Ann Marie stood up, and so did Bruce and Eddie.

"One moment," Riggs said. He took a gold watch out of his drawer and handed it to its rightful owner. Bruce took the watch and followed Ann

213

Marie.

Riggs turned to Mrs. Mooney. "And now, about your jewelry."

"Good heavens," she exclaimed. "I'd completely forgotten why I was here. Can you imagine? I was so caught up in all this excitement and finding out that pretty woman, Miss Baker, was actually a terrible murderer that my heirlooms slipped my mind! My jewel thief, Miss Pike, is a saint compared to that woman. Well then, should I finish describing my heirlooms to you, Inspector?"

Riggs smiled and shook his head. "I don't think you need to bother." He pulled out a cloth pouch from his drawer and opened it up. "Mrs. Mooney, can you identify these?"

Mrs. Mooney put her hand over her mouth and began to cry. "I never thought I'd see them again, and here they are! Oh, I'm so grateful to you, Inspector. Where did you find them?"

"In a hatbox. Fortunately for you, Sadie stole it from Roberta's boat before it sank."

"Well, I never!" Mrs. Mooney exclaimed happily. "My mother always said two wrongs don't make a right, but in this case, it was the second wrong that saved my jewelry!"

* * *

Ann Marie, Bruce, and Eddie stepped out of the police station. The late afternoon sun was still shining brightly, and the streets were busy with people making their way home for the weekend.

Eddie looked up and down the street and sighed. "Well, I'm glad they caught the murderer. Ruby's friend. I never would have believed it." He held out his hand to Bruce. "No hard feelings, Mr. Steele?"

Bruce shook his hand. "No hard feelings, Mr. Pike. I guess there's nothing like an unknown murderer to put everyone on guard. About those things I said, well, it was pretty rotten of me."

"Don't mention it," Eddie said. "I understand wanting to protect someone you love."

Bruce smiled and put his hand on Ann Marie's shoulder. She looked between the two and said, "I'm glad you're both behaving like civilized men."

Eddie Pike shrugged. "Well, I guess I'd better get going. Goodbye, Mr. Steele. Goodbye, Ann Marie."

Eddie turned and started walking up the street. Ann Marie watched him for a moment while Bruce smiled down at her. The two men were as different as night and day. Bruce stroked a wisp of hair from her face and tucked it behind her ear. "Well, Annie, this whole mess is finally behind us. We'll have a fresh start, and this time I promise to do everything right."

Ann Marie stood up on her toes so that she could reach Bruce's cheek. She kissed him, smiled, and whispered, "Goodbye, Bruce. I'm sure you'll find a wonderful girl who's thrilled with your charm, and I hope for both of your sakes, you treat her better than you treated me."

Bruce's mouth opened, but he quickly smirked and said, "Oh, Annie, you don't really mean that."

"Yes, I do," Ann Marie said. "I could never be happy with a man I couldn't trust. Oh, this is for you," she added, handing him her paper parcel. "It's all the gifts you've ever given me."

"Keep them. They were presents," Bruce insisted. "In fact, I have another one for you." He reached in his pocket and took out the small velvet-lined jewelry box.

Ann Marie looked at the box and shook her head. "I'm afraid your gifts don't bring back happy memories," she explained. "No, Bruce, this whole mess is over, and we're over, too. I really do wish you all the best, darling. Goodbye."

Ann Marie turned away from Bruce Steele for the last time. She hurried down the sidewalk. It took her half a block to catch up with what she was after. "Oh, Eddie, wait up, will you?"

Eddie Pike turned around and smiled as Ann Marie came up to him. She took his arm with her hand and said, "Why, Mr. Pike, did you forget that I invited you up for some tea? And did I mention that I have some cookies, too?"

Eddie looked doubtfully at her and back in the direction she'd just come from. "But Ann Marie, aren't you going with Bruce? I think he really does love you."

She shook her head happily. "It's not the kind of love I'm after," she said. "I'd rather be alone than have a love that's inconsistent. Besides, Eddie, there's a couple things I've been meaning to ask you." She stepped closer to him.

Eddie looked down at her and tried not to grin. "What's that, Ann Marie?"

"First, will you call me Annie?"

"It would be my pleasure, Annie. And second?"

"Will you teach me how to bowl?" she asked. "I've always wanted to learn. You could teach me, and then we could go out to dinner. And when the weather is nice, we can take a picnic to the waterfront and when it's bad, we can either go bowling or we can go to the cinema. Well, what do you think, Eddie?"

Eddie stepped close to Ann Marie and slipped his arm around her waist. "Annie," he said with a broad smile, "I'd love to teach you how to bowl."

* * *

Back in the office, Victoria pulled her hair back up into a bun. Fisher came back in and said, "Okay, Miss Glocke. The coast is clear. Most of the department has already gone home, but you'd better hurry before the Chief hears about the arrest."

She nodded. "Or one of Jenison's telephone calls tip off the reporters."

The telephone on Riggs's desk started ringing, but he ignored it. "I owe you one, Bell, I really do."

"Yes, you do," she agreed as she put her hat back on. "And you can pay me back by never mentioning it again."

Riggs raised his eyebrow. "But it was fun, wasn't it?"

"Yes," Victoria grinned as she pulled down a piece of lace from her hat so that it covered her eyes. "It was fun, but this was absolutely the last time. Now, I'm going to go home to my husband and pretend that none of this ever happened. And you should get home to your wife and oh — maybe you should buy her some flowers."

"Flowers?" Riggs repeated.

"Just in case," Victoria nodded. Then she grabbed her handbag and asked, "All right, how does this look?"

"Well…" Fisher considered. He vacated his post at the door so that he could re-adjust the lace of her hat.

"That's better," he said. "Now, come on, I'll get you out by the back staircase."

Fisher stepped into the hallway, but an approaching commotion blocked him. It was all he could do to retreat back into the office and push Victoria behind the door.

The door burst open, and the police chief barged into the office. "Well, Riggs, what's this I hear about the Pike case being solved?" he demanded happily. "Some reporters are downstairs asking questions."

"Well, we—uh, we made some good progress," Riggs stammered as he tried not to look past the chief to Victoria. Fisher signaled Victoria to sneak behind the chief's back.

"Progress, my foot!" the chief roared. "Inspector Reilly said you made an arrest! A woman, no less. Now, don't be coy with me, Riggs! I want to hear all about it!"

Victoria crept toward the door, and Fisher tried to move so he could block her from sight just in case the chief looked behind him.

"Well, you, you, you, see," Riggs stuttered, "it's a…it's a touchy sort of business, Chief. We're pretty sure. That is. I might need to clear up a couple points before I write my report."

"To hell with the report!" the Chief said. "I want to know the same thing all those reporters downstairs want to know! Give me details. Did you use our secret weapon?"

"Our secret weapon?" Riggs asked. Victoria was almost to the hall.

"What's the matter with you, Riggs? I'm talking about that woman, Bell! She was the juiciest police sensation this Department's ever had! She made our jobs seem downright glamorous! The newspapers want the sex angle. And boy, did Victoria Bell have it!"

Victoria froze in the doorway and stared.

But the chief was rubbing his chin, happily unaware of her. "What did they call Bell last time? Oh, right, 'Seattle's Sultry Sleuth.' Oh, that was fun, wasn't it? Oh, and do you remember 'Victoria, the Delicious Detective'? Oh, I could use some more excitement like that." The Chief grinned at the possibility of more scandals.

"Well, unfortunately, Bell didn't have anything to do with this case," Riggs insisted. "Absolutely nothing."

Fisher was closing the door when the chief snapped his fingers. He held up his hands to make a marquee. "I got it!" he shouted. "Next time you get Bell to help you, I'll get the newsboys to print: 'Victoria Bell, the Titillating-Truth-Tracker'!

Victoria's jaw fell open, and Inspector Fisher decisively swung the door shut in her face.

* * *

An hour later, Michael Riggs stepped out onto the sidewalk and put on his hat. Part of him felt guilty for taking all the credit. And part of him was just grateful for the success. He ducked into a telephone booth and dialed his own number. Riggs told his wife the same story he'd already told the chief. Amy was delighted with the good news. It wasn't until Riggs was driving home that it occurred to him that Amy might know the truth. It was suspicious the way she hadn't asked any questions. Michael Riggs laughed at himself; Amy was far too busy with their five children to pay that much attention. He turned into his neighborhood. Still, Amy often had a funny way of knowing things. Riggs stopped at the corner market and bought a bottle of wine. He was just getting back in the car when he paused. Michael Riggs turned around, went back to the corner florist, and bought half a dozen roses.

Acknowledgements

My deepest appreciation to Naomi Johnson, Lisa Tschannen, Cornelia Schmitt, Kirstin Johnson, Cheryl Barnes, and Christine Bearden for feedback and editorial expertise. A huge thanks to my family for their endless support, encouragement, and endurance. And lastly, I would like to thank my wonderful publishers, especially Verena Rose and Shawn Reilly Simmons, for giving the Elliott Bay Mysteries a home at Level Best Books.

About the Author

Jennifer Berg is a historical mystery writer from the Pacific Northwest. She studied history at the University of Washington and worked in Seattle's tourism industry before moving, with her family, to San Diego, California. She is the author of two historical mystery series and her short stories have been featured in the 2020 and 2023 Bouchercon Anthologies. Jennifer is a member of Sisters in Crime, the Crime Writers Association, and Mystery Writers of America. She currently lives in a hamlet in the Bavarian foothills.

SOCIAL MEDIA HANDLES:
  Twitter: 1950sMysteries
  Facebook: 1950sMysteries

AUTHOR WEBSITE:
  jenniferberg.me

Also by Jennifer Berg

The Charlatan Murders

The Blue Pearl Murders

Milton Keynes UK
Ingram Content Group UK Ltd.
UKHW012219090923
428401UK00004B/46